CRY HAVOC

DAVID WHALE

OCTOSQUID

Publisher's Note: This is a work of fiction. Names, characters, places, and incidents are a product of the author's imagination. Locales and public names are sometimes used for atmospheric purposes. Any resemblance to actual people, living or dead, or to businesses, companies, events, institutions, or locales is completely coincidental.

Book Layout © 2017 BookDesignTemplates.com

Cry Havoc / David Whale. -- 1st ed.
ISBN 978-0-9958100-6-8

<u>**Also by David Whale**</u>

Radko's War
Out of the Black

Cry "Havoc"! and let slip the dogs of war

- Williame Shakespeare, Julius Caesar

Robesombel.

The moon had, in days past, been a favoured vacation spot of wealthy icarans. Crystal clear lakes, towering plantlife featuring cascades of blue and yellow and orange flowers when in bloom, impressive - but mercifully vegetarian - megafauna that featured prominently in both advertisements and souvenirs.

Brigadier Arysis of the Icaran Votol Commandos had never had the means to visit Robesombel until the war with the ril-ga-las had sent her there. While she had no doubt it was a beautiful place to rest and relax, her current situation was not amenable to either.

Standing on a high ridge, knee deep in the wide-bladed, pale orange grass, the Brigadier intently scanned the valley below. Running north-south, the valley was wide and flat, easy to traverse and dotted with ponds and streams of fresh water where she and her team could allow their mounts to drink.

The valley could not have been a more perfect path forward if Arysis had designed it herself.

It was a trap, of course.

It was always a trap.

Narrowing her three good eyes, she focused on the far treeline, before the other wall of the valley rose up in a sheer, ivy-covered face of rock. Though she could see no movement, she discerned dark spots just inside the treeline that, from the position of the suns, could not have been shadows cast by trees. And were much too small to be the native megafauna.

"The same trick?"

Arysis turned as her second in command, Eltraar stepped up beside her. One of the tallest icarans she'd ever encountered, Arysis had to look up to meet his gaze. He'd brought both of their mounts -- tall, lithe beasts covered in thick fur, that the Commandos called kyroos, after the sound they made, because none of the soldiers could pronounce the indigenous name.

"It would appear so," said Arysis, absently stroking the snout of her mount, Otyro. "Which concerns me."

"They are becoming predictable."

Arysis bobbed her head and scratched at the ever-itchy socket of her missing eye.

"They've stopped trying," she said. "Which is very different. What have you noted about their number in our last two encounters?"

Arysis was testing him, and he knew it. He had stiffened ever so slightly, and she noticed a small nerve twitching beneath his primary left eye -- a sure sign he was annoyed. Not that she was trying to annoy him, but Eltraar had only just been given the place of second in command, and it had been over Arysis's objections. She needed to test him.

"They are fewer every time," he said finally. "As we are thinning their numbers."

"They are fewer in number, but not entirely of our doing. The enemy no longer tries to defeat us, but delay our progress."

Without waiting for a response, Arysis swung herself up on Otyro's back and scratched the kyroo between her shoulder blades just the way she liked.

"Bring up the others," she said, detaching one of the two *vayan* pistols affixed to her chest plate. "We need to spring the trap and find out what's beyond it."

Eltraar mounted his own kyroo and left Arysis alone, returning moments later with the remaining six members of Arysis's team.

Though the path into the valley was steep, the wide, six-toed, clawed paws of the kyroos, with their near-opposable first and sixth digits, were perfectly designed for difficult ascents and descents. The team was on the valley floor within moments.

And Arysis saw movement within the trees.

Small shapes, and larger ones.

Broad heads, waving slightly back and forth.

"Foot soldiers," said Eltraar.

"And stalkers," said Arysis, adopting the nomenclature for the smaller, more agile ril-galas that had come through in the shared information packets from the humans.

Significantly smaller than the typical ril-galas foot soldier, standing roughly six feet when fully upright, the stalkers had a similarly manta-shaped head, though like everything else about them, it was sleeker, more streamlined. They were also leaner, their digitigrade legs ending in almost bird-like feet. Their smaller, secondary arms were the ones ending in canons, unlike the foot soldier, and these were kept tucked close to their chest while the primary arms, ending in long, sharp talons, served as the stalker's primary weapon. Between the claws on their primary arms and those on their feet, stalkers were excellent climbers and the perfect units to use in an ambush. Perhaps the most unsettling difference between the foot soldier and the stalker was the latter's inclusion of a wide mouth full of row upon row of sharp teeth. The foot soldier's mouth wasn't visible, if it existed at all, while the stalker's was clearly weaponized.

Ril-galas foot soldiers were slower than an icaran, mounted or not, but the stalkers were both remarkably fast and, with their knife-like claws, remarkably dangerous. A ril-galas stalker had, in the Brigadier's very first encounter at the start of the present war, taken her eye. By any measure, Arysis had more than exacted revenge: she'd successfully lead the defense of Ballesaan Station, liberated the colony of Jessik, and, after having been cut off from the rest of the icaran armed forces, fought her way single-handedly through the Battle of Heetraphaar.

One in six had died in that battle.

"They're coming."

Bursting from the treeline, the ril-galas charged the icarans. The enemy had broken cover too soon for the trap to have been effective and were now wasting time crossing open space.

The stalkers came first, loping across the open field with an unnerving sideways gait, their taloned hands hanging loosely at their sides. Stories had reached Arysis that the silence of the stalkers had terrified some humans, but so too had the faceless battle helms worn by icarans once terrified humans. Arysis was not so arrogant as to say she never felt fear, but she could say without hubris that she'd never experienced terror.

As the stalkers charged, a low rumble rolled up from Otyro, and her head crest flashed in bursts of yellow and red bioluminescence.

Be warned, she appeared to be saying, *I am not easy prey.*

Raising her *vayan* and nudging Otyro onward, Arysis took aim at the leading stalker and fired a superheated projectile through the creature's head, and a second through its chest as it fell. A second stalker lunged at her and she shot it out of the air and suddenly Otyro reared up on her hind legs and slammed downward, driving her armoured head crest into a ril-galas foot soldier, driving its head down and crushing its chest cavity.

And as Arysis spun to find her next target, her heavy pistol sweeping the battlefield, she found no more targets. While a handful of ril-galas lay dead or dying, at least twice as many were disappearing back into the trees.

Re-affixing her pistol to her chest plate, Arysis patted Otyro's shoulder while she opened up a communications channel to the icaran naval task force in orbit around Robesombel.

"Yes, Brigadier Arysis -- you have news?"

"The enemy tactics have changed, Commodore Orenphaar. I believe them to be covering a retreat."

A moment of silence followed before the Commodore voiced what Arysis herself had been thinking.

"The ril-galas do not retreat. If they..."

"Commodore...?"

"One moment," said Orenphaar.

Arysis could her a smattering of voices in the pause that followed, but nothing clear enough to understand.

"Brigadier," said the Commodore. "We have confirmation of ril-galas pods leaving the surface of Robesombel and docking with their carrier ships. By all appearances, they are abandoning the moon."

Once again, Arysis's three good eyes narrowed. She glanced around the valley, scratched Otyro's neck, looked up into the sky. Though it was still daylight, she could see some of the brighter stars above.

"Commodore," she said finally. "The ril-galas wouldn't be abandoning this moon unless they were called to be someplace else."

Though the deck plates shook violently beneath her feet, Lieutenant Commander Amira el Bahari stood her ground, hands clasped behind her back, stubbornly refusing to hold onto a railing to steady herself. In a moment, it would be over, she reminded herself. The ril-galas battleship before her was already rupturing with dozens of small explosions over its hull, and the glow from its primary beam weapon was fluctuating angrily.

In her peripheral vision, el Bahari saw the engines of the badly-damaged HMCS Goose Bay finally flare to life as the ship began to move away from the attacker that had very nearly destroyed it.

An attacker that had very quickly turned its attention to the ship that had intervened in the fight.

The ril-galas vessel wasn't allowed a final salvo.

"Forward rail guns, fire," said el Bahari.

Almost immediately she felt the thrum through the ship and saw the projectiles tear into the enemy. The ril-galas ship became a large, brief sphere of fire, and then became nothing but small pieces of flotsam.

The HMCS Vimy Ridge had added another chapter to its growing legend, though this time under a different commander.

The left corner of el Bahari's mouth twitched upward ever so slightly in a fleeting ghost of a smile. The destruction of a single ril-galas battleship was hardly as impressive as the victory against the so-called Hornets' Nest - the alien command station that had been the lynchpin of the ril-galas occupation of Earth - that victory had been achieved under the command of Finn Radko. She knew she was his equal, but the crew of the Vimy

Ridge... they were fiercely loyal to Radko. If she was to command them, she would need to prove herself to them.

And to do that-

"Commander, incoming communication from the Venn Shakara."

El Bahari nodded.

"Put it up here," she said, stepping over to the secondary sand table.

She was in the observation dome of the command deck, a reinforced transparent dome ringed and crossed by catwalks, with a platform in the centre holding a mirrored version of the holographic display interface - the sand table - that sat at the centre of the main command deck below.

"Admiral Rhekar," said el Bahari, when the channel flashed active in the small holographic window hovering over the table. "What can I do for you?"

"Commander. Have you any word on the condition of Commander Radko?"

Trying to hide her annoyance at being asked the same question - yet again, by yet another person - el Bahari forced a smile.

"Nothing yet, Admiral. I'm sure we'll have more information soon. Is that all?"

"We have reports from icaran space. The ril-galas appear to be in the process of a massive redeployment."

"Redeployment to where?" she asked, already knowing - or at least strongly suspecting - the answer.

"We compiled reports from several locations, once the pattern was first noticed on Robesombel," said Rhekar. "All of the retreating forces are following similar paths."

"To Earth."

"To Earth," said Rhekar.

"We dealt them a serious blow in destroying the Hornets' Nest," she said slowly. "But they still have a massive force."

"Our greatest advantage was that they had begun to spread themselves too thin. It was one of the reasons our assault was so successful."

Rubbing at her temple, el Bahari swore under her breath. It was amazing how quickly a stress headache could come on.

"If they consolidate and reinforce their occupation force on Earth, it will be just like the victory over the Hornets' Nest never happened. Thank you, Admiral, I'll be in touch shortly," she said, quickly ending the communication.

Just as quickly, she picked up her personal tablet and tapped in the code to activate one of her private channels. She sincerely hoped Ironhorse was available to pick up.

"Yes?"

She let out a breath she didn't realize she'd been holding.

"We don't have as much time as we thought. The ril-galas are pulling out of icaran space and heading here. What's your status?"

"Radko's going to be arrested once he's cleared to leave the hospital. Could be any time now, from what I hear."

"Keep me posted."

"Of course. The other situation seems to be moving forward as well."

"Damn it. How quickly?"

"Hard to tell. She plays her hand very close to the vest," said Ironhorse. "Honestly Amira, we may not know until it's already happening."

"I'm getting stress headaches again."

"I've had one for two fucking years."

"Fair. Take care of yourself," she said, and disconnected.

Giving herself a moment to breathe, and to close her eyes and calm herself, el Bahari locked her tablet - there were too many secrets there to leave it open - and headed down to the main command deck.

"Owens," she said, "we need to call back the fleet."

As she half expected, he didn't execute the order, but instead looked up at her questioningly. With self-control that amazed even her, el Bahari explained the information provided by the ic-arans before re-stating her order.

"We need to do this quickly, Owens. We have to assume they're redeploying from other, closer areas as well."

"Understood."

"Thank you. I'll be in my office, seeing if I can get anything out of Thor's Hammer," she said.

In what had almost become tradition, the connection sat idle for several minutes before Upshaw picked up.

Head of the private military contractor ATC Castle, newly-appointed Deputy Prime Minister of the Commonwealth, and unofficial overseer of the Commonwealth Armed Forces, Bianca Upshaw looked even more imperious than usual. Her hair and makeup were flawless, and while el Bahari couldn't help but marvel at the woman's ability to expand her own influence, the career naval officer disliked Upshaw more every time they spoke.

"Congratulations Amira," said Upshaw, with a smirk. "I told you I'd see that you got your own command when Radko was out of the picture."

"We need more ATC Castle resources deployed," said el Bahari, ignoring Upshaw's gloating. After all, she was commanding the Vimy Ridge because of Radko's injury, not because of anything Upshaw did.

Upshaw's eyes narrowed.

"The Deputy Prime Minister doesn't take orders from a Lieutenant Commander in the Commonwealth Navy."

"We're spread too thin out here, Bianca-"

"Commander el Bahari. We have icaran and udukiin warships on our doorstep. I will not pull resources from the defense of Thor's Hammer with those hostiles ready to pounce. Not to mention the continued threat of the Soviet presence," said Upshaw. "Honestly, Amira, I recruited you because I *thought* you could see the bigger picture. Was I wrong?"

"No," said el Bahari, shaking her head. "I do see the bigger picture. I'm just starting to feel that the picture you're seeing is from a paint-by-numbers book."

Upshaw's face reddened.

"You-"

"The ril-galas are preparing a counter-attack. The Vimy Ridge is sending you an information packet. We need to act on this, Bianca, or *none* of our plans are going to come to fruition," she said. "Resources. Ships. Soldiers."

But Upshaw had terminated the transmission.

Chaos.

It was both the best and only word Commander Finn Radko could conjure to describe the aftermath of what people had already begun to call the Battle of the Hornets' Nest. The battle itself had been mere hours old, and when the Hornets' Nest itself -- the orbital facility used by the ril-galas invaders to support their occupation of Earth -- had exploded in a spectacular, if brief, fireball, it seemed no one on either side of the conflict had known what to do.

For the ril-galas, destruction of their spaceborne stronghold had likely been unthinkable.

And though he was loathe to admit it, for many in Joint Task Force One - the name given the combined human, icaran, and udukiin fleet - Radko was certain that victory had been equally unthinkable.

Now, for the first time in the entirety of the war against the ril-galas, humanity had dealt the invaders a massive, destabilizing blow. Their ships had zoomed about aimlessly, without a specific target to defend, but JTF1 was similarly discombobulated, without a specific target to attack.

Though much of the immediate aftermath was a blur to Radko, owing to the injuries sustained to his left eye and head, he did remember el Bahari ordering some ships to fall back for defense of Thor's Hammer and for others to press the attack on the ril-galas forces. He also remembered her ordering someone to get him to a shuttle and then on to the medical facilities at Thor's Hammer.

Which is where he had awakened, groggy due to drugs, and feeling little pain for the same reason. The left side of his head, including his eye, was heavily bandaged.

"How long have I been out?" he asked the nearby nurse.

At least, he thought that's what he'd asked, but it came out more like a cross between a grunt and a belch, so he tried again.

The nurse, a young man who looked barely old enough to drink and likely only had to shave once a month, smiled and approached Radko's bed.

"Only about twelve hours, Commander," he said. "Your injuries weren't as bad as they first looked."

The young man hesitated.

"But...," said Radko, encouraging the nurse to continue.

"I... should probably get the doctor to-."

"Nurse..."

"Krogstad. Emil Krogstad."

"Nurse Krogstad," said Radko. "If it's just that I've lost my eye, you can tell me."

Krogstad nodded and Radko did the same.

"I could feel the damage. I knew it was a longshot that it could be saved. I should ask an udukiin for one," he said, smiling slightly. "They have six each, kind of unfair."

The nurse glanced uncomfortably to Radko's left, and then a familiar voice cut in.

"I would be happy to arrange that, though it would take some time – I do not currently have an inventory of udukiin biomatter."

"Doctor Frankenstein," said Radko, chuckling, then wincing because chuckling hurt. "Thanks for the offer, but it was a joke."

"Should it become a serious request, I will of course be at your service."

Though he'd spent time with the brill before – not much, and certainly not as much as Freyja – Radko was still in awe of the doctor. Not only was Frankenstein a highly intelligent isopodic life form about the size of a watermelon, piloting a mechanical exosuit, but he was doing so with enough dexterity to perform surgeries. The single, large photoreceptor in the head of the exosuit pulsed with soft blue light as Frankenstein spoke.

"I suspect you wish to enquire about the health of Freyja Sigurdsson. She is doing well, Commander. Her physical health remains optimal, though the stress of the war and more recently your injuries have had a negative impact on her mental health."

"Yeah, I suspect the Commonwealth is going to find itself in dire need of therapists when this is over."

Frankenstein bobbed his head in his approximation of a nod, but the kid – Nurse Krogstad – just stared.

"I know it wasn't that funny, but-"

"Sir... what's going on out there?"

It was Radko's turn to stare.

"What do you mean?" he asked.

"We're just hearing bits and pieces," said Krogstad. "We heard your ship came back. We heard that the icarans had made an incursion into Commonwealth space, and some people even said they saw an udukiin ship. And then the Royal Sovereign took off without clearance, and-"

"Stop," said Radko, wearily holding up a hand. "Just stop. What the hell do you mean the icarans *made an incursion?*"

Krogstad handed him a cup of water and Radko took a sip.

"Just that," said the nurse.

"It seems," said Frankenstein, "that information available on Thor's Hammer is... of questionable veracity."

Seeming confused by the statement, the nurse looked to Frankenstein, then back to Radko, then back and forth again before continuing.

"We're fighting for our lives and the icarans sound like they're trying to take advantage of that. And who knows what the udukiin are up to?"

"I do. I fucking know," said Radko. "This whole place is run by goddamned idiots."

"What do you... wait what are you doing?"

Tossing aside the bedsheet, Radko was relieved to see he was at least still wearing his pants.

"I'm getting up. Where are my boots and jacket?"

"You shouldn't be up and about!"

"And yet I'm doing it anyway. That's what happens with me, generally," said Radko.

"Yet another trait you and Freyja Sigurdsson share," said Frankenstein.

"So, we have two choices here, Krogstad. We can work together and you make sure I have whatever meds I need to keep functioning while I heal on the go, or I can leave without getting any meds and see what happens."

Again the nurse hesitated, and Radko sighed and slowly -- gingerly -- swung his legs over the side of the bed.

"In a perfect world, I'd rest here until I'm healed, but as I'm sure you've noticed, this isn't a perfect world. It's not even a world, it's a space station -- our actual world is still very much at risk, and people need to know the truth about that. They need to know the icarans and udukiin aren't invading, or using this crisis to snatch territory."

"They're not...?"

"They *joined* us. They fought alongside us, along with some pirates and some Soviets, and we took out the Hornets' Nest.

The Royal Sovereign helped as well, so what does that tell you about the people who wouldn't give it clearance to launch?"

Krogstad didn't answer, but Radko hadn't expected him to.

"We have an opportunity here to liberate Earth," he said. "But we'll miss our chance if we can't get past our own bullshit."

"We can't... we can't trust them, sir. They, I mean the udukiin *and* the icarans, have invasion fleets right on our doorstep."

Closing his eye, Radko tried his best to summon the faint shreds of patience that remained somewhere in the deep, dark corners of his soul.

Those shreds failed to respond to his summons.

"Krogstad, don't be a fucking tool. Do you think I'm just making this up? That I'm, what, trying to hide an alien invasion *while actually fighting an alien invasion?*"

In that instant, Radko could see the young nurse shut down. His mouth tightened into a thin line, he stood up a bit straighter, and an arrogance that Radko hadn't seen before settled into his eyes.

"I know what Deputy Prime Minister Upshaw says-"

"Oh, for fuck's sake..."

"I'm sorry sir," said Krogstad. "I'm going to have to-"

And then his eyes rolled back into his head and the nurse dropped to the floor with a thud. Behind him stood Frankenstein, a now-empty syringe in his hand.

"Sedatives can be very useful."

"I'll keep that in mind. Now, how about those medications that will keep me functional? I need to get the hell out of fantasyland here and back to the real world."

"I have already packed the necessaries here," said the doctor, handing Radko a small medical bag. "However, you cannot leave at the moment."

"And why is that?"

"There are ATC Castle guards outside who are under or-ders to arrest you as soon as you are well enough to be discharged. I believe Nurse Krogstad was about to advise them of your ambulatory ambitions."

3

As the ril-galas battleship erupted in an explosion that tore it in half along its spine, there was no cheering from the crew of Her Glorious Vengeance -- only nods, and low grunts of satisfaction.

Standing on the command deck with the German Shepherd Jaeger at her side, Freyja Sigurdsson clenched and unclenched her fists repeatedly, and fought constantly to stop herself from pacing like a caged animal. Though this was her ship, in her new role as Kaigor Kai Rii -- the Matriarch of the Three and supreme commander of the udukiin armed forces -- command of the vessel really belonged to Gholl Kai Rendrek. Despite the organic armour over her shoulders and arms, despite having inadvertently become bonded with an udukiin Matriarch, and despite her apparent embodiment of the centuries-old legend of the Kaigor Kai Rii, a War Matriarch who would lead the udukiin to their rightful place in the universe, Freyja Sigurdsson was out of her element aboard a starship.

She was a soldier. She belonged on solid ground, with a rifle in her hand. It was there that she knew she could do the most good, where her skills, honed over years in the Commonwealth Army before being forced out, could be best applied.

On the ground.

Yet there she was, in space.

Essentially doing nothing but watching events unfold.

The desire to do something herself, to lead a squad into the fray, was near to causing physical pain.

She badly needed to cause some damage.

"Any word on Radko?"

She knew the answer before it came from the udukiin responsible for communication with the rest of Joint Task Force One.

"Not yet, Kaigor Kai Rii."

Of course not.

It had only been ten minutes since she'd last asked.

Taking a deep breath, Sigurdsson let it out slowly, and forced herself to unclench her fists.

If Radko's surgery had gone badly, someone would have got word to her. She had to assume, then, that surgery had gone well and that Radko was resting. And as much as she may have wanted to return to Thor's Hammer to check on him herself, the continued presence of the three udukiin dreadnaughts in the vicinity of the wreckage of the Hornets' Nest played a major role in preventing the ril-galas from regrouping enough to threaten Thor's Hammer.

Like it or not, Sigurdsson had to stay where she was.

The question of whether she'd even be allowed to set foot on Thor's Hammer was moot, for now. The current government of the Commonwealth, in the persons of Prime Minister Rocco de Freitas and his newly-appointed Deputy Prime Minister Bianca Upshaw -- who still also ran the private military contractor ATC Castle, despite the obvious conflict of interest -- still considered both the icarans and the udukiin enemies, despite both having joined the fight against the ril-galas. With Sigurdsson having bonded with an udukiin Matriarch, and with the aptly named brill Doctor Frankenstein having replaced Sigurdsson's failing cybernetic arms with living icaran arms... her status with the Commonwealth was somewhat questionable. Being at once human, icaran, and udukiin had both given her the immense power of being anointed the Matriarch of the Three, but had potentially made her an enemy in the eyes of the very government she had served for most of her adult life.

Jaeger leaned against her leg and she smiled as she reached down to run her fingers across the top of his head the way he liked. Somehow, he always knew when she needed him.

"Thanks, pal," she said.

"Freyja Sigurdsson," said Gholl, the only crewmember of Her Glorious Vengeance to actually follow through on her request to be addressed by name rather than title. "Her Divine Retribution and Her Infallible Judgement report the ril-galas forces appear to be retreating from Earth orbit."

"Retreating, or regrouping for a counter-attack?"

"Unknown at this time. Though presumably, given their forces still planetside, they are re-grouping."

"For an attack against Thor's Hammer."

"It is what I would do in their place."

Sigurdsson nodded.

"Her Glorious Vengeance will pull back to Thor's Hammer and take up defensive position there," she said. "Tell the others to maintain their positions -- strike when able, but don't pursue. I don't want anyone getting caught in an ambush."

4

"We're almost in a worse position now than when the ril-galas blockade was in force."

Prime Minister Rocco de Freitas rubbed at his reddened face, then took another long sip of his drink.

"At least then we knew we had one enemy," he continued. "Now we've got icaran warships in Commonwealth space, the Soviets lurking around - even living on this station for fuck's sake - and those massive udukiin ships just sitting there. Hovering there, like they're staring at us. I've heard the udukiin eat their enemies."

Before Khaifa could attempt to inject some common sense, Upshaw stepped in to make things worse.

"It's also clear that we have enemies within, trying to destroy the Commonwealth. All three of those forces have tried to destroy us in the past."

"We've never been at war with the udukiin," said Khaifa with a sigh.

Though she was Director of the Ministry of Health and therefore part of the extant Commonwealth government, Nasrin Khaifa wasn't sure why she bothered with her continued attendance at these strategy meetings. Invariably, they were just de Freitas being paranoid and Upshaw stoking the fires.

"All three have tried to destroy us," repeated Upshaw, as if Khaifa hadn't spoken. "And won't hesitate to try again."

Seated at a large boardroom table, the attendees of the strategy meeting were de Freitas, Upshaw, Khaifa, and Admiral Mahoney. And, of course, various security, including Khaifa's personal security in the form of Captain Maximillian Ironhorse. Mahoney's presence was partly punitive. His decision to, without clearance, launch the Royal Sovereign - the largest warship in the Commonwealth fleet - to assist Radko's assault on the Hornets' Nest had cost him his role as commander of the armed forces. That role was now Upshaw's, and she enjoyed reminding him of it.

"I shouldn't need to point out," said Mahoney, "that the icarans and the Soviets both suffered serious casualties to eliminate that station and to create an opportunity for us to retake Earth."

He leaned forward, spreading his hands flat on the table.

"An opportunity we are currently letting slip by."

"Your opinion is noted, Admiral," said de Freitas with a dismissive wave. "But I have to think bigger. Fate of the Commonwealth. The sort of thing that's above your pay grade."

"With all due respect, Mister Prime Minister," said Khaifa, with very little respect evident in her tone, "the Commonwealth includes those people trapped on Earth by an alien occupation. What do you suppose *their* fate will be if we continue to just fortress ourselves inside the bulkheads of Thor's Hammer?"

"Doctor, your military experience is-"

"Essentially nothing, much like your own, Mister Prime Minister."

"I can assure you," said Upshaw, "that my own experience is-"

"Is coming up through the ATC Castle ranks as a PR representative, isn't it?"

Though she said nothing, the deep crimson creeping up Upshaw's neck was answer enough.

Khaifa stood.

"I apologise, I thought this was a strategy meeting not a verbal masturbation session."

"You're out of order, Doctor Khaifa."

"But her point isn't," said Mahoney. "We've all questioned his methods, but the fact remains that Radko has handed us a prime opportunity - maybe even a chance to win this war. We need to take it. We need to act, before the window to do so closes."

"And what, Admiral? Launch a full-scale assault on Earth?" said de Freitas. "Leave Thor's Hammer to the Soviets, and expose our backs to the other aliens?"

"It's naïve to think the icarans or the udukiin - especially the udukiin - are here out of some selfless desire to liberate Earth," said Upshaw, in the haughty tone that was quickly becoming her standard. "They are here to benefit themselves."

De Freitas nodded vigorously.

"They're here to move against the Commonwealth while we're at our weakest."

"I think we'll adjourn for today," said Upshaw, sliding her chair back from the table.

Her office door had barely closed behind them when Khaifa let loose.

"Every time I think those two can't possibly get any more stupid, they prove me wrong," she said, tossing her tablet onto her desk with a clunk. "No, you know what? I take it back. They aren't stupid. They're half willfully ignorant and half manipulative egomaniacs."

Truus Van Der Berg, former director of intelligence for the Commonwealth, sipped a coffee from her vantage point in a large armchair in the corner of the office. Khaifa had stopped asking how the spymaster had consistently been able to gain access to her private office.

"The meeting went well, I take it?" said Van Der Berg, one perfectly sculpted brow inching upward in amusement.

"Exceptionally."

"The doctor didn't ask me to kill anyone," said Ironhorse, crossing his arms and leaning up against the doorframe. "So that's something."

"It was close," said Khaifa. "They're still grasping so tightly to the idea that everyone is out to get us. I honestly don't think they'll be happy until they can build a metal sphere around this station and cut us off from the wider universe."

"They've even started ignoring Mahoney now," said Ironhorse.

Van Der Berg nodded and took another sip of coffee.

"Expected," she said. "Mahoney helped Radko. In their minds, he sided with their enemy, so he's not to be trusted."

Khaifa paced behind her desk.

"There seems to be a lot of that going around."

She stopped pacing and leaned forward, fingertips splayed on the surface of her desk.

"This can't continue," she said.

"Politics can be-"

"This isn't politics, Truus. Politics is just people being assholes to each other to score points with the electorate. This is far bigger than that."

"I concede the point," said Van Der Berg, nodding. "In which case, perhaps someone should do something about it...?"

Straightening up, Khaifa tugged at the hem of her jacket, then turned to look out her window into space. The rotation of Thor's Hammer was such that she could see Earth then. It was only about the size of a very large apple - she really missed apples - but it was there, hanging in the black, almost staring accusatorily at the station in which the de facto leaders of humanity remained safely ensconced. Treading water, too afraid of currents that didn't even exist.

No one knew yet how many humans had survived the initial invasion of Earth by the ril-galas, nor how many of those survivors had managed to survive until now. However, it was certain that those numbers dwindled daily as the ril-galas processing plants continued to turn captured humans into a food source for their army.

A chill went up Khaifa's spine every time she thought about it - which was frequently.

And yet the Prime Minister and Deputy Prime Minister were too afraid to act.

"Truus," she said, "any further word on Radko?"

"Recovering. The eye wasn't salvageable, but he's not medically ready for cybernetic replacement yet. He's expected to be cleared to leave the hospital shortly..."

"At which time ATC Castle will arrest him," said Khaifa.

"Yes."

Khaifa's tablet beeped, but after a quick glance she ignored it. Within an hour of the assault on the Hornets' Nest, Upshaw had begun station-wide news broadcasts at least twice a day. Propaganda, really, more than news. Normally she'd listen, just so she knew what spin Upshaw and de Freitas were putting on recent events and in what light they were painting the actions of the various parties, but she had no stomach for it that day. She knew that Van Der Berg had every broadcast transcribed in real time, so if anything important-

"Upshaw just announced formal charges against Finn Radko," said Van Der Berg.

For a long moment, Khaifa said nothing. She slowly sat down at her desk and steepled her fingers. Closing her eyes, she took a deep breath before opening them again.

"Truus, we're going to need access to those station-wide channels," she said. "Ironhorse, if you would be so kind as to fetch Mister Babacar?"

5

The flash in the night sky had been bright enough that Harley Ransom had known what had happened even before Sergeant Hobson had come to confirm -- the Hornets' Nest had been destroyed.

Word had spread quickly through the survivors and freedom fighters within the walls of Edinburgh Castle, and the hope that had begun to stir with the return of the lone surviving member of the British monarchy, the young King named Arthur, had begun to blossom. The Hornets' Nest was gone. The blockade around Earth was broken. Help might be coming.

The relief that Ransom felt was only partly due to the potential for help in fighting the ril-galas on Earth. The other part was due to the initial surge of hope being based on lies.

It wasn't just that Arthur wasn't King -- he was a Prince, and while no one else in his family remained among the living, the mechanisms for formal coronation were long gone.

No, the problem was that Arthur wasn't Arthur. The real Arthur was dead, and the Arthur that had presented himself as a symbol of hope to the denizens of the castle was an imposter.

Ransom ran a hand through her short red hair. She missed her long mass of curls, behind which she could easily hide her face and her emotions. But Arthur had short hair, and so she'd cut hers to suit.

She was lying to people, but it was for the right reasons. At least, that's what she told herself every minute she wore her disguise. Only a handful of people knew the truth, and they also knew the necessity of the lie: Arthur had wanted to surrender to the ril-galas. The people needed a symbol of hope, not a coward who would have destroyed what little hope they'd had left.

A handful of people knew why Arthur needed to be replaced after his death, but only one other person knew Ransom had killed him.

Leaning back in her chair, she looked over at the cot on the far side of the room, where Hunter lay sleeping, curled in the fetal position, facing away from Ransom, and covered by a heavy woolen blanket.

Ransom smiled. The blanket was hunter green. She hadn't noticed before.

The smile disappeared as quickly as it had come.

Hunter.

Poor, broken Hunter, who had given so much to keep people safe.

"I can hear you," said Hunter, wearily.

"I'm sorry," said Ransom. "I'll think quieter."

Hunter rolled over to face her friend and smiled slightly.

"It's okay, I know I'm broken."

Standing, Ransom crossed the room and lowered herself to sit on the floor beside Hunter, her back resting again the frame of the cot.

"We're all broken," she said. "It's just how much at this point."

"It feels like... something has broken off inside my mind," said Hunter after a lengthy silence. "It's floating around. Sometimes I can feel it and sometimes I can't."

"They say that people who lose limbs can sometimes still feel them itching. The limb they lost, I mean."

Hunter was again silent for a few moments before speaking.

"I still can't block anything out," she said. "I can hear everyone's thoughts. All at once, all the time. I can't control it anymore, it's always there. Sometimes I can't tell whether a thought is mine, or yours, or belongs to some person passing by in the hallway."

"Did you sleep at all?"

"A couple hours. Then I woke up wondering if now that the Hornets' Nest was gone, whether my husband would be one of the soldiers who comes down to help us."

Ransom frowned.

"I'm sorry, I had no idea you were married."

"I'm not. I don't know whose thought it was, but it felt like mine for a while," she said. "I feel like I may lose myself soon."

Ransom turned herself to face Hunter, feeling tears pricking at her eyes but determined not to let them win.

"Hunter, if ever you feel like you're losing yourself, you do what I told you. You find me. Wherever I am, you reach out and find me," she said, taking Hunter's hand and squeezing gently. "Because I know who you are. Maybe better than you ever have."

Hunter squeezed Ransom's hand in return, but said nothing.

The sun was almost up, which meant it was near time for Harley Ransom to disappear. Outside the four walls of the room she shared with Hunter, Harley Ransom no longer existed. Outside was the domain of Arthur, and while Arthur had placed Sergeant Walter Hobson in charge of defense, the King himself needed to make regular appearances -- a symbol was useless if no one ever saw it. And so it was time for Ransom to transform.

Which was, thankfully, a fairly straightforward process.

"Let me help," said Hunter, sitting up slowly and swinging her legs over the side of the cot, her bare feet resting on the cool stone floor.

"No, you need to rest."

"Too noisy to rest," said Hunter, tapping her temple. "Everyone is waking up."

Grudgingly, Ransom accepted the help.

First, the impossibly tight undershirt that would keep Ransom's chest as flat and static as possible. Then the pants into which Greaves had -- with a chuckle -- sewn an old pair of socks to give the appearance of a bulge at the front. Then a slightly loose shirt that would help disguise body shape, though her broad shoulders and athlete's build helped a great deal in supporting the illusion.

Clearing her throat several times, Ransom accepted a lukewarm mug of tea from Hunter -- what remained of the mug she herself had brought Hunter earlier -- and took a sip.

When she spoke again, Ransom was gone.

"Thank you, Hunter," said Arthur.

Hunter forced a smile.

"Long live the King."

6

When el Bahari's tablet buzzed in her hand - the telltale three quick vibrations that indicated a secure call from Ironhorse - she almost ignored it. Freyja Sigurdsson, the Kaigor Kai Rii of the udukiin, and her honour guard had just arrived aboard the Vimy Ridge and el Bahari had enough on her plate to brief them on what was happening with the ril-galas. But she also knew that Ironhorse wasn't prone to frivolous communication.

She activated the link.

"Yes?"

"It's happening," he said.

The transmission, as always, was audio-only, but she could tell he was moving through the station and moving quickly.

"Damn it. How much time do we have?"

"Time's up, Amira. Upshaw just showed her hand - the charges against Radko have been made public."

El Bahari swore.

"For an intelligent woman, she can be remarkably stupid," she said. "Khaifa's reaction?"

"As expected. I'm on an errand to get the lawyer now."

"Make sure your people are in place. We'll only have one shot at managing this."

"Don't worry, we're ready."

Closing the connection, el Bahari took a moment to compose herself before leaving her office. When she'd first set this plan in motion, it had seemed solid, almost foolproof. But now, she was beginning to realize just how much of it was predicated on everything going right - and odds were against that.

"Mister Owens, you remain in command while I brief the udukiin," she said as she passed through the command deck.

As she made her way through the ship to the largely abandoned officers' lounge where the udukiin were waiting, a crew member stepped into her path forcing her to stop.

"Commander el Bahari," he said. "I need a word."

She wanted to glare at him - maybe even swear at him - but she was the commanding officer of the Vimy Ridge, and had to behave like it.

"Certainly. Specialist... Kidd, isn't it?"

"Yessir."

"What can I do for you, Specialist?"

Whatever it was, she dearly hoped he'd be quick about it. Aside from her own, more secret plans, she did have a war to wage after all.

Kidd glanced around in a way that made el Bahari suddenly pay much closer attention.

"Miss Upshaw isn't happy with you right now."

Of course.

Why hadn't she thought that ATC Castle wouldn't settle for having one set of eyes and ears on the Vimy Ridge to keep track of Radko?

"Why would Bianca Upshaw's moods matter to me, Specialist Kidd?" she said, adding a dash on impatience to her tone. "And why would you be aware of her mindset?"

"I think you know the answers to both of those questions," he said with a smile el Bahari immediately disliked.

It was a smile she saw all too frequently throughout her career. The smile of a white male, secure in his superiority over a brown woman. She fought the urge to punch him physically, instead doing so verbally.

"*Specialist* Kidd, as commanding officer of the HMCS Vimy Ridge I would strongly recommend you choose both your words and your next course of action with extreme caution. Whatever interactions I may have with Bianca Upshaw are none of your concern, and I shouldn't need to remind you that we are currently fighting a war."

Without giving him a chance to respond, she stepped in close enough that his smile turned into an uncomfortable frown.

"I should also not have to remind you that I am not a person of which you wish to make an enemy," she said. "Now, Specialist Kidd, get the fuck out of my way."

Thankfully, he did. Frankly, the Commander wasn't certain what her next move would have been otherwise - Kidd was nearly a head taller than her and outweighed her by a fair margin. El Bahari would never have been able to beat him in a fair fight if it came to that - not that she would have fought fairly - and she was still uncertain as to how much the rest of the Vimy Ridge crew would have her back in an altercation.

But that was a problem for another day.

"I apologise for the delay," she said as she stepped into the lounge. "A crew member had an issue that required my attention."

Only four other beings were in the lounge. Kestrel Cagliari was there, at el Bahari's request - though technically a civilian, Cagliari was in charge of the Commonwealth's advanced starfighter group known as Outlaw Squadron, but more importantly to the current situation, was a friend of Freyja Sigurdsson and Finn Radko who could act as a buffer between el Bahari and the Kaigor Kai Rii. There were two udukiin, of course, whose names el Bahari didn't know.

And there was the Kaigor Kai Rii herself: Freyja Sigurdsson.

El Bahari imagined that Sigurdsson had been an imposing figure even before the events of the last two years had transformed her into something... something slightly more than human. Now, with her irreparably damaged arms having been replaced with those of an icaran, and her psychic bonding with an udukiin Matriarch, Sigurdsson had, by all accounts, fulfilled an ancient prophecy. Kaigor Kai Rii. The Matriarch of the three - udukiin, icaran, and human - a War Matriarch who would lead the udukiin to their rightful place in the universe.

Most were not particularly excited to see where that thought process landed.

For now, it was enough that the War Matriarch was on the side of the Commonwealth.

"You said you had news," said Sigurdsson, her voice tight with stress. "But it was best delivered in person."

"Yes," said el Bahari, but then realized what Sigurdsson must be thinking. "Oh, no, I'm sorry - Radko is fine. I mean, he only has one eye, but he's recovering."

"Fucking balls," said Sigurdsson, running a hand over her face. "You almost gave me a heart attack."

"I am sorry. It didn't even occur to me... the information I wanted to discuss is related to the war effort," she said.

Cagliari sprawled out in one of the armchairs, one leg dangling over an arm.

"We couldn't have just sent an info packet?"

"Some of this information... is sensitive. And cannot leave this room."

She tried not to be intimidated by Sigurdsson's narrowed gaze.

"I'm listening."

El Bahari nodded, then began going through in detail the ril-galas redeployment witnessed by the icarans, and backed up by data from the outermost Commonwealth patrols.

"I would ask you to reach out to your armed forces as well," she said. "It seems clear the ril-galas are pulling back to reinforce their occupation of Earth, but I'd like to know if they're retreating from everywhere."

"They are," said Sigurdsson, gazing out the window toward Thor's Hammer for a brief moment. "They left the Shattered World a few days ago, but we just got confirmation about an hour ago that the small fleet they had within the Udukiin Priex had left at high speed. We have a scout ship shadowing them."

"They're heading toward Earth," said el Bahari.

Sigurdsson just nodded.

"We need to pull back ourselves," said el Bahari. "Create a tighter fleet."

"Agreed. But we also need to start talking about what no one seems to want to talk about," said Sigurdsson.

"Taking back Earth," said Cagliari, running a hand through her blue hair. "That was supposed to be the endgame here."

"Agreed," said el Bahari, nodding. "But in order to have success down there, we need to be secure in our positioning up here."

There was silence for a moment, and Sigurdsson sat down on a couch, brow furrowed in thought. After a moment, she looked up at el Bahari and raised a brow.

"None of this was sensitive enough to require a face-to-face meeting."

"No," said el Bahari with a small sigh. "I wanted to tell you in person that an arrest warrant has been issued for Radko. The moment he's discharged from medical, he'll be taken into custody."

Sigurdsson shot to her feet and el Bahari took an involuntary step backward.

"What? The fuck would he be arrested for?"

"Currently, dereliction of duty and willful destruction of Commonwealth property, though I think we can safely assume that we're heading along the Cortez path here. He hasn't been arrested yet," said el Bahari. "But from what I understand, the order has been given."

"There's no way I'm letting this happen."

"There would be a chance to fight the charges, right?" said Cagliari.

"Did Cortez get a fair shot at that?" said Sigurdsson, through gritted teeth. "I'm going in there and getting him out. Like Radko wanted to do with Cortez."

El Bahari shook her head slowly.

"No."

"What do you mean no?"

"You can't do that."

"Who the fuck are you to give me orders? The only reason you're even in command is because Radko's in the hospital. Or it that the reason you don't want me to march in there and get him out? You want to stay in command."

Through her short time in command of the Vimy Ridge, el Bahari had kept so much frustration bottled up, tried so hard to *not* give anyone reason to think she wasn't up to the challenge. But this was not the time to keep things bottled up, and her encounter with Kidd had put her in a mood, so she let it all loose.

"Whether I'm in command of the Vimy Ridge or not doesn't change the fact that what you're proposing is moronic," she said, jabbing a finger into Sigurdsson's armoured chest. "As the War Matriarch I would expect more strategic thinking from you, and less blundering around, throwing furniture.

While you may be human - mostly - you are also the military leader of an alien civilization. The level of paranoia and mistrust at the upper levels of the Commonwealth government is precarious, Sigurdsson. The continued presence of the Soviets was already having an effect, but now with icaran and udukiin warships inside the Solar system? The situation is a powder keg, and I would thank you to not start tossing around lit matches."

"So, we should leave Radko to those same paranoid shitbags, to prevent them from becoming *more* paranoid? Whose side are you on?"

"The question that will be asked," said el Bahari, sharply, "is whose side *you're* on, Sigurdsson. If you lead an armed group of udukiin in what is essentially a military action against the last stronghold of the Commonwealth - of humanity, really - how do you think that will look? Not just to de Freitas and Upshaw, but to humanity in general?"

Sigurdsson just glared, but Cagliari answered.

"The udukiin taking advantage of us. Kicking us when we're down."

"And because of the paranoia, it will be considered an act of war, regardless of your actual intentions."

El Bahari took a deep breath and rubbed at her eyes. She was tired, physically and emotionally, and she was tired of having this conversation.

"We are barely gaining ground in the war we're currently fighting, Freyja," she said, softening her tone. "Please don't give those morons an excuse to start a second one. Humanity will not survive it."

"The udukiin wouldn't start a war with-"

"This is how wars start. One faction does something ill-advised and the other faction has to respond."

She paused, hesitating. Then sighed. She was going to have to discuss it sooner or later - it may as well be to prevent a second war.

"I have agents on Thor's Hammer. People who have been keeping me apprised of the situation, and who have been... working on my behalf, unofficially," she said. "I need you to trust me when I say that the Radko situation is in hand."

For a moment, Sigurdsson just stared and el Bahari thought there might be a fist heading in her direction. Thankfully, there wasn't.

"In hand how?"

"You'll know the details soon enough," she said. "In the meantime, we need to focus on the war, and the redeployment of the ril-galas. Can we continue to count on udukiin military support?"

Sigurdsson nodded.

"Of course," she said, then paused for a moment. "Have you spoken to him?"

"Radko? No, I haven't had time to try."

"I tried to visit him, but they wouldn't give me clearance to dock."

Suddenly Sigurdsson seemed a different person. More human, less Kaigor Kai Rii. More like the somewhat lost soul el Bahari had first met on the Vimy Ridge when Sigurdsson had been involuntarily discharged from the Commonwealth Army.

"They don't even want the Soviets there," said el Bahari. "I'm not surprised they refused you. I can try to get a message to him if you like."

"Just tell him... nothing. Never mind."

Her demeanour became more formal and she nodded once.

"I'll have our dreadnaughts pull back into tighter formation. But we also need to start talking about making planetfall on Earth. Sooner or later, this has to be a ground war."

"Agreed. Once we've set our new defensive formations, that should be priority one," said el Bahari. "And since you have more experience in ground-based combat, I'd appreciate you spearheading those plans."

Sigurdsson nodded.

"I can do that."

7

"So that's where we stand," said Khaifa.

It wasn't a question so much as a statement, though she still made eye contact with each person in the room, inviting any questions they may have had. Van Der Berg was there, as was Mahoney. Amadou Babacar, the constitutional law expert, had come, and Ironhorse had, after a brief absence which had, to everyone's delight, included obtaining another bag of cookies, returned.

"It is," said Mahoney.

Van Der Berg nodded.

Babacar sipped his coffee, then also nodded.

"Our arguments are legally sound," he said.

"And morally justified," added Mahoney.

Khaifa picked up a cookie then set it down again. The idea of eating was more attractive than the reality of it - her stomach was in knots.

"If we proceed," she said, still keeping up the pretense that the decision hadn't yet been made, "how much push-back can we expect?"

"The civilian population of Thor's Hammer has been spoon-fed Upshaw's propaganda for months," said Van Der Berg. "My people have been trying to counteract its influence, but I will be honest, it's hard to say what traction we've had in such a short period. The good news is that by all accounts, it appears that the Commonwealth Armed Forces would... not be opposed to our actions."

"I can confirm that those I have spoken with are not comfortable with the current direction," said Mahoney.

"I know this stuff is above my pay grade," said Ironhorse from his vantage point in the corner, "but I'm not sure it was ever the Commonwealth military we needed to worry about."

"ATC Castle," said Khaifa.

The operators employed by the private military contractor would likely rally behind Upshaw, but there was precedent to think otherwise. Dozens of ATC Castle operators had abandoned their contracts to join the war effort under Radko. Khaifa had to believe that would be the case again, partly due to her faith in humanity's ability to come together in times of need - though that faith seemed misplaced recently - and partly due to her need for it to be true. No one could afford a civil war.

"We will hope for the best," she said. "But plan for the worst. With that being said... are we ready for this?"

"My assets are in place and ready," said Van Der Berg. "And we have access to the broadcast channels whenever you're ready."

"Security is taken care of," said Ironhorse.

"And I've taken care of a contingency plan," said Mahoney. "Just to be safe."

Khaifa frowned.

"What kind of contingency plan?"

"Thanks to some programming advice from Miss Cagliari, the Royal Sovereign is experiencing cascading system outages. Currently its airlocks will not open," he said with a small smile. "So my hand-picked crew is not able to allow the ATC Castle maintenance teams on board."

Khaifa nodded, then closed her eyes and took two deep breaths.

"I don't want this," she said softly.

Mahoney leaned forward.

"That's exactly why it's you that must do it," he said.

"I know," she said with a heavy sigh. "I know."

8

"I can't stay here forever," said Radko.

The nurse, Krogstad, said nothing, as having only recently awoken from the tranquilizer Frankenstein had given him. But regardless, he replayed Upshaw's announcement of the charges against Radko.

Looking to Frankenstein, Radko pointed to Krogstad.

"Can we sedate him again?"

"I will prepare another dose."

"No," said Krogstad, backing up a few steps, suddenly more alert. "You can't do that!"

"Then go sit in the corner and shut up," said Radko. "Doctor, I can't stay here forever."

"That is true," said Frankenstein, as Krogstad retreated sullenly to flop into a chair across the room. "Yet the fact remains that you will be arrested upon discharge."

"And if you don't formally discharge me...?"

"There would still be ATC Castle personnel outside the medical facility. Whether formally discharged or not, your departure would no doubt be interpreted as a discharge."

Radko's sigh turned into a growl of annoyance. A war. A significant victory. A small opening, a chance that they could retake Earth. And still bullshit and petty vendettas were the rule of the day, keeping humanity from achieving something truly meaningful.

Voices in the hall.

Radko and Frankenstein looked toward the door, Radko frowning.

Krogstad looked up hopefully, and didn't bother supressing his grin when the doors parted to reveal two fully armoured ATC Castle operators, visors down to obscure their faces. Two other members of the military contractor – presumably the ones who had been standing guard, as neither was as well-armed or armoured as the newcomers – disappeared around the bend in the corridor, on their way elsewhere.

The pair of operators entered the med bay, and stopped directly in front of Radko, standing rigidly, almost as if they were actively trying not to salute.

"Commander Radko," said the taller of the two. "We'll need you to come with us, sir."

While it was good of them to use his rank and address him as 'sir,' Radko still didn't move.

The two ATC Castle soldiers exchanged glances, seemingly unsure how to proceed.

"Commander," said the one clearly designated as the spokesman, "I need you to come with us. Now."

The urge to tell the pair of operators where he would suggest they store their orders was strong; Radko closed his eye and took a deep breath to quell it. These were, after all, soldiers following orders; they were people doing the job they'd been hired to do. Stability in the overwhelmingly unstable times they'd all found themselves was something every one of them – except maybe Sigurdsson, who seemed at times the embodiment of chaos – desperately clung to. Many ATC Castle people over the course of the war had traded in their contractor status to join the Commonwealth Armed Forces, but many had stayed for that stability. Stability of the day-to-day, but also of the pay-to-pay, which, despite everything, was still important to people who had families to feed.

That ATC Castle employment did not automatically make someone an equivalent to Upshaw was something of which Radko frequently reminded himself.

"Fine," he said, finally, "let's get this bullshit underway."

Again, el Bahari found Specialist Kidd standing in her path.

"Kidd. You're in my way again."

"I've been talking with Upshaw again," he said, after a quick glance around to make sure he wouldn't be overheard. "She has questions."

"I'm sure."

Stepping around Kidd, el Bahari continued on her way through the corridors of the Vimy Ridge. Kidd, unfortunately, kept pace, and even less pleasantly, kept talking.

"She wants to know why you haven't returned the ship to Thor's Hammer."

"I should think that would be obvious, given that we've been in combat almost continually since the Hornets' Nest was destroyed. Unless I've missed some sort of peace agreement being reached with the ril-galas, we are still at war," she said. "Is that the case, Specialist? Has Upshaw been negotiating with the occupation force?"

Kidd scowled.

"Upshaw isn't the one who was negotiating with enemies of the Commonwealth - that was Radko," he said. "And that's her next question: you sent our ships on a wild goose chase."

"That isn't a question."

Of course, she knew exactly what he was talking about. The info she had passed along to Upshaw - the purported rendezvous site Radko had arranged for what would become the task force he led against the Hornets' Nest - had been incorrect, and intentionally so. She'd directed the ATC Castle strike force, intended to take Radko into custody and place el Bahari in command of the Vimy Ridge, to an abandoned pirate base. It also wasn't lost on el Bahari that Kidd, a career enlisted man in the Commonwealth Navy, had referred to a group of ATC Castle vessels as *our ships*.

"You know what I mean," said Kidd, anger creeping into his voice. "She wants to know why you lied. She feels you may have lost sight of-"

Suddenly she spun on him and shoved him hard up against the bulkhead. He was larger than her, but her anger had grown larger than them both.

"Choose your next words very carefully, Kidd, or you may find yourself floating home."

"I just-"

"I lied because Upshaw is letting her vendetta against Radko cloud her judgement, and yes, you go ahead and tell her I said that. Whatever agreement I had with Upshaw, I was never going to sabotage the Commonwealth or its defense," she said.

"So, you're a liar and a traitor," said Kidd.

At that, el Bahari actually laughed.

"I've been called much worse by much better people."

She started on her way again, but Kidd called after her.

"She's not going to be happy about this!"

"I suspect that very shortly, there are going to be many, many things Bianca Upshaw is unhappy with," she said.

"What's that supposed to mean?"

"Fuck off, Specialist Kidd."

Understandably, el Bahari was in a foul mood when she reached the command deck and, after a cursory round of greetings, retreated to the observation dome. Generally, the dome was empty, an area for the commanding officer and first officer to see things from a different perspective, while the bulk of the actual ship operations took place on the main command deck. El Bahari was glad to be the only occupant of the dome for the time being. Events were unfolding much faster now than she'd anticipated, and Kidd having inserted himself in the equation added another wrinkle. He was in the unique position of being able to speak of her involvement with ATC Castle, regardless of how tenuous that relationship may have become. Doing so would reveal his own deception, but if Upshaw was backing him the prospect of being kicked out of the Navy to land a cushy job at the military contractor may embolden him.

Regardless, that wasn't something she could worry about presently.

The developments on the station and with the ril-galas were a more pressing concern.

"Commander. A word?"

Owens had approached without her notice. It was unusual for el Bahari to be so unaware of her surroundings. She'd have to find a way to regain her focus.

"Of course, Owens. What can I do for you?"

Tablet in hand and concerned look on his face, Owens seemed to weigh his words before speaking.

"One of our communications techs came to me a few hours ago. He found some...," he paused for a moment, frowning, then shrugged, "I can't remember the terminology - an irregularity in our comms array. Basically a tiny signal being sent out intermittently through our array, but hidden."

With much effort, el Bahari was able to keep her body language and facial expression under control.

"Not hidden well enough, apparently."

"No, but almost. The signal was encrypted, but we've tracked its destination."

"Thor's Hammer," said el Bahari.

Owens didn't react, which struck el Bahari as both odd and concerning. He'd been expecting her to know, which means they'd likely have also traced the origin point of the transmissions. If so, the next portion of this discussion could be difficult, to say the least.

"Yes, Thor's Hammer," he said. "We also traced their origin point aboard the Vimy Ridge."

El Bahari sighed.

"Mister Owens, I have neither the time, nor the patience, to play a game of twenty questions. If you have information to share, do it."

It was then that she noticed the two soldiers positioned at the entrance to the command deck.

How many times had she told herself that keeping as many secrets as she was, working as many angles as she was, that an accident was bound to happen? That no matter how careful she tried to be, one mistake could sink the entire plan. Her consolation was that the events she had helped set in motion - or had helped push along - were already beyond the point of being stopped. Owens could do whatever he wanted to her and it wouldn't matter in the slightest.

So, she thought bitterly, fuck it.

"I'll save you the trouble," she said, waving a hand dismissively. "I have been in touch with individuals aboard Thor's Hammer since being assigned to the Vimy Ridge. And yes, those individuals include ATC Castle personnel - first Edward Vossek, and then Bianca Upshaw directly."

His face darkening, Owens tapped a command into his tablet and the two soldiers began moving toward the observation deck level. Though they were moving at a casual pace - she presumed so as to not attract undue attention - el Bahari noticed that both rested a hand on their holstered sidearm.

"You sold us out," said Owens. "For what? To get command of a ship again? To get a lucrative contract with Castle?"

"I don't owe you an explanation for my actions, Mister Owens," she said, impressing herself with how calm and reasonable she sounded. "But no, despite what I'm sure you and everyone like you would love to believe, I'm not nearly that self-serving."

"I find that hard to believe."

"Of course you do. You're very good at your job, Owens, but you lack imagination."

The soldiers had reached the observation deck. Very shortly, she'd be arrested on suspicion of... what, exactly, she wasn't sure. Upshaw was the Deputy Prime Minister, so could el Bahari really be accused of treason?

"I didn't trust Radko," she said, knowing it would buy her some time to hopefully find a way out of the situation. "I didn't trust his apparent cozy relationship with our traditional enemies, and I was concerned about his willingness to operate outside his authority. Even you would have to admit that from the outside, what he had been doing could look like an attempted power grab."

Owens said nothing, but that was what el Bahari had expected. He was good at his job, but he was also a blind Radko loyalist. Though from what she'd heard, that certainly wasn't the case originally.

"So, yes, I was reporting back to Upshaw about Radko-"

"You admit you sold us out."

"Open your fucking eyes," she said, slamming her palm down on the edge of the sand table. "Has ATC Castle made any moves against the Vimy Ridge? Have they blocked anything we've tried to accomplish? When I had the information about where Radko was assembling Joint Task Force One, did the ATC Castle strike group intercept us?"

"No."

"And where, pray tell, did that strike group go, Mister Owens?"

"The old pirate base at Cassandra Hajek."

"Which is *hours away* from our actual rendezvous site," she hissed. "Did you think they just got lost along the way? They went to the pirate base because that's where I told them the Vimy Ridge was headed."

There was a soldier on either side of her then, and several members of the crew had noticed.

"So," said Owens, "you expect me to believe you've been feeding them false information, then? There are several of these transmissions every day, Commander. That's a lot of false info."

"Not all of it would be false," she said, feeling her heartrate increasing. "If it was all false, the game would have been up too quickly. It's also not all me, as I'm sure your trace would indicate."

"They don't all originate on your tablet," he conceded. "But the remaining ones don't have a clear origin source, so they could still have been sent by you."

Suddenly, something clicked. El Bahari blinked twice, then narrowed her eyes.

"A communications tech brought you this information. And I'm assuming he is also the one who traced the one set of transmissions to me, and determined the other transmissions were untraceable?"

Though he said nothing in response, el Bahari took it as confirmation.

"Specialist Markus Kidd," she said.

Owens blinked.

That little bastard.

"He's confronted me several times," she continued. "Asking questions on Upshaw's behalf. You can ask some of the crew – our encounters weren't private, nor were they particularly friendly. I'm sure the stories are spreading in the mess hall as we speak."

Processing this new information seemed to take Owens longer than should be necessary, in el Bahari's mind.

"You're trying to tell me that Kidd is working for ATC Castle, and he's giving me this information as what? Some kind of revenge for you going against Upshaw?"

"I'm not *trying* to tell you anything - I'm giving you facts. What you do with them is your own problem," she said. "As is Specialist Kidd. Because while I have been feeding selective misinformation back to Thor's Hammer, you can rest assured he has not."

Owens was hesitating now, trying to parse all the new information she was giving him. Which was excellent news for her.

"Commander Owens!" someone shouted from below. "ATC Castle has just arrested Commander Radko!"

"What?"

"It was just on the feed we get from Thor's Hammer-"

"The propaganda feed," said el Bahari.

"-that ATC Castle personnel acting on orders from the Commonwealth government have arrested Finn Radko."

Spinning back to el Bahari, Owens wore a look of pure outrage.

"This was your endgame all along, wasn't it? Get Radko out of the way so you could take command of the Vimy Ridge. You had this whole thing planned out with Upshaw."

"ATC Castle has not arrested Radko," she said, as evenly as possible given that the soldiers on either side of her were gripping their holstered sidearms rather than simply resting their hands on them.

Before Owens could speak again, his tablet bleeped. He frowned as he read the message, then looked back at el Bahari with narrowed eyes.

"Armed ATC Castle soldiers just lead Radko away from the hospital," he said, tapping an accusatory finger on his tablet screen. "We have a source inside the hospital who confirms it."

"ATC Castle has not arrested Radko," repeated el Bahari.

Her projection of outward calm was starting to falter. She'd balled her left hand into fists at some point without realizing it, and her right, clutching her tablet, was damp with sweat. Her heart was beating so fast she could feel it in her chest.

And then el Bahari's tablet buzzed three times in rapid succession.

As she lifted the tablet to answer, Owens grabbed for it. El Bahari held on, but then the soldiers yanked her back - but not before she'd activated the link.

"Who are you contacting?" said Owens.

"Who the fuck is this?" came the disembodied voice of Ironhorse.

"It's all right, Max, I'm here," said el Bahari. "This is Lieutenant Commander Owens, my second in command on the Vimy Ridge."

She stared at Owens for a moment, daring him to contradict her but banking on him being too confused and too curious to do so.

And she was correct.

"Owens, this is my brother-in-law, Max."

"Captain Maximillian Ironhorse, Revelstoke Rangers of the Commonwealth Armed Forces," said Ironhorse.

"Max, if you would be so kind as to advise Mister Owens of your current situation...?"

"We have Commander Radko."

"What... what do you mean you have Radko?" said Owens.

He was clearly struggling to understand what was happening, and el Bahari - if only for a brief moment - felt sorry for him.

"Intercepted the ATC Castle goon squad and replaced them with my own men," said Ironhorse. "Radko was never arrested, because ATC Castle never got to him. Just looked like they did."

"Stolen armour," said el Bahari, just to make sure everyone was on the same page.

"It's okay, Owens."

This time, it was Radko's voice filtering through the tablet.

"I'm fine, el Bahari is telling the truth," he continued. "Ironhorse just saved my ass."

Though she shook her head in derision, el Bahari couldn't help but smile slightly at the vindication. But the smile disappeared as quickly as it came, and she directed the scowl that replaced it at first the soldiers flanking her - who rightly backed off - and then at Owens.

She snatched her tablet out of his hands.

"Max, proceed as planned. And stay safe."

"Understood."

The connection terminated, and el Bahari looked up to see Owens opening his mouth to say something.

"No," she said, and he closed his mouth. "Have Kidd taken into custody. I will advise Sigurdsson of recent developments. Then we plan our next steps."

"And then you-"

"And then you shut the fuck up and do your job, and I pretend not to notice that this is the *second time* you've tried to remove the rightful commanding officer of this vessel."

"Commander el Bahari!"

She looked down into the main command deck with a frown. It was the same crew member who had shouted about Radko's arrest.

"We're getting another transmission from Thor's Hammer... *on all channels*, sir," he said, visibly confused. "And Commander, it's Doctor Khaifa."

10

"Where the hell is this coming from?"

Storming into the ATC Castle command centre, Bianca Upshaw threw glares around like daggers, her face reddening in anger beneath her makeup. Her eyes finally settled on Vossek, who weathered it better than most.

"We don't know," he said. "But we're totally locked out of the system."

"What do you mean locked out? We can't cut her off?"

Vossek just shook his head and returned his attention to the video feed.

"...clear to me that, as we have learned time and time again over the course of human history, dangerous times call for difficult decisions to be made," Khaifa was saying. "And to be clear, this is neither a decision I want to make, nor is it one I make lightly."

Approaching one of several screens displaying Khaifa - a simple head-and-shoulders shot, with a nondescript background that could have been anywhere on Thor's Hammer - Upshaw leaned in closer, as if proximity to the image would give her some insight as to how to terminate it.

"Is it pre-recorded?"

"It looks to be going out live," said Vossek. "On every single broadcast channel."

Upshaw spun to face him, her eyes wide.

"All of them?"

That would mean not just Thor's Hammer, but every-where. Commonwealth ships, Soviet ships, the few human colonies that remained, even the icaran and udukiin ships would be able to pick it up. Even... even Earth.

"What the hell is she about to do...?"

"We are facing a crisis the scale of which we have never seen," said Khaifa, her voice clear and strong, but her face carrying a look of concern. "And when I say we, I mean all of us. Commonwealth, Soviet, icaran, udukiin... we have all been touched by this crisis, this invasion. We have all lost friends and family, and humanity is in danger of losing its homeworld. The ril-galas invasion has pushed us to the brink, with the very real possibility that without further action, Earth will never belong to humanity again, and that those who remain trapped there will be killed. And processed. And consumed."

The doctor paused for a moment, but no one in the control room spoke or moved at all.

"This is not political spin. This is not propaganda. These are facts," she said. "And yet in the face of these facts, Prime Minister Rocco de Freitas has, rather than focus his energies on fighting the ril-galas occupation, become a puppet to ATC Castle executive Bianca Upshaw as she pursues corporate interests and her personal vendetta against Commander Finn Radko."

Upshaw jerked backward as if she'd been shot. Her mouth began moving, but no sound came out.

And still Khaifa continued.

"After appointing Upshaw to the position of Deputy Prime Minister in contravention of the Constitution he was elected to uphold, the Prime Minister has repeatedly and knowingly directed resources away from the war effort and, in conjunction with Upshaw, launched a full-blown propaganda campaign to foment mistrust between the Commonwealth and the other people affected by this war, and even within the Commonwealth itself," she said, her voice rising slightly in her indignation. "Even going so far as to label Finn Radko - a man whose bravery and determination to protect us every single one of you knows very well - an enemy of the state. You heard it from Upshaw's own lips not an hour ago, the announcement that Radko was being arrested. Radko, who liberated this station from the ril-galas blockade. Radko, who led the assault that destroyed the Hornets' Nest. Radko, who, until not long ago, was resting in our hospital after losing an eye fighting for us. But despite what de Freitas and Upshaw would like you to think, this is not now, nor has it ever been about Finn Radko."

"Vossek," said Upshaw, her voice barely a croak. "Vossek, I need you to kill her."

Vossek turned to her, his eyebrows jumping upward.

"I beg your pardon?"

"Find her and kill her," said Upshaw.

"What this is really about is the future," Khaifa was saying. "Our future. The kind of future in which we would like to live. The Prime Minister and the corporate executive pulling his strings would have you believe that the Commonwealth is besieged on all sides, that we are an island, surrounded by aliens who wish us harm. That even our fellow humans, the Soviets, have us in their crosshairs, just waiting to strike. But you are being lied to."

Khaifa paused then, to allow the statement to sink in. Not even Upshaw spoke. Not because she didn't want to, but because no words would come.

"The Commonwealth is besieged only by the ril-galas. As are the Soviets. As are the icarans and the udukiin, and others. They have all come here, to our home system, to help us break the ril-galas grip on Earth. Together we defeated the Hornets' Nest; together we created an opening for us to take back the home planet of mankind."

"Fuck," said Upshaw.

"But instead, our leadership has chosen to isolate us, to try to break apart the alliance that was built, to wield power like a club over petty grievances. And that, my fellow citizens of the Commonwealth, *is not leadership*."

"Oh, fuck..."

"It is paranoia. It is, at best, selfishness. At worst, it is a betrayal of humanity."

"Somebody fucking do something!"

"Prime Minister de Freitas and his unconstitutionally appointed Deputy Prime Minister Bianca Upshaw, through their extreme paranoia, have weakened the war effort and abandoned Earth and in doing so, are no longer fit to govern. As the legally-appointed Director of the Ministry of Health, I am invoking Section Four, subsection G, clause seventeen of the Commonwealth Constitution."

"Someone bring up that clause," snapped Vossek.

"It's a coup," said Upshaw, her lip curled in a snarl.

"Someone get me that fucking info," yelled Vossek, but he didn't have to wait for someone to explain it.

"Should it be determined that the Prime Minister of the Commonwealth, due to physical or mental malady or disorder, be no longer fit to carry out the duties of his or her office," said Khaifa, reading from her tablet. "The office of the Director of the Ministry of Health shall serve notice and, with documentation of their findings, apply this clause to effect the temporary removal of the Prime Minister from office."

She carefully set down the tablet, then looked back into the camera lens.

"We cannot allow paranoia and obsession to chart the future of mankind."

And then the screens all went black.

The feed had finished.

The announcement had been made.

Nasrin Khaifa had launched a coup.

11

Very few things could make Lieutenant Kerry Stanton-West break her British calm, and even fewer could make her swear. But, while standing on the expansive command deck of the HMS Royal Sovereign with a handful of Mahoney's crew, she watched Doctor Khaifa's address projected by the Sovereign's state of the art holographic interface, she could think of but one response.

"Fucking hell."

Once the moment of shock passed - or at least lessened by a degree - Stanton-West rapped a knuckle on the edge of the sand table.

"Right then," she said. "All systems online, I want us ready for departure at a moments' notice. But no airlocks yet - I don't trust those contract chavs."

After a round of 'yessirs,' one of the younger crewmen approached the Lieutenant.

"Are we expecting to get clearance to leave, Sir?"

Stanton-West chuckled.

"I suspect we'll be leaving shortly, with or without clearance."

12

"Now is the time," said Major Vasily Petrenko. "If ever we were going to strike at the Commonwealth and take Thor's Hammer for our own-"

"No."

"But they are in a state of-"

"I said no," repeated the older man, calmly, but firmly. Broad-shouldered, he wore the uniform of the Soviet Army though it was barely visible beneath all of his medals.

Seated around a stainless steel table repurposed from what had once been one of the mess halls aboard Thor's Hammer were five men and two women. The Soviet equivalent of the Commonwealth's clearly now-defunct advisory council.

"Comrade General," said a third man. He was of similar age to the General, but wore civilian clothing and a perpetually amused expression. "That is not a decision for the armed forces to make. It is for our leaders to decide."

General Antonovich leaned forward.

"But it would be for the Soviet military to carry out such action," he said. "And should our leaders ask this of us, Comrade Khudobin, I am uncertain they would be pleased at our response."

The civilian's amused expression suddenly seemed less amused. He opened his mouth to speak, but the grey-haired Chinese woman in a crisp naval uniform cut him off before he began.

"Politics is your speciality, Khudobin," she said. "But our counterparts in the Commonwealth have just shown us what can happen when a government places political gamesmanship above the welfare of its citizens."

Khudobin shot to his feet, his face turning as red as his politics.

"This is an outrage, Admiral Chu," he said. "This is treason!"

"No," said Chu. "This is our new reality."

Chaos once more.

Or, perhaps, it would have been more accurate to say chaos continued.

Thor's Hammer was in a state of upheaval. ATC Castle soldiers ran everywhere, both trying to keep order and, based on very shrilly relayed orders from Upshaw, to find Khaifa.

De Freitas was nowhere to be seen, but rumours were already beginning to spread that he'd barricaded himself inside his personal quarters, surrounded by ATC Castle security.

Upshaw was also nowhere to be seen by the public, as she issued a continual stream of orders from her control room, from which she also monitored efforts to regain control of the broadcast systems.

From the makeshift war room Khaifa's team had set up in an unused cargo bay, Radko watched and listened as Thor's Hammer tried to find its footing. Tried to make sense of the accusations against de Freitas and tried to figure out exactly what Khaifa had done. On the latter front, Amadou Babacar had been helpful, Radko thought. A constitutional law expert who had worked for several administrations, he was relatively well-known on the station due to his years of providing legal commentary on news networks - and having been involved sporadically with several of the non-governmental news sources that had tried, and mostly failed, to sustain themselves since the ril-galas invasion. Though lawyers were not usually known for speaking plainly, Babacar had a knack for boiling complex legal jargon down to almost childlike simplicity, and based on the information filtering through Truus Van Der

Berg's surprisingly robust network of informants as well as things overheard by Ironhorse's men, the population of Thor's Hammer appeared to understand what was happening. That Khaifa was stepping in as Prime Minister on a temporary basis.

And more important, they seemed to take Khaifa's rationale for her actions at face value.

But, odd as it seemed, Radko had even more important concerns on his mind.

"We need to reinforce our line before they complete their redeployment," he said to Mahoney, waving a hand over transcripts of the information packet sent by el Bahari.

Spreading a plasticoated system map over the cargo crate serving as their low-tech - or more accurately, no-tech - sand table, Radko picked up three grease pencils Ironhorse had somehow obtained; red, blue, and green. He began to draw on the map, red X's indicating the approximate position of known ril-galas forces within the Solar system, blue circles indicating forces Radko continued to call JTF1 - Joint Task Force One, his amalgamated fleet of Commonwealth, Soviet, udukiin, and icaran ships. With the green pencil, he drew several arcing lines from the edge of the map and drawing inwards: the projected paths of several groups of ril-galas retreating from the Udukiin Priex, the Icaran Colonial Systems, and the Ota of Krellin.

As he drew the last green arc, one of Mahoney's staff approached and handed the old man a tablet. Squinting at the screen for a few moments, Mahoney grunted, then looked back up at Radko.

"Reinforcements," said the Admiral. "The krellin have just sent advance word that they have two corvettes in pursuit of the retreating ril-galas and will continue pursuit into the Solar system if we'll allow them to join our war effort."

"I'm assuming we'll say yes?"

"We'd be idiots not to," he said, then smiled and chuckled. "I'm starting to sound like you."

Radko nodded absently, rubbing his chin as he stared with his remaining eye at the map.

"We need to make our own blockade, so we can land troops on Earth," he said. "Who's in charge of the Army now, Admiral?"

Leaning back in his chair, Mahoney grunted.

"Until that broadcast went out, it was Upshaw. Now? I don't know."

"You are."

Both Radko and Mahoney looked up, startled by the sudden appearance of Khaifa. Neither had heard her approach.

"You are, Mahoney," she said, nodding, possibly only to herself. "I'm reinstating you as Minister of Defense."

Mahoney stood, nodded solemnly, and saluted.

"I'll do my best, Doctor. Or should I say... Prime Minister?"

"Let's not do that right now," said the Doctor, wincing. "If I start using the title, people might think I actually want it."

Turning her attention quickly to Radko, she tapped a finger beneath her own left eye.

"How are you doing, Commander?"

"It hurts, but I'm managing. And thank you for not letting me get arrested."

"That wasn't actually me," she said. "My plan was just to release you once we'd finished with this whole process."

She waved a hand around the room, where a mix of civilian and military personnel made valiant efforts to reign in the chaos and establish lines of communication with all of the areas, people, and entities required to run a government. And then she nodded over to one side, where Ironhorse and a few of his men were gearing up.

"It seems that some people weren't convinced I'd actually go through with it," said Khaifa. "So contingency plans were made."

When Van Der Berg called out for Khaifa, the doctor smiled apologetically and left the two naval officers on their own.

"As much as this change in leadership was necessary, the timing could have been better," said Mahoney, returning his attention to the system map. "The resources we're spending right now..."

"Let's not fool ourselves, Admiral," said Radko. "If Khaifa hadn't stepped up like this, Upshaw wouldn't have given us *any* resources. You'd still be tucked off to the side with no authority, I'd be in prison, and who the hell knows what would have happened with our alliance. What we're looking at now is far from a worst-case scenario."

He glanced around the cargo bay.

"It may not be pretty, but we don't need pretty. We need people willing to work together for the common good. We have that now."

The Admiral's tablet beeped.

"Speaking of," he said, before activating the connection. "Commander el Bahari, how are things aboard the Vimy Ridge?"

"Nearly as exciting as things aboard Thor's Hammer, Admiral," she said.

"I understand you had a hand in events over here, Commander," said Mahoney "From the sounds of it, I should have assigned you to military intelligence."

"I'm fairly certain Mister Owens came close to having me shot, so perhaps spy work isn't my calling, Sir."

"Wait, he what?" said Radko, confused.

"Radko, welcome back into the fold," said el Bahari. "I take it you've nearly recovered enough to start being a pain in the ass again?"

"He doesn't need to recover for that," muttered the Admiral.

"I concede the point, Sir."

"Have you guys been practicing that? Yes, I'm doing all right, considering. And once we've got all this shit squared away, I want to hear the whole story about you and Owens," said Radko.

"It makes him look bad, so I'll enjoy telling it," said el Bahari. "In the meantime, we need to find a way to get you safely back aboard the Vimy Ridge, Commander. Since Khaifa detonated her political warhead, ATC Castle fighters have been running patrols around the station. I'm not sure a shuttle would be allowed to come or go at this point. We may have to come and pick you up ourselves."

Mahoney was already shaking his head.

"Negative, Commander. With this information you've given us, we can't afford to take any ship, especially the Vimy Ridge, away from the line."

"Admiral, as much as it pains me to say this - and believe me it does - we need Radko on the line," she said. "He is the most visible symbol of our combined fleet. He's the one who brought all this together. And frankly..."

There was a pause, a lengthy one, and both Radko and Mahoney frowned, thinking the connection may have been terminated. Had Upshaw succeeded in jamming external-

"Frankly, he's also our best tactician."

Radko smirked and shook his head. He could imagine the sour facial expression as she choked out those words. With Herculean effort, he managed not to point it out.

"Mahoney's right though," he said instead. "We can't pull any defenses right now. I'll just have to take my chances in a shuttle."

"I think I have a better idea," said Mahoney. "After commanding the Royal Sovereign against the Hornets' Nest, I came to realize that my days of being a ship captain are well behind me, and should stay well behind me. I'm not too proud to admit I felt out of my depth, nor too proud to stand aside for a more capable officer to take that role."

Locking eyes with Radko, Mahoney raised a bushy brow.

"The HMS Royal Sovereign needs a new commanding officer," he said. "She's fully crewed, and she's right here at Thor's Hammer."

"Not that I have any say in this decision," said el Bahari. "And being fully aware this may sound to most that I'm simply trying to hold onto command of the Vimy Ridge, it makes sense, Commander. The Royal Sovereign would be a significant asset... and though once again it's causing physical discomfort for me to admit, she'd be an even greater asset with you in command."

Rubbing his chin and then almost - almost, before he caught himself - rubbing his eyes, Radko managed to avoid sighing. Both Mahoney and el Bahari were right. Taking command of the Sovereign was both the logical step, given that the ship was right there and in need of a CO, and a significant tactical advantage in the coming conflict. But it would mean giving up the Vimy Ridge, the ship that had become almost an extension of himself. Crew members had come and gone, friends had been reassigned, friends had died, but from the first moments of the ril-galas attack until now, it had been Finn Radko and the HMCS Vimy Ridge. The two of them, inseparable despite everything.

Leaning forward, Mahoney put a hand on Radko's shoulder. The Admiral wore a look that was both sympathetic and wistful.

"I understand," he said quietly. "For me, it was the HMS Protestant Caesar. Commanded her for six years, and served on her for six before that. Never went through anything like this, of course, but still. I understand."

He sat up again, still smiling, but shrugged.

"We've all made sacrifices for the greater good of those we've pledged to protect."

Radko chuckled.

"I probably shouldn't be looking at an assignment as CO of the largest and most advanced ship in the fleet as a sacrifice," he said.

"No," said el Bahari. "But you're not known for being reasonable about things."

Though he said nothing, Mahoney pointed to the tablet from which el Bahari's voice was emanating, and nodded dramatically.

"All right," said Radko. "I appreciate the vote of confidence, Admiral."

"There is one small issue," said Mahoney. "The HMS Royal Sovereign is the flagship of the Commonwealth Navy."

Reaching into his pocket, the Admiral retrieved a small object, set it on the crate and slid it across to Radko.

"We can't have our flagship sail under a Commander," he said. "Congratulations, Captain Radko."

Taking the small box, Radko opened it to reveal a shining gold Captain's bar. Back in the old days, when he thought about being promoted to Captain, he'd imagined a full ceremony, all kinds of pomp, maybe even a band. It was amazing how going through a crisis could change your perspective on what really mattered. Pinning the Captain's bar to his uniform, he placed his old silver Commander's bar in the box.

"Thank you, Admiral."

"Normally we'd have a more formal presentation," said Mahoney, as if reading Radko's mind. "But the times being what they are..."

"We just need to get back to work."

Mahoney nodded.

"And get you to the Royal Sovereign."

Now that the opportunity to do so had passed, Radko was wishing he had taken the painkillers. The empty socket of his left eye, now covered by a bandage and a patch, was beginning to throb.

"You ok?" asked Ironhorse as he waved the rest of his squad forward.

"I'll be fine."

Ironhorse nodded, glanced down the corridor, then turned back to Radko.

"She'll probably never tell you this herself," he said, "but this was all her. This plan. Getting you out, supporting Khaifa."

"What? She meaning who?"

"Amira."

"You were working under el Bahari's orders? I thought you were working for Van Der Berg."

Shaking his head, Ironhorse quickly signalled two of his men to proceed forward to ensure a safe path.

"She had me watching things. Watching Upshaw, really, and keeping an eye on Khaifa," he said. "After the Cortez thing, everything shifted."

"Yeah, it did," said Radko, a familiar sensation of heat building in his chest. It came every time he thought about Anna

Cortez - and more specifically, about how he'd been unable to prevent her death.

"Amira kept saying that with Upshaw and de Freitas, she was the more dangerous one," said Ironhorse.

"True, and probably even an understatement. So, you've been working on this grand plan all along? Even before I was hospitalized?"

"I wouldn't call it grand," said Ironhorse with a dry chuckle. "But it was a plan. Had to keep adjusting it, but we're all still alive."

A gunshot rang out down the corridor, and then another.

Ironhorse raised his rifle to his shoulder and Radko drew his REV1 pistol.

"Report," said Ironhorse.

Several more shots rang out and something pinged off a bulkhead not far from the pair.

One of the other Rangers responded, her voice filtering through Radko's earpiece. He was glad Ironhorse had allowed him access to the Revelstoke Rangers' comm channel.

"PMCs," she said - Radko was fairly certain her name was Vickers. "Six of them."

"Search party," said another voice. Possibly Khundra?

Whether this ATC Castle search party was looking for Khaifa or himself, Radko didn't know, but likely it was both. He would not have been surprised if Upshaw had placed a bounty on one or both of them, a significant bonus paid to the team who either brought one of them back or provided proof of their deaths. That was an action that would fit Upshaw's mercenary mentality perfectly. When she and Radko first met, had he known what kind of a sociopath she'd been he never would have left her in a position of power aboard that ATC Castle training facility.

"Keep low and stay close," said Ironhorse.

Nodding, Radko followed as they quickly headed down the corridor to meet up with Vickers and Khundra. The pair were a study in opposites - Maz Khundra tall and lanky, Bethany Vickers built like a tank.

And by the time Radko and Ironhorse had arrived on the scene, the six mercenaries had become five, with one of their number sprawled lifelessly on the corridor floor.

A bullet pinged off the wall not far from the Rangers and all of them – Radko included – returned fire. A cry of pain told them they'd hit a target, but the string of swearing in the same voice told them it hadn't been a kill shot.

"Getting shot hurts, eh? Been there," said Ironhorse, speaking loudly enough to be heard down the corridor. "Since Khaifa would want me to, I'm giving you the option of not getting shot anymore. Lay down your weapons and walk away, and we'll act like none of this happened."

There was a brief silence, and Radko fought the urge to sigh. But then a voice called out from behind a bend in the corridor.

"And if we don't?"

"I think you already know the answer to that," said Ironhorse, who then glanced at Radko before continuing. "We have more important shit to worry about right now than whether you're alive or dead. So, stand in the way of us doing what needs to be done, and we won't hold back. I trust you understand what that means."

"Yeah."

The was a soft clattering sound of weapons being placed on the floor.

"Weapons are down, we're taking our wounded to medical," said the voice.

"Best of luck," said Ironhorse, nodding for Khundra and Vickers to move ahead and confirm.

Carefully moving forward, rifles ready, the pair disappeared around the bend, and Radko took the lack of gunfire to be a good thing. An even better thing when Khundra came back around the corner with her rifle in her left hand, and six Caliburn SMGs cradled in her right arm.

"They left their sidearms as well," she said. "I'm just not enough of an octopus to carry them all."

With a small smile and a nod, Ironhorse waved the team forward.

"Let's get to the Royal Sovereign," he said.

Unexpectedly, the airlock was not guarded.

"Poor planning?" said Vickers.

"More likely extreme paranoia," said Radko. "If there were any guards here, Upshaw probably either sent them after me, or sent them after Khaifa, or called them back to wherever she's holed up, for additional protection."

Vickers nodded, but her attention was already elsewhere as she took up a defensive position to watch the corridor behind the group. Ironhorse did the same while Radko retrieved a tablet from his satchel and keyed in the code Mahoney had provided for the direct connection to the Royal Sovereign.

"This is Radko," he said once the connection was accepted. "I'm at airlock nine."

The responding voice didn't identify itself, but told him to wait a moment. Which he did, but when 'a moment' stretched to more than thirty seconds, Radko prepared to activate the connection again. But then the three red lights above the airlock flashed yellow, then green, then the telltale hiss sounded and the airlock door slid open.

Standing in the open doorway was a young, dark-skinned woman in a naval uniform, her mass of dark curls barely controlled by a headband. At her side was an enlisted man carrying an old Trondheim Arms GNK - which was considered borderline obsolete when Radko was given his first assignment out of the academy. The man had to be in his sixties based on his appearance, but still scowled well enough to appear threatening.

The young woman smiled. The enlisted man did not.

"Captain Radko," she said, first saluting, then extending her hand. "Lieutenant Kerry Stanton-West. This is my personal assassin, Crewman Smiley."

Shaking hands with Stanton-West, Radko shifted his gaze to Smiley, who very much wasn't, and Radko thought the young Lieutenant might be yanking his chain both about the man's job - clearly he wasn't an assassin - and his name, but that was a question for another time.

"We need to get underway before the Upshaw loyalists figure out what's happening," he said, then turned back to Ironhorse. "Good luck."

The Ranger nodded.

"You too, Radko."

Closing the airlock, Stanton-West and Smiley led him onward, into the ship that was now his to command.

The HMS Royal Sovereign.

Though for a long time the Sovereign had been the butt of jokes within the Navy, given how long its launch had been delayed, Radko had found out the truth from Kestrel Cagliari. The delays had been due to ATC Castle taking over the naval contract from the ship's original designers, Cagliari Aerospace. Launch was delayed while ATC Castle tried to reverse engineer some of the technology created for the project that was beyond what they could produce themselves.

"Wait, hold on," he said, stopping their progress long enough to take a painkiller.

"No worries," said Stanton-West. "I'm surprised you're already up and about to be honest."

"I keep hearing that. I'm too stubborn to lay in a hospital bed for too long."

"Funny, I keep hearing that about you."

The command deck of the Royal Sovereign was vastly different from that of the Vimy Ridge. For starters, it was in the dead centre of the ship, not dorsally positioned, like an enormous cockpit. It was also brighter. As much as the Vimy Ridge's command deck had been his home for the past two years, it had been a home with very dim lighting, designed to prevent glare on the multitude of screens being used by the crew. Incorporating much more of the holographic technology used in the sand table of the Vimy Ridge - but much newer versions of it - nearly every crew interface on the Sovereign, beyond their individual tablets, was holographic.

One of the largest differences was the structure. Where the Vimy Ridge command deck had been two levels - the main command deck and the second level observation dome - the Royal Sovereign command deck was a single level. But it was suspended within a sphere of curved composite panels of an almost impossibly deep black.

One of the delays, Radko knew from the discussion with Cagliari, was that ATC Castle hadn't been able to get those panels to function properly.

"We had some outside assistance," said Stanton-West, smiling again as she followed Radko's gaze up toward the panels. "It turns out that the final bit of programming hadn't been installed by Cagliari Aerospace when the contract was transferred to ATC Castle. We very recently had a sympathetic soul forward a copy of the completed coding."

Radko smiled.

The dark panels were, from what Cagliari had told him, a massive version of the interior setup of the Argentavis Starfighters.

The sphere in which the command deck was situated was an enormous Universal HUD, an interface that utilized exterior sensors to build a complete and realistic holographic representation of the surrounding space, giving the crew a near complete three-hundred and sixty degree view of their surroundings. It would be like the Royal Sovereign had become transparent around them. Overlay systems could track and label friendly and enemy ships, could magnify portions of the screen...

Shaking his head, Radko's smile broadened. It would be like his entire command deck was a sand table.

"Shall we light it up?" said Stanton-West.

"Absolutely."

"Deng, if you would be so kind?" she said, nodding to the extraordinarily tall man standing at one of the several circular control stations placed throughout the command deck. From what Radko knew of the Royal Sovereign, those control stations were multifunctional, and could serve interchangeably as controls for any ship function normally controlled from the command deck. The holographic interface would simply reconfigure itself depending on what was required of the crewmembers to whose tablet the console was tethered.

With a nod, Deng brought up a new set of controls, and Radko realized a major advantage to the holoscreens over traditional consoles - they self-adjusted based on the user's height. With a traditional console, Deng, who was nearly as tall as an icaran, would have needed to hunch forward to use it. The control station on the Sovereign simply projected its interface higher, allowing him to stand normally.

And then Radko stopped thinking about consoles and tall Sudanese crewmembers and everything else.

The Royal Sovereign's UHUD blinked to life, the matte black curves dissolving into...

Space.

And Thor's Hammer to port.

And everything else. The command deck was floating in space, or appeared to be, and the illusion was so real that Radko had to place a hand on the sand table to ground himself.

"Mind-blowing, isn't it?" said Stanton-West quietly. "The first time we turned it on, I think we all just stood and stared for twenty minutes."

"I wish we had twenty minutes so I could do the same," he said, reluctantly turning back to his new Executive Officer. "But we need to get underway before Upshaw figures out what's going on."

Stanton-West nodded and brought up the ship-wide broadcast channel on the sand table. Reaching out her hand, she stopped before activating it.

"Would you like to give the order, Captain?"

Having been aboard for under fifteen minutes, Radko was inclined to let Stanton-West handle it - the crew knew her, and since the ship had docked after the Hornets' Nest, Stanton-West had been acting CO. But while the crew of the Royal Sovereign may not yet know him personally, they would certainly

know of him, and though Radko was loathe to use the un-
wanted fame now linked to his name, he felt he owed it to the
crew - now his crew - to hear directly from their new commanding officer.

He nodded to Stanton-West, and she activated the channel.

"Attention crew of the HMS Royal Sovereign," she said.
"Our new commanding officer would like a word."

"This is Commander Finn Radko," he said, then immediately chuckled at himself. "No, apparently I'm a Captain now.
So, this is Captain Finn Radko, and we're off to a wonderful
start."

Much to his relief, everyone on the command deck was
smiling or chuckling. It had been an accidental slip of the
tongue, but the last thing Radko wanted was this crew to see
him as a symbol, up on a pedestal. He was human just like
them, and it was important for him that they understand that.

"I'd like to promise that the next few days will go more
smoothly than my opening statement, but I'd be lying," he said.
"Nothing about this war has been easy, and while the events
transpiring on Thor's Hammer are necessary, they also compli-
cate things for us. But not enough for us to lose sight of what
really matters: the liberation of Earth."

He paused then, partly to allow the statement to sink in
and partly to collect his thoughts. The assignment to the Royal
Sovereign had been so sudden that he hadn't given much
thought as to what he would say in his first address to the
crew. So, he kept it simple.

"We're all here for a reason. Every single one of us - myself
included - were hand-picked by Admiral Mahoney to crew the
largest, most advanced, and most powerful ship in the history
of the Commonwealth Navy," he said. "So let's go write our

names in the history books. All stations make ready for launch."

Thankfully there was no cheering, but Radko noticed some determined smiles and nods, including from his XO.

"Well said, Captain."

"Thank you. We should probably bring some of our lower-powered weapons online right away."

"Just in case the Upshaw loyalists try to pick a fight," she said, nodding.

"All stations report ready, Captain," said Deng.

"Remote disengage docking clamps," said Radko.

"Docking clamps disengaged," confirmed Deng.

Without prompting, and in a small enough window that no one else saw, Stanton-West brought up a crew roster and highlighted the name of the pilot on duty.

"Petty Officer Wharton," said Radko, with a nod of thanks to Stanton-West "Take us out."

No sooner had Wharton confirmed than the tactical display on the sand table sprung to life. A scale version of the Royal Sovereign hovered over its surface, showing the ship pulling away from Thor's Hammer, but it also showed three smaller ships approaching along the axis of the station.

"Onyx interceptors," said Stanton-West, raising a brow. "ATC Castle superiority fighters."

"Well, they're not messing around, are they?"

"Did you expect any less?"

"I try not to underestimate their attempts to overcompensate."

Turning to the side, Radko watched the UHUD as the trio of Onyx fighters emerged from behind the station. Automatically the Sovereign's defensive AI logged their position, tagging each with a circular overlay of information.

"Weapons are online?"

"They are, Captain."

"Captain Radko," said Deng. "Incoming transmission from the fighter group. Audio only."

"Attention HMS Royal Sovereign, Thor's Hammer is currently in lockdown. You are ordered to return to your berth at once," said the voice. "I repeat, you are ordered-"

"By whom?" said Radko.

"Return to your berth, Royal Sovereign, by direct order."

"Yeah, heard that part - I'm asking who's giving that order."

"I am a Colonel with the joint ATC Castle-"

"We don't work for ATC Castle. Fuck off."

Glancing at Deng, Radko sharply drew a finger across his throat and Deng, understanding, cut the transmission.

"They're giving their people ranks now?" muttered Stanton-West.

There wasn't time to respond, as the red overlays on the fighters suddenly began to glow orange. The Onyx fighters, against all common sense, had locked weapons on the Royal Sovereign.

"They can't be serious," said a young woman to Radko's left. Again, Stanton-West came to his rescue with a slyly provided bit on information. Kennedy Bell, Sub-Lieutenant. Logistics officer.

"Lieutenant Bell," said Radko, "they're always serious. That's what makes them such a pain in the ass. Stanton-West, please fire a warning shot."

The order was given and Radko watched the projectile fly harmlessly between the fighters, but close enough that they took evasive action.

"Attention Royal Sovereign. You have fired on an official government patrol. You will stand down immediately and return to your berth or risk reprisal."

Before Radko could respond, the voice continued.

"Lieutenant Kerry Stanton-West, as commanding officer of the Royal Sovereign, you will be held personally responsible-"

"I'm sorry Colonel, but you've been given incorrect information if you believe I'm commanding officer here," said Stanton-West, as she quickly typed something into her tablet, the corners of her mouth twitching upward in a smile.

Radko's tablet pinged and he looked down to see a text-only message... from Stanton-West.

They don't know you're here, it said. *Dramatic reveal time...?*

With a smile of his own, Radko nodded.

"To whom do we have the pleasure of speaking?" he asked.

"My name is none of your concern."

"Ah. Well, I guarantee mine will be of concern to you," said Radko. "This is Captain Finn Radko, commanding officer of the HMS Royal Sovereign. So, I likely won't have to explain to you how excellent an idea it would be, my nameless Colonel, for you to back down."

There was no immediate response. The UHUD overlays continued to pulse orange.

Shaking his head, Radko muted the channel and turned to Bell.

"Bring the rail guns online."

She was young, and despite the blonde hair she reminded him a little too much of Anna Cortez. But she did what he asked with commendable efficiency.

He re-activated the link to the fighter group. The Colonel, whoever he was, would have seen the heavy weapons systems start up.

"Go ahead and test me, Colonel," said Radko.

Nothing.

And then...

The overlays stopped pulsing orange, settling in to the usual basic red, and then all three Onyx fighters peeled off.

"Look at that," said Stanton-West. "Gave the poor man a hint of what we could do and he ran off without a goodbye."

"Sound like our love lives, eh Kerry?" said Bell with a grin.

Stanton-West laughed and Bell immediately looked to Radko, eyes wide and cheeks flushing.

"I'm... I'm sorry Captain. That was inappropriate of me."

"It's okay Bell, I didn't hear anything," he said, pointing to his bandage. "You were speaking into my bad eye."

Bell grinned, but then Radko rapped his knuckles on the sand table.

"Wharton, do we have a fix on the Vimy Ridge's battle group?"

"Yessir. Right here."

A green triangle overlay about the size of Radko's hand appeared on the UHUD. Three small lines of text accompanied it:

HMCS Vimy Ridge

Outlaw Squadron

SS Azrael's Tear

The battle group was running lean, he realized. While the Ridge could hold its own - if anyone knew that it was Radko - having only light support like Cagliari's fighters and Singh's pirate ship had to mean that the ril-galas were ramping up attacks elsewhere, drawing off ships that would normally be part of the various battle groups. It had always been part of the post-Hornets' Nest plan that if they were successful, battle groups would always be a minimum three offensively capable vessels.

"All right," he said. And what about the udukiin?"

A second triangle popped into existence not far from the first, but then a third sprang up much closer. It was the far one that kept his attention.

Her Glorious Vengeance.

Sigurdsson's ship.

Radko sighed.

First things first.

"Set a course for the Vimy Ridge battle group," he said. "And Mister Deng, please advise Admiral Mahoney we're on our way."

"Yes, Captain."

Turning to Stanton-West, Radko forced a smile. He'd just realized how exhausted he was.

"Do I have an office, by any chance?"

"Yes. It even has a cot, if you were so inclined," she said with a sympathetic smile. "Straight through the front of the command deck."

Following her pointed finger, Radko saw a doorway built into the curved wall of UHUD panels. Picking up his satchel, Radko headed toward the door.

"Let me know when we're in range of the Vimy Ridge," he said. "You're in charge again, Lieutenant."

"Aye, Captain."

Closing the door behind him, Radko was pleased but not surprised to find the office was both larger and better fur-nished than his old office aboard the Vimy Ridge. Cleaner, too - either Stanton-West was more organized than him or she just had simply not used the office. The shelves were largely empty, aside from the usual hard copies of naval manuals to be used as a reliable backup in the event of digital library failures, and a brass lamp on an armature.

It felt like a luxury hotel compared to his cramped space aboard the Vimy Ridge.

To one side was a second doorway leading to a small room just big enough for a cot and a side table.

Dropping his satchel on the office chair, Radko retrieved his tablet and left the rest to be dealt with later when he'd had some time to rest. As he set his tablet on the small side table and lay down on the cot, he chuckled to himself. Rest was likely going to become a foreign concept again very shortly.

14

"We're going to need help very soon," said Hobson.

The three of them - Hobson, Hunter and Ransom in her Arthurian disguise - stood atop the Half-Moon Battery looking out into what remained of the city. Edinburgh had fared better than a lot of cities across the world, as they had found out via the sporadic contact they'd made with other groups of survivors, but it still smouldered in places and there were still many buildings that had either fallen or were in such a state that they could fall at any moment.

In amongst the ruins, and skulking through the intact but abandoned buildings, Ransom could see ril-galas stalkers. It seemed they had been seeing more of those than the bulkier foot soldiers of late, and their speed had required a significant shift in tactics from the defenders of Edinburgh Castle. But more to Hobson's point, the enemy was becoming bolder in its attacks, and those attacks were becoming more frequent. In the prior twenty-four hours, the ril-galas had done three hit and run attacks at various points around the perimeter.

"They're looking for weaknesses in our defenses," continued Hobson. "We're spread thin and not enough of us have military training. Sooner or later, they'll find a weakness."

Ransom nodded and ran a hand through her short red hair. She really missed the mass of curls she'd cut off to become Arthur. Her shield from the world.

She felt very exposed.

"This isn't all on you," said Hunter, placing a hand on Ransom's forearm.

"No, of course," said Hobson. "I hope you don't think that's what I was implying."

Forcing a smile, Ransom shook her head.

"No, I know you didn't. I'm just...," she paused, looking around to make sure the three were alone. "This is harder than I thought it would be."

"Leadership often is," said Hobson.

"Remember what the mood here was like before we brought back Arthur," said Hunter. "And what it's become since we returned. You're making a difference just by playing this role."

"I know. Doesn't make it much easier, but I do know it."

About to reply, Hobson stopped at the sound of running footsteps approaching. Ransom reflexively changed her posture and slid back into her role as Prince Arthur. Around the corner barrelled a tiny teenage girl, her jeans and leather jacket battered and filthy, her hair not faring much better. A dark streak crossed her face horizontally in such a way that Ransom questioned whether it was intentional or accidental.

The girl skidded to stop, breathing heavily.

"Oh. Hey," she said.

"Hello there," said Ransom, in Arthur's voice. "Karina, isn't it?"

"Yeah. I mean, yes your Majesty? Right? Um, yeah, Karina Jennings."

Ransom smiled, hoping to put the girl at ease. Despite her young age - Karina was barely thirteen according to Hunter - she was also a very good scout, small enough to sneak in and out of areas other scouts couldn't.

"So, two things, right?" said Jennings. "First, that lady doctor, whose name I don't remember? She totally just gave the

Prime Minister a big fuck you and she's in charge now. Second, I think the skrags can regenerate."

The three listeners - Ransom, Hobson, and Hunter - just stared for a moment, trying to parse what they'd just heard. All of them knew that "skrags" had somehow ended up as the derogatory slang name for the ril-galas among the younger denizens of the castle, mostly because Ransom herself was only seventeen and the name had been in use well before she'd taken on the mantle of Arthur. But the rest of her statement...?

"Do you mean Nasrin Khaifa?" said Hunter.

Jennings looked at her, then looked away and nodded. Most of the under-twenty set were nervous of Hunter, given the rumours about her abilities. Then again, thought Ransom bitterly, the same was true of the over-twenty set.

"Khaifa has pushed out the Prime Minister?" said Hobson, the incredulity clear in both his voice and his face. "There was a coup?"

"No, it was like... um... oh wait."

Face scrunched in concentration, the kid dug through her pockets, pulling out a fistful of dirty hair elastics, some gum wrappers, a pair of brass knuckles, and finally, a neatly-folded but still crumpled piece of paper.

"Here," she said, handing the paper to Hobson. "Grieve wrote it down because he has the nice handwriting."

Unfolding the paper, Hobson read it to himself, his eyebrows inching higher with each line. It seemed to Ransom that if the note were any longer, his eyebrows might meld into his hairline.

"Hobson...?" she said as he refolded the paper very carefully, his eyebrows quickly dropping.

"It seems Doctor Khaifa invoked the infirmity clause to temporarily remove the Prime Minister from office," he said. "Due to his unwillingness to help those of us still on Earth."

"And that means she's in charge now?"

"Temporarily."

"Does that mean the Prime Minister could come back?"

"I guess it's possible, but I doubt it based on this," he said, handing the paper over to Ransom.

Ransom read the paper.

"Oh shit," she said.

15

Seeing the Vimy Ridge from the outside, from the vantage point of another vessel, and knowing that someone else commanded her, turned out to be worse than Radko had expected. He'd expected disappointment, maybe some wistfulness, but this felt more like seeing the ex you were still in love with making eyes at her new husband.

"Are you all right, sir?" said Stanton-West.

"The eye has dulled to just an insistent throbbing," he said. "So it's either getting better, or a brilliant mixture of meds and adrenaline have kicked in."

"Good to know. Also not exactly what I meant."

He sighed, still staring off at the Vimy Ridge, the holographic version of it being generated by the UHUD slowly getting larger as the Royal Sovereign approached.

"I was trying to avoid the topic."

"Fair enough. The Royal Sovereign is an excellent ship, Captain," she said.

Sensing a mild note of defensiveness in her words, Radko turned to the Lieutenant and smiled.

"I know, Stanton-West-"

"You can call me Kerry," she said. "My last name can be a mouthful."

"Kerry, then. I know this is an excellent ship, and despite how it may look, I'm both proud and honoured to have been put in command. But you know how you have a favourite shirt, or pair of shoes? They've been with you forever, they're comfortable. You have newer shirts, newer shoes - nicer ones, better quality, not nearly as battered and worn - but you still keep going back to those old shoes. That old shirt. They're comfortable. They mean something to you, so you have a hard time giving them up."

Stanton-West was nodding, but she was also frowning, and seemed ready to object.

"The new shoes, you'll work them in. You'll wear them enough that they eventually become comfortable old shoes that you won't want to let go," he said. "But that takes time."

"I understand," she said, then smirked. "And you haven't even figured out how to tie the laces here yet."

"Exactly."

"I've had the conference room prepared - I took the liberty of arranging a meeting here with the key players," she said, tapping a command on her tablet.

Radko blinked as a floating screen popped to life in front of him.

"Sorry," said Stanton-West. "I forget you're not used to the features of the UHUD yet. We can send screens to various points if we need to, it's just generally more logical to keep it free of clutter."

"This really is going to take some getting used to," said Radko as he reviewed the screen.

It was a list of names; people Stanton-West had invited to the Royal Sovereign.

Amira el Bahari, HMCS Vimy Ridge - confirmed

Jagat Sohal Singh, SS Azrael's Tear - confirmed

Rhekar, Venn Shakara - confirmed

Kestrel Cagliari, Outlaw Squadron - confirmed

Freyja Sigurdsson, Her Glorious Vengeance - confirmed

There were several other names on this list, but Radko stopped reading at Sigurdsson. And his eyes drifted back to the Vimy Ridge.

"Admiral Mahoney will try to join via comm," said Stanton-West. "But it will depend on the situation on Thor's Hammer. However, he's given you the authority to make decisions on behalf of the Commonwealth Navy in his absence."

Reluctantly tearing his gaze from the Vimy Ridge, Radko walked to the sand table just as a pair of circular red overlays popped into existence on the UHUD, directly behind the Royal Sovereign. Back in the direction of the station.

Ships, two of them, that the defensive AI had flagged as hostile.

"Someone identify those ships. And give me a mag window."

The magnification overlay appeared almost immediately, and though they were still small, Radko knew the lines of the two vessels.

"Soviet," he said.

"Confirmed," said Bell. "The Hangzhou and the Potemkin. Captain, they're on an intercept course."

"Of course they are," said Radko with a sigh. "Open a channel to them, please."

"They're already requesting a channel," said Deng.

"Then by all means..."

"HMS Royal Sovereign, this is Admiral Chu Zhang-Yi of the Soviet cruiser Hangzhou."

Radko and Stanton-West exchanged frowns, and the Lieutenant quickly muted the channel.

"Chu? Isn't she in command of the whole Soviet fleet?"

"Last I heard, yes," he said, then unmuted the communications. "Admiral, this is Captain Finn Radko of the Royal Sovereign. How can I be of service?"

"Captain Radko, I was unaware you commanded the Royal Sovereign. I believe congratulations are in order."

"I appreciate the sentiment, Admiral, but I'll celebrate another time."

"Understandable, Captain," said Chu. "Especially given the current political developments within the Commonwealth. These are indeed trying times."

"Has there ever been a political situation that *wasn't* trying, Admiral?" he said, looking back at the ships on the UHUD as it generated information about their speed and projected time to intercept. "And I hate to be rude, but we have a war going on - could we maybe cut the banter and get to the point?"

"I had heard you could be quite rude."

"Admiral, with all due respect, I have more important concerns than whether I've offended you."

"Many say the same of me, Captain," said Chu. "I am here to lend support to the war effort. As I believe a friend of yours once said, this is no longer about the Commonwealth and the Soviets, it's simply about humanity."

Radko smiled, remembering the first time he'd heard that sentiment back aboard the Leonid Gorshkov, when Captain Kovalenko had agreed to set aside years of Commonwealth-Soviet animosity for a greater good. And Radko was glad to see the red overlays vanish, the AI no longer classifying the Hangzhou and the Potemkin as hostile. Someone on the crew was really quick. Stanton-West caught his eye and nodded almost imperceptibly toward Bell.

"I'm glad to have the assistance," said Radko, giving Bell a quick thumbs up for a job well done. "We're just organizing a strategy session here and would be happy to have you join us."

"I would be honoured," said Chu.

After the connection had closed, Radko turned to Stanton-West.

"I'd better start preparing."

Less than sixty minutes later, their guests began arriving.

The first to arrive was Sigurdsson, which was exactly how it had been planned. Elgraphaar, the icaran commando who had once served under Locaris, was with her, as was an udukiin called Udrach Kai Togru. And, of course, Jaeger was there.

Smiling, Radko knelt as the big German Shepherd padded up to him, tail wagging.

"Hey pal, thanks for taking care of everyone," he said.

Jaeger put his nose right up against Radko's and then his tongue darted out for a quick kiss. Giving the dog a scratch behind the ears, Radko stood and saw that the rest of the group had moved off to the far end of the conference room to give him and Sigurdsson some space. The two embraced, and it felt to Radko as if it had been years since they'd been together.

"How are you doing?" said Sigurdsson, as they released one another reluctantly.

"I'm okay."

"I can tell when you're lying."

Radko nodded.

"I need rest," he admitted. "But that's not likely to happen in the near future. You?"

She did that thing she did, a half smile and a light shrug.

"I'd really like to not have to be thinking about warfare every waking moment. I'm just...," she paused, rolling her eyes at the fact they were tearing up.

In the years before the two had met, Radko knew that Sigurdsson had spent a lot of time and energy cutting herself off from people, insulating herself against emotion, against caring about things. Her job in the Commonwealth Army was her life and little else mattered. She'd been, in her own estimation, a cold and unapproachable person. But as with Radko himself, though in a different way, the invasion had changed both her outlook on the universe and her way of interacting with it. Though she still retained her combative nature, rather than being fired off in every direction, it was honed with laser-like focus, and her overriding motivation had little to do with her own wants or needs.

And like Radko, responsibility weighed heavily on her shoulders.

"I'm just so fucking tired," she said. "Physically, emotionally. Down to my core, Finn."

Taking her three-fingered blue hand in his, Radko squeezed it gently. Her lopsided smile came back, but the weariness in her eyes remained. One of the first things they had shared early on, when each was just a tinny voice on the other end of a low-quality comm channel, was their fear that neither of them was up to the task they'd been handed. That fear had never really left, Radko knew, despite all they'd accomplished, despite all the good they had done. Despite all the lives that they'd saved. He knew that Sigurdsson still felt inadequate for the role into which she'd been thrust, because he felt the same about his own role. That it was only a matter of time until someone realized he was just making it all up as he went and that there were far better people to lead than him.

"We'll be all right," he said, as much for his own benefit as Sigurdsson's.

"And when this is all over, we both badly need to get help," she said, tapping her temple. "Because when this is over, I don't want anything to get in the way of us living our lives."

"Definitely," he said, raising her hand to his lips and kissing it. "It will be nice to not be a War Matriarch and whatever the hell I am."

Sigurdsson smiled.

"Let's be honest, Finn, you're a War Matriarch with a penis."

"I don't get the cool armour, though," he said, tapping a finger on the chitinous armour plates covering her shoulders, biceps, and forearms - armour that was actually the udukiin Matriarch with whom Sigurdsson had bonded.

By then the remaining guests had begun to arrive and Radko had to tear himself away and play host, despite wanting nothing more than to steal a few more moments with Sigurdsson. They were, it seemed, always short on time.

Once the last of the guests arrived, they gathered around the conference table. Like the room itself, the table was circular, and its centre was a holographic sand table. Hovering above the sand table were numbers, nearly a foot tall each. A countdown.

09:47:22

"Welcome aboard the HMS Royal Sovereign," said Radko, remaining standing while the rest of the attendees sat. Stanton-West had joined them moments before, leaving Bell in charge on the command deck.

"No pre-amble here, I'll get right to the point," he said. "The countdown you see in front of you is the projected timeframe until the first wave of ril-galas reinforcements arrive in Earth orbit."

"Under ten hours," said el Bahari, "to coordinate a defensive strategy among three species and four militaries."

"Though I am loathe to point out the obvious," said Singh, the old pirate interlacing his fingers as he leaned forward and looked around the table before meeting Radko's gaze. "The Commonwealth is in chaos. Will we even have support from your government?"

There was a chuckle from across the room and everyone's attention turned to Cagliari, who leaned back and put her feet up on the table.

"Singh. Dude, come on," she said. "Exactly what support did we have from the Commonwealth when we hit the Hornets' Nest?"

"This ship," said Stanton-West. "That's it."

"And it wasn't even one hundred percent operational," said Cagliari.

"Singh is right," said Radko. "The Commonwealth is, to be blunt, a shitshow right now. Khaifa is banking on Constitutional arguments, while Upshaw is banking on the might of her private army. Honestly, I don't know who will come out on top and that's the truth. But you know what? Right now I don't care. I can't, not yet.

"Yes, I consider Khaifa a friend and Upshaw an enemy - only one of them has tried to have me arrested, after all - but they have their battle and I have mine."

He looked around the table, meeting everyone's eyes as he spoke.

"We're all here because we've decided that politics is for the politicians, and we've chosen serving the greater good over serving the whims of isolationists and petty dictators."

"We're above politics now," said Sigurdsson. "Look at what the people around this table have accomplished. For decades, even centuries, we've all been told how different we are, how our differences make us enemies. How we can't trust each other. Some of our leaders are still trying to beat that drum, but we've already proven that it's bullshit. Everyone here has been touched by this war in a different way, but every one of us has realized that whatever differences of opinion or belief or genetics or culture, we are stronger and better together."

Radko nodded emphatically.

"Admiral Chu and I can't change the fact that our respective flags are painted on our hulls," he said.

"But we can elect to ignore them," said Chu.

"And declare ourselves not members of our militaries," said Admiral Rhekar, "but members of a United Defense Fleet?"

"United Defense *Force*," said Sigurdsson. "Because we'll be landing troops on Earth."

To Radko's relief, all he saw around the table were nods of agreement.

"Then," said Singh, "we should get on with it."

Taking that as her cue, Stanton-West stood and, tapping the commands into her tablet, brought up a projection of the current and expected ril-galas deployment.

"As you can see, the ril-galas reinforcements appear to be converging on two distinct headings," she said. "The first is bringing ships directly at our current thinly-defended line here."

An overlay popped up indicating a small section of space defended only by the HMS Newcastle and the HMCS Haida Gwaii.

"The second projected path brings a larger number of enemy vessels into roughly the same area of Earth orbit as the debris field from the Hornet's Nest."

Another overlay popped into existence, but most at the table hadn't needed to be told where the remains of the Hornet's Nest floated.

Taking her feet off the table, Cagliari stood, frowning at the sand table display and leaning forward.

"So what are you fuckers looking for...?" she said, more to herself than the assembled group.

"You believe them to be looking for something?" said Chu.

"They have to be. The Hornets' Nest is destroyed, so there's nothing left there to defend, and we have ships in that area constantly, so it's not an easy entry point. There has to be a reason they're going there."

"I agree," said Rhekar. "This area of space is of no strategic value if we assume there is nothing there for them. Therefore, there must be something there for them."

"And they have to know that Thor's Hammer is our base of operations," said el Bahari. "Yet based on these projections, they're completely ignoring it."

"They want to keep Earth," said Radko, nodding slowly. "And there's something in the wreckage of the Hornet's Nest that they need."

El Bahari stood, turning to Stanton-West while nodding toward the projection.

"May I?"

With a nod, Stanton-West turned over control of the sand table to el Bahari.

"This appears to be a feint," she said, highlighting the ril-galas path to the Newcastle battle group. "Those ships will arrive before the main reinforcement fleet and no doubt begin attacking immediately."

"Hoping to draw ships away from their real target," said Radko, nodding.

"Trojan horse," said Cagliari.

Once again everyone looked at her.

"Sorry, thinking out loud here," she said. "My fighters are stealth fighters, and we know the ril-galas, with whatever detection technology they use, can't track them very well. But they're also insulated and pressurized, and while it might get chilly, they can stay in low power mode in space for several hours without the pilot having any issues."

"I'm not following," said Sigurdsson.

"The story of the Trojan horse. These dudes hid inside a giant wooden horse, and when their enemy took it inside his fortress, they came out and killed everyone," said Cagliari. "Except instead we hide Starfighters in a debris field."

"As advanced as your fighters are," said el Bahari, "we'll need capital ships if we're going to stop them."

Drumming his thick fingers on the table, Singh frowned at the projection in front of them.

"This must be a series of quick strikes," he said. "Not a line of warships the enemy will see from a great distance. We cannot give them time to adjust. The hidden Starfighters is a start, but will not be enough."

As Radko stared at the display, he narrowed his eye. Singh was right, the ruse with Cagliari's fighters, while an excellent idea, wasn't going to be enough. If the United Defense Fleet was already in position when the ril-galas arrived, they'd be able to adjust their attack and maybe even see through the ruse - which could prove disastrous for an Outlaw Squadron drifting in low-power mode. The bulk of the fleet needed to be nearby, but hidden from the ril-galas approach. And even then, would it be enough? Would the enemy be distracted enough by the debris of the Hornets' Nest to not question the lack of defensive presence?

Unlikely.

"We need a diversion. We can hide the fleet here," he said, a green triangle appearing beside the moon, directly opposite to the ril-galas approach vector. "But we need to keep their attention away from us and keep them from looking too closely at the debris field."

He turned to el Bahari.

"The HMCS Goose Bay. What's her condition?"

"She's not in great shape," said el Bahari with a shrug. "I'm not going to sugar coat it - we should keep her as far from the battle as we can. I doubt she could take much punishment."

"What if we don't need her to survive?" said Radko. "What if we use one of the enemy's own strategies against them?"

"The ghost ship," said Rhekar.

Radko nodded. Though he expected they'd tried it elsewhere, Radko had only encountered the situation once. The rilgalas had gutted an icaran cruiser and concealed their own battleships and fighters within the shell of its hull in an attempt to get closer to the enemy. It had nearly worked.

"Given our timeline, I do not believe it's feasible to gut a ship," said Rhekar.

"I don't want to gut it, I want to fill it with nuclear warheads."

"If we are able to get it close enough to the invasion fleet before it detonates," said Chu, nodding, "the combination of the warheads, plus the reactor, could be devastating."

"You'd need to ask for a volunteer to pilot it," said Sigurdsson.

Cagliari shook her head.

"No, the computer system on the Goose Bay is the same one that's on the Vimy Ridge," she said. "I can install a module with a rudimentary AI that can pilot a basic course, fire weapons, and blow the warheads and reactors when the time comes."

"You can do that in the small window we have left?" said Chu.

"I programmed my first AI when I was nine," said Cagliari with a wink. "This one I could do in my sleep."

"All right. Freyja, can you send one of your dreadnaughts to reinforce the Newcastle?"

"Yeah, of course," she said, nodding.

"Thank you. We'll also shift the INS Chennai from its patrol zone, and Admiral Rhekar, if you would be so kind as to send one of your ships to that engagement zone as well?"

"I will assign the Vir Lorocasis," said Rhekar.

"The remainder of the fleet will conceal itself on the far side of the moon, with Outlaw Squadron hiding in the debris field," said Radko. "The Goose Bay will engage and detonate, hopefully causing serious damage to the enemy, but more importantly causing enough of a distraction that they don't notice us until it's too late."

"And at which point, Outlaw Squadron will have already engaged," said Cagliari.

"One way or another," said el Bahari, "we'll be hitting them from the front and the flank."

"Is everyone in agreement?" said Radko.

Slowly, he looked around the table, meeting everyone's eyes in turn, and they all voiced their agreement.

"All right," he said, quickly glancing at the countdown.

09:03:51

"While we're fighting in orbit, we also need to begin our ground assault. For that, I'm going to defer to the Kaigor Kai Rii."

Typing a quick command into her tablet, Sigurdsson stood as the orbital and deployment projection was replaced with a larger holographic representation of Earth. A multitude of small red dots sprinkled the surface of the planet, along with a dozen larger ones.

"These dots represent concentrations of the distinct radiation signature generated by ril-galas technology as of four days ago," she said. "Our assumption is that the smaller dots are outposts and the larger ones are either command hubs, or... processing plants."

All the humans in attendance shifted uncomfortably.

"But we noticed changes within the last twenty-four hours," said Sigurdsson.

Tapping out another command, the display changed. The larger red dots grew in size by nearly twenty five percent, and while the overall number of smaller dots decreased, their concentration around the larger dots increased.

"They're consolidating their forces," said Rhekar.

"They're expecting us to attack," said el Bahari.

"If they weren't, they'd be idiots," said Sigurdsson. "They're probably shocked we haven't tried anything already."

"Just like the rest of us," said Cagliari.

"It may not look like it, but this is good news for us," said Sigurdsson. "The spacing between deployment zones now means they'll take longer to send reinforcements between them."

"We land an overwhelming force and crush one of these 'zones' before they can react," said Chu.

Sigurdsson shook her head.

"No. We have to remember, just like here in space, we're fighting a guerilla war," she said. "If we march a giant army on one of their command hubs, the entire occupation force knows where we are. They can send reinforcements because they know our whole force is in one spot."

Four green triangles appeared on the Earth's surface.

"So, we land four forces, four different locations. Places we know that there's an active resistance movement we can count on to have our back, but also places that can be easily defended if things go badly. Qala'at Sanjil in Tripoli, Lebanon; the Commonwealth Armed Forces survival training facility in Santarém, Brazil; Jiayuguan Fortress in Gansu, China; Edinburgh Castle in Edinburgh, Scotland."

"We absolutely need Edinburgh Castle," said el Bahari. "The Prince Regent is there, and Doctor Khaifa's role as leader of the Commonwealth is only until such time as a member of the Royal Family can take over and call an election."

"I was born in Quanhuxiang, which isn't far from Jiayuguan, so I approve of that location - the fortress was in excellent condition when I last visited," said Chu. "However, these landing sites are spread very far apart."

"That's the idea. With the current ril-galas deployment on Earth, they're also spreading themselves out. With four separate attacks, they won't be able to just send their forces to a single location, they'll have to either split their forces or choose to abandon some positions," said Sigurdsson. "We'll have several quick-strike teams in reserve - if they abandon a position, a strike team will swoop in to either claim that position for us, or hit the ril-galas from behind."

As Radko had expected, there was very little discussion. It was a good plan, a plan that the ril-galas would likely not be expecting. And it was, if he was being honest, the only workable plan that anyone had come up with.

"I would like to ask you all for a favour, though," said Sigurdsson. "I'd like us to all split our forces. Not me commanding the udukiin, and one of Chu's people commanding the Soviets, and one of Rhekar's people commanding the icarans. I want each of the four assault groups to have members from all of our armies. We need to show the people trapped on Earth what we're showing right here, right now."

"That we're all together on this," said Radko, nodding.

"Agreed," said Rhekar for the icarans.

Chu also nodded her agreement on behalf of the Soviets.

"All right," said Radko as he stood. "We all know what we have to do. No speech, let's just get this done."

08:42:17

One of Radko's biggest concerns about the plan to use the HMCS Goose Bay as a decoy ship - essentially an enormous missile - was the reaction of the Goose Bay's commanding officer, Lieutenant Commander Yvonne Keyootak, to giving up her ship. As it turned out, he needn't have worried. With the shape the Goose Bay was in, Keyootak didn't have much confidence taking her into battle again.

"Every time they try to bring their electro-reactive armour online," said Radko, "life support starts to shut down."

All the other attendees having departed, he was alone in the conference room with Sigurdsson. She'd sent her own entourage - with the exception of Jaeger - to the shuttle to wait for her.

"I guess since an AI doesn't need life support, Cagliari can shut that down to get the armour going?"

"Hopefully," he said, then paused for a moment, staring at the holographic Earth still hovering above the conference table. "We didn't cover this, but I assume you'll be leading one of the assault groups."

She nodded.

"I have to, Finn. I'm the War Matriarch, it's what I'm supposed to do. I'll have Aylaar and Elgraphaar take command of another. They won't like it, but they're smart and I trust them. And I think they'll be happier together than apart."

"I can understand that."

"Me too. But we don't really have that option right now."

"Yeah. And we don't have enough time right now either," he said, glancing at the countdown.

08:21:01

"It's a theme with us," she said, forcing a smile she clearly didn't feel.

He did the same, and neither spoke for what seemed like a very long time. But both were watching the clock and knew it had only been seconds.

"We could win this war today, Freyja," said Radko.

Nodding, Sigurdsson stared off into space for a moment.

"I know. If you'd told me, back when I was hunkered down on Van Daniken's Landing, just trying to survive, that we'd be in this position...," she said. "I don't know. I feel so disconnected from the person I was back then. Sometimes I can't remember what I felt in those early days. Sometimes I can't even remember what it was like to have human arms, or have five fingers."

Holding her hands in front of her face, she slowly moved the two fingers and thumb on each hand. Frankenstein had earned his name by replacing her failing cybernetic arms with the arms from a deceased icaran. With all that had happened since, it seemed like a dream to think back to the days when she was entirely human.

Reaching out, Radko took both of those blue hands in his own.

"I have a hard time remembering how I felt about most things," he said. "Because mostly I was just numb. I was just scrambling from one crisis to the next, no time to feel anything. And if I did start to feel it, I had to shove it away and not deal with it, because I had another crisis on my hands. But there was always one point of light for me."

"At the other end of the comm line," said Sigurdsson, and this time her smile was genuine.

"Then it got closer."

Leaning in, she kissed him, but then reluctantly pulled away and sighed.

"Having that clock counting down right beside us is a real fucking buzzkill," she said. "I need to go."

"I know."

Releasing her hands, Radko wished he could think of something inspirational to say, something that would reinforce that they were doing the right thing, that nothing would stop them. Something that would tell her to fight hard, but also to keep herself safe; to do whatever it took to secure the victory, but to not risk her life unnecessarily. Only one simple phrase came to mind and Sigurdsson was nearly at the door by the time he managed to say it.

"Freyja. I love you."

She turned, but only slightly, and he saw her smile.

"I love you too," she said, and then she disappeared through the door.

16

Edinburgh Castle was remarkably quiet given the number of survivors living within its walls, and as they sat huddled together in the small stone room that served as their war room, Ransom, Hunter, and Hobson were glad of it.

"If true, it changes everything," Hobson said.

Frowning, Ransom poured a cup of water and handed it to Hunter before standing from the table and pacing beside it.

"I still don't really understand what she was telling us," said Ransom, speaking of the young scout, Karina Jennings. "They go into this chamber and, what, get healed?"

"Essentially," said Hobson, rubbing his chin. "We have noticed that wounded foot soldiers - or damaged, whatever you prefer - disappear from the battlefield. The ones where we haven't killed the pilot. Based on what Jennings saw, the damaged units are placed inside these pod-type structures and they come out fully repaired."

"But just the units, the vehicle or whatever, right?" said Ransom.

They'd learned early on, thanks to the broadcast of an autopsy performed by Nasrin Khaifa, that the actual ril-galas were little more than brains with eyes and tentacles sitting inside the chest of what everyone called the ril-galas. The foot soldiers, the bats, the stalkers, and presumably the Starfighters and even capital ships were biomechanical constructs. Suits of armour worn by the ril-galas.

"Presumably."

Running a hand through her hair Ransom swore.

"This is really bad," she said.

"No," said Hunter. "It isn't."

Her first words since they'd sat down for the meeting caused both Ransom and Hobson to frown in her direction. Hunter continued to stare at the pitted surface of the wooden table, focusing on small details.

"It's not a bad thing that our enemy can heal their troops?" said Hobson.

Hunter nodded, but closed her eyes and massaged her temples before replying. Reaching across the table, Ransom put a hand on Hunter's forearm, but the older woman shook it off.

"I'm fine," she said, but realized how unconvincing it was. "I'm fine, let's just... I mean, yes, it's bad they can regenerate, but it's also good news."

Pausing again, she sipped the water Ransom had given her. The others simply waited, and while Hunter appreciated that they knew how hard it was becoming for her to pluck her own thoughts out of the psychic soup constantly flowing through her mind, she wished they would stop worrying so much about her. Hunter worried enough as it was, and the waves of worry from elsewhere just made the feeling worse.

She knew she was slipping.

"If they have these regen facilities, if they have to keep healing their soldiers," she said, "their occupation force might be smaller than we thought."

There was silence for a moment, and Hunter began to wonder if she'd actually said anything or if she'd just formulated the thought in her head but failed to convey it.

"We've been assuming they had a massive force," said Hobson finally. "Because they never seem to be depleted. But if the only reason they seem so strong is because of their regen..."

"If we were to take out those regen pods, we could really weaken them," said Ransom.

In spite of everything, Hunter smiled. Though she knew the girl would never admit, and would probably profess the exact opposite, she was growing into her role well. Not the role of Prince Arthur, but her role as a leader. In there with just the three of them, she was completely Harley Ransom, but she was becoming just as much a leader behind closed doors as she was in her public persona. And Hunter felt pride in that growth, proud that she'd helped someone else do what she had fought so hard to do herself - to grow beyond what she had been, and to make a difference.

If Ransom was to be her legacy, Hunter could leave this universe content.

The others were still talking, but Hunter wasn't listening. She could feel another wave coming. They were happening more and more frequently now, sudden crashes where the continual buzz of minds - the entire population of Edinburgh Castle - rose to a deafening roar in her skull.

Leaning forward, she clenched her teeth, gripped the arms of her chair

It came.

Hundreds of minds suddenly in her head. Yelling. Loving. Hating. Longing for love. Longing for death. Feeling betrayed, feeling defeated, feeling delirious. And the pain. The pain was like her skull was too small to contain it all, that it would split open at any moment and spill the jellied pulp of what remained onto the table in front of her.

But by far the worst of it was losing herself. In the torrent of thought and emotion, she became unmoored, not knowing what was her and what was someone else. Memories that belonged to someone else often lingered and in the worst cases replaced memories that were authentically hers.

She had lost the memory of her parents somewhere between when she'd damaged her mind and then, had them replaced by memories of someone else's parents. They seemed nice. Schoolteachers on one of the Lunar colonies. Supportive parents. Hadn't sold their daughter to the government like Hunter's own parents had, but now the two people who had sold young Quon Li-Chen to Project Nightwatch due to her natural abilities had been replaced by Linda and Theresa Morton. Replaced almost completely. That she was given up by her parents she remembered - it was ingrained into her identity in Nightwatch - but their names, their appearance? Gone.

Oddly, she took comfort in Linda and Theresa. They were good people, she was sure, and she was trying to be a good person herself. She wished she knew in whose memory they really belonged, so she could find out if they'd survived the invasion. Maybe even let their real child know how much of a comfort they had become to her.

"Hunter?"

The voice was Ransom's, loud and panicky.

"I'm here," she said, her voice sounding weak even to her own ears.

Somehow, she was slumped over the table, her cheek resting against the pitted wooden surface. The wave had passed, leaving behind the usual throbbing headache, but as she lifted her head and felt the small puddle of drool at her cheek, Hunter realized it may not have passed as quickly as she'd thought.

"You scared us," said Ransom, kneeling at Hunter's side, a hand on her shoulder.

In that moment, the girl looked far older than she had a right to in Hunter's eyes. Far more mature.

"Did I pass out?"

"For nearly nine minutes," said Hobson.

He was watching her closely, but the warmth and worry in his eyes made Hunter smile a little - at least inside.

"I'm back now," she said with a small smile. "Did we win the war while I was out?"

A feeble attempt at humour, she knew, but it made Ransom chuckle, so it worth it.

"Not yet," said Ransom.

"Then we'd better make some plans. We should... probably try to take out one of those...," Hunter paused. The word she wanted wasn't coming to her. "The re..."

"Regeneration?"

"Regeneration pods. Yes."

Hobson nodded at first, but he was frowning in a way that telegraphed his thoughts so clear that Hunter didn't need to try to separate his from the jumble of others drifting through her head.

"Shortly, but not yet. Two of our other scouts came in after Jennings," he said. "They saw a large number of ril-galas on the move."

"Another attack?" said Ransom.

"No, they all appeared to be converging on the processing plant in Holyrood Park. With so many ril-galas all headed to the same place, I'm not sure we'd be able to launch an attack of any significance."

"We'd have to get through a horde just to hit our target," said Ransom, dropping heavily into a chair.

The disappointment radiated off Ransom with such intensity that Hunter had to grit her teeth and force it down, lest it take over her own emotions. If she could determine what those even were.

"We don't have the numbers for that," she said. "But we could..."

She winced at a sudden sharp pain in her left temple that was gone as quickly as it arrived.

"We could launch small strikes. Distract them from whatever they're trying to do," she continued. "At least keep them occupied until help arrives."

Neither Hobson nor Ransom responded at first, nor did she need them to. Even in the cacophony swirling in her mind, Hunter could pick out certain thoughts and feelings being projected by those in closest proximity to her. Practicing doing so, focusing on those strands of other peoples' thoughts that drifted through her mind, had become the only way to prevent completely losing herself to whatever mental injury she'd sustained in focusing - weaponizing - her abilities into the mind of a ril-galas attacker. She was unquestionably unmoored, but focusing on the thoughts of those to whom she was closest - Ransom, in particular - had kept her from drifting away.

And so she responded to the young woman's unspoken fear.

"Yes, there will be help coming," she said, nodding as much to herself as the others. "Doctor Khaifa is in charge of the Commonwealth now. Which probably means Radko is in charge of the war effort."

"But...," Ransom said, hesitating.

Hunter nodded as if Ransom had continued the thought. She had, but not verbally and as Hunter began to respond she realized she wasn't sure anymore how much of the recent conversation had been spoken aloud and how much was just her responding to unspoken thoughts.

"He didn't try to liberate Earth the first time because it wasn't possible with the resources he had," she said.

"And based on what we know about the destruction of the Hornets' Nest," said Hobson, "there are a lot more assets in play now."

"Khaifa won't hold back support like the ATC Castle woman did," said Hunter.

"Which brings us to another point," said Hobson, frowning in Ransom's direction.

"We had no way of knowing," said Hunter.

"And we've taken this too far to tell people now," said Ransom. "I mean, they'll fucking riot. But at the same time, I sure as hell can't be head of a government, even temporarily."

Taking another sip of water, Hunter nodded. Her head felt like it was filled with cotton-wrapped concrete - fuzzy, but extremely heavy.

"Getting ahead of ourselves," she said, beginning to slur her words slightly. "We need... First step is to get help down here. Prince Arthur being temporary leader of the Commonwealth will be a moot point... if we never get out from under the occupation."

"And when we do get free, I think there's only one option here," said Ransom. "Arthur has to die again."

17

"Prince Arthur will be taking over as interim leader of the Commonwealth the moment we're able to either secure the planet or get him to safety," said Khaifa. "Whichever we can do first."

Assembled in the small restaurant, amid heavy security provided by Ironhorse and his Revelstoke Rangers, were key members of the Thor's Hammer community, officials from the Commonwealth government - who had not been coopted by Upshaw's money - and representatives of the Commonwealth Armed Forces. The latter had been brought in by Mahoney, though he himself was not present. Also in attendance, to Khaifa's surprise, were two ATC Castle operators, vouched for by Ironhorse, who apparently represented a small group of the same who were, in Ironhorse's words, not entirely displeased with recent developments.

The meeting had been a very formal affair to that point, with plenty of discussion of the Constitution, and Khaifa was beginning to feel the crash of her adrenaline wearing off.

"Look," she said with a sigh, "let's set aside all the legal stuff and all the political stuff for a moment."

Some eyes that had glazed over were attentive once more.

"I really and truly did not want it to come to this. But something had to be done, and someone had to do it," she said, shrugging. "I hoped that it could be anyone but me... but here we are."

"Upshaw is calling this a coup," said one of the ATC Castle operators - a rough-looking man in his forties that Khaifa was fairly certain was called Winkler, "and is calling for you to be arrested for treason."

"And yet here you are," she said, spreading her arms wide.

"Maybe I'm just here to get a read on the enemy."

"The enemy of what, exactly, Mister Winkler? An enemy of ATC Castle? Yes, I'm probably an enemy of ATC Castle at this point, but then the claim of treason would be irrelevant - you can't commit treason against a corporation. An enemy of Bianca Upshaw? Absolutely. An enemy of Rocco de Freitas? Certainly. He and Upshaw have been fighting two wars, but only their private war of personal grudges has been getting their full focus and full support, while the real war was treated as some annoying side concern," said Khaifa. "Treason? Everything I've done has been according to the letter of the Commonwealth Constitution, while Upshaw's very appointment to the role of Deputy Prime Minister contravenes that same Constitution, and de Freitas's willful disregard for his responsibilities to the citizens of the Commonwealth laid out in that Constitution is an unforgivable dereliction of office."

"...unforgivable dereliction of office."

It may have been the applause that followed that set Upshaw off the deep end. It wasn't clear if Khaifa knew the meeting was being broadcast, but Upshaw had to assume no one else did - otherwise the traitors Winkler and Santoro wouldn't have been so brazen in their attendance. Or maybe they would have. Maybe this was their way of putting on a public show of support for Khaifa? Or was it a subterfuge to get close to her?

Neither one was well enough known to her to decide.

"Vossek," she said, "why aren't they moving against her? We have a standing order."

Looking first at Upshaw then back to the screen, Vossek reached out and tapped the screen in several spots, indicating men Upshaw didn't recognise. No, wait. She did recognize one - the soldier who had been guarding Khaifa for the last several weeks.

"These men," said Vossek, "are members of the Revelstoke Rangers. Highly trained, highly capable, and highly dangerous. Winkler and Santoro are decent operators, but they're outclassed by a fair margin in that room."

"You have a lower opinion of our training programs than I would have expected."

"ATC Castle training programs are good," said Vossek, apparently unaware he was further darkening Upshaw's mood. "But the Commonwealth Ranger program is the best there is. We have a long way to go before we can consider ourselves on equal footing."

Of course. Vossek himself had been a Commonwealth Ranger before she'd recruited him, so it made sense he'd try to build them up to near-mythical status.

"Where the fuck is de Freitas?" she said.

One of her newer hires, whose name she hadn't cared to learn, spoke up.

"He's in his quarters, refusing to leave."

"Under guard?"

"Of course, Ma'am."

"Fucking coward. Vossek, we know where this meeting is taking place," she said. "So why is it *still taking place?*"

It took Vossek a second longer than she liked to turn his attention back to her from whatever the hell he was doing on his tablet.

"I'm not sure what you're asking, Bianca."

She clenched her jaw. Fucking underlings calling her by her first name.

"I want you to send in operators. Two fire teams," she said through clenched teeth. "I want Khaifa either in custody or dead within the hour."

"All right," he said, hesitating. "But there are civilians there. And, as much as I hate to say this, we've double-checked and her Constitutional argument-"

"Fuck the Constitution. Fuck the civilians. Fuck Nasrin fucking Khaifa. I will double the annual salary of whatever operator puts her in a jail cell or puts a bullet in her head. I'll be happy with either," she said. *"Get it fucking done, Vossek."*

His pause was only the briefest of moments, but Upshaw knew she'd cowed him.

"I'll relay the order," he said, tapping his tablet again.

"Good," she said.

The sooner they re-established control over this mess the better.

18

06:39:51

As Sigurdsson had expected, Elgraphaar and Aylarr protested the idea of leading their own assault group rather than staying under her command, though their reasons were not what she'd expected. While the strategy meeting had been going on, a new icaran ship had arrived to assist, carrying aboard it a team of Commandos. The commandos were led by Brigadier Arysis, who had been Elgraphaar's commanding officer for years prior to him joining the commando unit led by Brigadier General Locaris. Though she had initially pushed back on the idea, Elgraphaar and Aylarr had convinced Sigurdsson that with the experience and command ability Arysis brought to the table, she was the ideal candidate to lead one of the assault groups. And though she would never admit it, Sigurdsson was relieved she'd been convinced – having the two icarans continue to be at her side gave her some comfort.

With the udukiin dropship rattling its way through Earth atmosphere, Sigurdsson did her best to relax, but while she was projecting an outward calm - she'd had plenty of practice - inside, her stomach was doing somersaults. This operation, making planetfall on occupied Earth, had been the goal for what seemed an eternity. It was what most human soldiers she knew talked about in hushed tones in the back of the pub, or in louder tones depending on alcohol consumption, but though none would have admitted it then, they all thought it was a fantasy. They'd not seen any way to make it a reality.

But then the Kaigor Kai Rii had come, and the dream was about to become real.

And now she had to just make sure they didn't fuck it up.

Glancing down at the wrist-mounted data receiver Cagliari had given her, Sigurdsson almost wished she hadn't.

06:32:23

Six hours. No one knew what to expect when the enemy reinforcements arrived, but they had to work on the assumption it would be an all-out assault, both in space and on the planet. Sigurdsson, Arysis, and the two other strike team commanders – Captain Orlov from the Soviets and Major Guinness of the Commonwealth – and their teams needed to have made significant gains before then. The assault groups were substantial forces thanks to the combined Commonwealth, Soviet, icaran, and udukiin armies, but if they couldn't make the operation a success, there was no guarantee for safe passage back to their points of origin. Those ships would be engaged with the enemy. And if that part of the battle went poorly, then Sigurdsson and all the ground troops would be trapped on Earth.

19

The first sign of trouble had been when the ATC Castle operators in attendance - Winkler and Santoro - both put their hands
to their earpieces, frowned, and then looked up at Khaifa in
such perfect unison it may have been comical under different
circumstances. By the time the pair drew their concealed weapons, Ironhorse had already drawn his REV2 pistol and placed
himself between Khaifa and the hostiles.

Their weapons were little snub-nosed pistols, not designed
for combat. One of many ATC Castle firearm products targeted
to the civilian consumer, the Starling was a compact, light-
weight self defense pistol. Its magazine contained only three
rounds, and while accuracy at a range outside ten feet could be
questionable, its short-range effectiveness was strong.

"Stop," said Ironhorse, raising the barrel of his REV2 and
aiming directly at the chest of Winkler, the closer of the two.

"Winkler, stop," said Santoro.

It was then that Ironhorse realized that while Winkler had
been raising his weapon in Khaifa's direction, Santoro's was
pointed at his compatriot.

Winkler froze and two members of Ironhorse's Rangers
swooped in, disarmed him, and hauled him toward the back of
the restaurant. Santoro slowly set his Starling on a nearby table
and raised his hands. Gun still trained on the man, Ironhorse
double-checked that Khaifa was all right before approaching
Santoro.

"That your only weapon?" he said, nodding in the direction
of the Starling.

"I have a knife in my boot," said Santoro, "but that's it."

Quickly ducking down and removing the knife from Santoro, Ironhorse holstered his weapon. The Rangers were on high alert and he knew at least two would be keeping a close watch on Santoro's movements - the man would be dead in a heartbeat if he tried anything stupid.

"You guys heard something," he said, tapping his ear to indicate the communication that had clearly precipitated Winkler's action.

Nodding, Santoro looked ashamed. As if to highlight the feeling, he began to pick at the ATC Castle patch stitched his shoulder, trying to work free the stitches.

"There's been a bounty placed on her," said Santoro, glancing over at Khaifa. "Double salary."

"Good money," said Ironhorse. "Why the change of heart?"

Frustrated with his lack of progress on the patch, Santoro tore off his jacket and threw it to the floor.

"Because I'm a soldier, not a fucking assassin. The bounty is capture or kill, and let's be honest, there are people on the payroll who'd be happy with the easy money that one bullet can bring."

Ironhorse nodded. It was sad but true.

"And that bounty was broadcast to all ATC Castle operators?"

"Yeah," said Santoro. "So, you guys need to get her somewhere safe, because everyone knows where she is right now."

Scooping up the Starling, Ironhorse went back to Khaifa and handed her the small pistol.

"What's this for?"

"Just in case," he said. "Upshaw's put a price on your head. Dead or alive."

For a moment, Khaifa just stared, mouth open and eyes wide, before gathering her wits and drawing herself up.

"Is it a lot of money?"

"Double salary."

"And to think my mother said no one would ever value me," she said. "Still, I'd appreciate it if you'd do your best to make sure no one collects."

"We need to move," he said, signalling the same to his Rangers.

"What about them?"

Ironhorse followed her gaze to Santoro, standing on his own looking angry - mostly at himself - and Winkler, tied to a chair near the back on the restaurant.

"He can stay here," said Ironhorse of Winkler, before directing his attention to the other man. "Santoro. Pick a side."

"Just did," he replied, kicking his discarded ATC Castle jacket aside with his boot.

"Good."

"Can I get a gun?"

"Fuck no."

"Fair."

Winkler was yelling obscenities, but Ironhorse wasn't sure if they were being directed at Khaifa or Santoro, and he had neither the time nor the inclination to find out.

"Captain, getting reports of PMC fire teams heading our way," said Sergeant Tangaroa.

"All right, let's move out," said Ironhorse, placing a hand on Khaifa's forearm. "Doctor, stay behind me. If we get separated for any reason, you stay with Tangaroa. Understood?"

Khaifa nodded as Tangaroa's massive frame slid in beside her. Two other Rangers appeared as well - Janz and Nomura - filling in the remaining two of four points around the doctor.

At Ironhorse's signal they began moving as a unit out of the restaurant and into the main corridors of the station.

Though he kept the muzzle of his gun low to avoid spooking the civilians, Ironhorse felt ready to take on whatever came. This was what he was good at, close quarters combat, and it felt like ages since he'd seen action. Even so, the Captain was conflicted about the situation - while he certainly felt ready to see action again, given the wider state of the galaxy, he wasn't thrilled to be seeing potential action against fellow humans, ATC Castle or otherwise.

That didn't mean he wouldn't shoot them if he had to.

20

05:55:40

The countdown continued.

For el Bahari, she didn't know what was worse - knowing how little time was left before the coming battle, or knowing how much time was left. The Vimy Ridge, now hers to command by Mahoney's orders rather than simply Radko's absence, would be in position on the far side of Earth's moon within twenty minutes, and after that, the following five hours would be a waiting game. A very tense waiting game, given that Cagliari's fighter squadron was going to be very exposed in the Hornets' Nest debris field.

And for all el Bahari's reputation as a heartless officer, she'd found - surprisingly - that she quite liked Cagliari. While her logical brain knew that the pseudo-Trojan horse plan could work, her emotional brain was struggling with it.

"Fleet status," she said, knowing that there was probably little more to be said on the matter since her last update.

"Outlaw Squadron is going through pre-flight checks," said Owens, who had kept his interactions with el Bahari to a minimum recently. "The Royal Sovereign confirms the AI Cagliari installed on the Goose Bay is up and running. The additional warheads are currently being loaded."

"Anything from Earth?"

"Not at this point, Commander."

Though she knew Owens wouldn't be looking at her, el Bahari nodded anyway. They both knew he'd need to be reassigned eventually, assuming that they survived the day and that she remained in command of the Vimy Ridge. Neither was a given, but the assumption that there was a future to plan for calmed her nerves, if only marginally.

"Incoming transmission from the Royal Sovereign," said one of the communications technicians.

"I'll take it in the dome," said el Bahari, making her way to the second level of the command deck to the secondary sand table.

Accepting the transmission, el Bahari watched in surprise as a window sprang to life over the sand table, a holographic Finn Radko within. The communications equipment aboard the Vimy Ridge wasn't usually strong enough for full holographic transmissions - the majority of calls el Bahari, or Radko before her, had taken aboard the ship had been audio-only due to technical limitations. As Commonwealth vessels went, the Vimy Ridge wasn't the oldest and was by no means outdated, but she was also not top of the line. In fact, prior to the invasion, the Ridge had been on a short list of ships to be docked at Thor's Hammer for an extended period of retrofitting. Clearly the equipment aboard the HMS Royal Sovereign was new enough and powerful enough to overcome the Vimy Ridge's technological deficiencies.

"Captain," said el Bahari. "I'm told progress is good with the Goose Bay?"

"Nothing currently on fire, so it's been a better day than most," said Radko.

El Bahari nodded in spite of herself.

"I find myself agreeing with you more and more these days," she said.

"That's disconcerting."

"Absolutely."

"I have two things for you," he said, becoming serious again. "First, we have krellin ships inbound. Two of them, following in behind the ril-galas."

"Krellin?" she said frowning. "Frankly, I had almost forgotten about them. I assume their system was hit by the invasion as well, then?"

"Yes, and apparently quite badly. The only reason they're able to send ships now is that the retreat of the ril-galas ended a complete blockade," he said. "I just wanted to make sure everyone's aware that we have some friendlies coming in directly behind the not-so-friendlies."

"I'll make sure everyone here is aware."

"Thanks," he said. "Next order of business is that I've just discovered I owe you a debt of gratitude."

Waving a hand dismissively, el Bahari chuckled.

"Our situation being what it is, I think we're past keeping tally of who owes who anything," she said.

"Even so, I appreciate it. I'm just in awe of the scale of it," he said. "Using ATC Castle the way you did, relaying false information, coordinating things with Ironhorse while were lightyears away? I think you missed your calling - you should have been in intelligence."

"Captain...," she said, sighing. "I'm glad it turned out the way it did, and I appreciate the kind words, but I should tell you that this wasn't always a grand plan to thwart ATC Castle."

Though she was planning to say more, Radko held up his hand to stop her, and smiled.

"Amira, not a one of us is an angel. The important thing is that when it came down to the critical decisions, you chose to do what you felt was right," he said. "But you even went one step further and you put things in place to prevent bad actors from kneecapping our ability to continue doing what's right."

El Bahari just forced a smile. The decision about which side to back in the Radko versus Upshaw situation had been more difficult than she was prepared to admit, both for how it would sound to others, but more important, how disappointed she was in herself with the benefit of hindsight.

"What was it that changed your mind?" said Radko.

"Cortez," she said without hesitation. "A good officer was railroaded for no reason other than revenge. That's when I knew - and told Max the same - that even though de Freitas could be dangerous in his position, Upshaw was the more dangerous of the two. If she was-"

She paused, frowning as her tablet bleeped with an urgent incoming transmission from Thor's Hammer. But not from Ironhorse. Not from anyone she could identify - the transmission was encrypted, the sender blocked.

The message itself was text only, but attached was an audio recording, a very short one judging by the file size.

Your people should be aware of this. Perhaps Khaifa can use it in a broadcast.

"Problem?" said Radko.

She quickly tethered her tablet to the sand table and tied it in to their transmission so Radko could see the text.

"Who sent it?" he said.

"I can't tell, the encryption is stronger than the tools I have available here," she said. "The audio file is just that - no red flags being raised about intrusion software."

As she played back the audio, both she and Radko frowned, their eyes narrowing in anger.

"I'm not sure what you're asking, Bianca."

It was a male voice, and one el Bahari recognized immediately.

"That's Edward Vossek," she said.

The second voice was obviously Bianca Upshaw.

"I want you to send in operators. Two fire teams. I want Khaifa either in custody or dead within the hour."

"All right," Vossek was saying. *"But there are civilians there. And, as much as I hate to say this, we've double-checked and her Constitutional argument-"*

"Fuck the Constitution. Fuck the civilians. Fuck Nasrin fucking Khaifa. I will double the annual salary of whatever operator puts her in a jail cell or puts a bullet in her head. I'll be happy with either. Get it fucking done, Vossek."

"I'll relay the order," Vossek said as the recording ended.

Both el Bahari and Radko stood in silence for a moment.

"She's gone off the deep end," said Radko, finally. "We need to warn Khaifa - and Ironhorse."

"I'm forwarding the message and the audio to Khaifa, Ironhorse, Mahoney, and Van Der Berg," she said, her finger flying over the surface of her tablet to get the task completed. "I don't know how long ago this was recorded, but clearly the orders have already been given."

An insistent alert began beeping on the sand table, unrelated to the message being relayed.

El Bahari saw Radko reacting to something similar on his end before he spoke.

"The Newcastle just picked up the first group of ril-galas ships," he said. "The first wave is almost here."

05:38:01

"Contact!"

Ironhorse was able to call out the warning a split second before the ATC Castle fire team – five men, all armed with the standard Caliburn submachine guns – opened fire.

As bullets pinged into the corridor wall, Ironhorse dropped to one knee and returned fire with short bursts from his 33A1. Behind and to his right, he heard another one of his team returning fire, and knew it would be Nomura, just as he knew that Janz and Tangaroa would have immediately taken up more defensive positioning around Khaifa. Firing another two quick bursts to keep the enemy at bay, Ironhorse signalled for Nomura to take his place at point, and once she did, he dropped back to Tangaroa and Janz.

As a utility and storage area, the corridor in which they travelled was dotted with alcoves and shelving areas, and it was within one of these alcoves, completely hidden behind Tangaroa, that Nasrin Khaifa has been placed.

"We haven't got time for this," said Ironhorse, firing again as the ATC Castle team made an attempt to move closer. Nomura had fired at the same moment, and by the yelp that echoed down the corridor, one of them had scored a hit.

Tangaroa nodded.

"We should keep moving. Longer we stay, the easier a target we are."

"Doctor, how are you doing?"

"This is the first time I've been shot at," she said. "But I'm sure I'll get used to it."

Her jaw was clenched, but her voice was steady and Ironhorse noticed a stubbornness set in her jaw that would rival Amira's.

He smiled slightly.

"Then we move and we move quickly. On my mark, we advance as a unit. Nomura and I in the lead, then Tangaroa and Khaifa. Janz, you bring up the rear."

Without waiting for acknowledgement – he knew his people well enough to know they'd all be on the same page – Ironhorse began his advance. Nomura fell in beside him and the pair moved forward at a quick pace, not quite running, but moving quickly enough to surprise the ATC Castle team, who poked their heads out of cover to find the Rangers nearly on top of them.

Squeezing his trigger, Ironhorse double-tapped one of the PMCs in the face and Nomura took out another as he tried to bring his own weapon to bear.

The remaining three were about to break – either surrender or run – Ironhorse could see it in their eyes, and for a moment, he felt hope that they could end this without any more human blood being spilled. But then he also saw the moment when all three realized how close they were to Nasrin Khaifa, and thus how close they were to a whole lot of Upshaw's money.

Almost in unison, like it was choreographed ahead of time, the three operators raised their Caliburns.

And so Ironhorse, Nomura, and Tangaroa squeezed their triggers.

05:20:37

The assault team had started taking fire the moment they entered Earth's atmosphere.

Swarmed by ril-galas bats, the dropships had to make liberal use of their gunners - ball turrets mounted fore and aft - and even still felt the continual impact of both weapons fire and physical collision with the bats until they dropped in low to the ground. Damage was minimal, certainly not enough to affect their landing, as the bats appeared designed more to attack soldiers on the ground as opposed to vehicles in the air.

But like the ril-galas ground troops, the bats appeared to be clustering in specific zones versus being an all-round presence. After the initial onslaught was weathered, the three ships that made up Sigurdsson's assault group skimmed low over the Scottish Borders and Lothian, and into Edinburgh.

It was dusk when the trio of dropships set down on Calton Hill, among the ruins of several monuments which Elgraphaar examined.

"Had you visited this place when these were intact?" he said, squatting by a pile of broken and scorched stone.

The stone was clearly very old, but the damage was clearly the opposite.

Sigurdsson sighted along the barrel of her gunstaff and scanned the area. A team of her udukiin soldiers had been assigned to secure the landing zone already and were no doubt doing so quickly and efficiently, but old habits die hard. Back at Fort Hathaway, Sigurdsson had been both first and last line of defense.

Lowering her gunstaff, she returned her attention to Elgraphaar, who held a piece of broken stone the size of an apple.

"No," she said, shaking her head. "Most of my travelling was with the army, and that was to other planets."

"It is a shame," said Elgraphaar, gently setting down the piece of rubble before standing. "It pains me to see history so poorly treated."

From across the hill Aylarr jogged up, *aoran* assault rifle in her hands.

"A perimeter has been established, but there is a large, open area in that direction," she said, pointing to the East of what looked like a small, truncated mountain. "Containing several ril-galas structures as well as a substantial ground force. A detachment appears to have already been sent in our direction."

Sigurdsson swore under her breath and reflexively looked at her timer.

05:14:11

"How many?"

"Difficult to say, but it does not appear substantial," said Aylarr, looking at their assembled force. "Certainly not what would be required, given the size of our assault group."

"But enough to potentially slow us down until they bring in reinforcements," said Sigurdsson.

"Likely their goal," agreed Elgraphaar.

After some discussion, it was agreed that Aylarr would remain at the landing site with the entire team from one of the dropships in order to keep the site secure. A trio of sniper teams, two from the Commonwealth Army and one from the icarans, were deployed at various points on Calton Hill facing what Sigurdsson learned was called Holyrood Park - where the udukiin appeared to be headquartered. The occupants of the remaining two ships followed Sigurdsson down a sloping path, past a tower-like structure broken off to half its height, and through a small wooded area.

The icaran commandos all had their *aoran* assault rifles to their shoulders, the Commonwealth soldiers were ready with their 33A1s, as were the udukiin with their gunstaves. The Soviet troops had their rifles at the ready as well, but Sigurdsson couldn't remember what model they were - she'd had so much new information come into her head recently, other facts were bound to have been pushed out. Apparently, the name of the Chinese-made assault rifle favoured by the Soviet Army was one of them. The more important aspect of her observations was twofold: first, every soldier, regardless of species or political affiliation was alert and ready and focused. Second, they weren't clustered among their own. Two Soviets were quietly chatting to an icaran, while several udukiin marched side by side with Commonwealth soldiers. She had assigned Udrach to take point as they'd headed out, but allowed him to select his own lead group. He'd chosen representatives of all four factions and it occurred to Sigurdsson as she looked at her assault group that the term 'faction' may not be appropriate any longer.

A Commonwealth Sergeant named Apone said something quietly to the Soviet Sergeant Major to his left, and the big Russian - his name was either Rustikov or Rusnikov - laughed.

An icaran commando and an udukiin warrior traded weapons, an *aoran* for a gunstaff.

Tatrex Kai Uro, one of the udukiin who had come with Sigurdsson along with Udrach from Her Glorious Vengeance, showed off to a Soviet Private the long knives she and most udukiin kept strapped to their chest.

Though she'd never had a high opinion of human nature, or the ability of any species to overcome its own ego, the United Defense Force was a reality.

Sigurdsson felt herself starting to smile.

And it wasn't just a name. It was an actual thing, it was physical and she could see it happening.

Then she saw Udrach raise one of his left fists while the hands of his lower arms gripped the hilts of his knives. Every single being stopped, crouched low and brought their weapons to their shoulders, scanning the area with their eyes.

Sigurdsson, with Jaeger at her heels and Elgraphaar at her side, quickly but carefully made her way to Udrach's side.

"What do you see?" said Sigurdsson, her voice low. However, she answered her own question a moment later - or more accurately, her passenger helped answer it.

In bonding with the Matriarch, Sigurdsson had gained increased strength, speed, and durability, but she had also gained some low-level psionic abilities than she neither fully understood, nor knew how to use. But the Matriarch, sentient despite being a symbiont, had a habit of stepping in to help. At first, Sigurdsson had hated and resented the intrusions, but as she and the Matriarch had spent more time bonded, the intrusions had become less about the Matriarch trying to direct Sigurdsson's actions and more about negating - or attempting to negate - Sigurdsson's weaknesses.

There were people approaching. Humans.

The knowledge slid into her mind in the way that Sigurdsson had come to recognize. Since there was nothing resembling conversation between her and the Matriarch, learning to tell the difference between her own thoughts and those that had been supplied to her had been one of the harder parts of the bonding, and had, at first, made Sigurdsson feel like the Matriarch was attempting to control her mind. She knew now that the Matriarch had no other way to communicate, and while an udukiin would have instinctively been able to differentiate between their own thoughts and those communicated by the Matriarch, the human brain was wired differently. The Matriarch knew now to 'flavour' the thoughts differently to assist, and it was that flavour that Sigurdsson felt now.

"How many?" she said, speaking to Udrach. If the Matriarch knew, that information would have been supplied automatically.

Udrach twirled his fingers in the udukiin equivalent of a shrug to indicate he was unsure.

"I can hear them," said Elgraphaar from behind his faceless helmet. "I estimate no more than twelve. Likely fewer."

Sigurdsson nodded. Between the udukiin senses and the icaran technology, they were well positioned to spot a potential ambush in advance. That the approaching group was human eased her mind somewhat, but despite how the UDF was developing, Sigurdsson wasn't prepared to give humanity a blanket pass. There was too much brutal history on that planet to ignore.

Raising her gunstaff, she took point with Jaeger and signalled the group to follow.

Slowly, they advanced, proceeding more quietly than Sigurdsson had hoped. The sun was beginning to set, and the light filtering through the trees would give them a natural camouflage... but it would do the same for the approaching group. Tapping her index finger against her temple, the connection between the two activation nodes - one in her temple and one in her finger - activated the optics mode of her cybernetic eye and cycled through to infrared. As always, doing so gave her an instant headache, but a little pain was better than falling for an ambush.

To be safe, Sigurdsson waved forward Elgraphaar and Otaris, one of the other icaran commandos. First pointing to her own eyes then pointing down the path, the commandos understood immediately and took up position on either side of her. The optics built into those faceless helms were far more advanced than the outdated technology in Sigurdsson's eye.

As she held up a clenched fist, the whole group stopped as one. Sigurdsson and the first few ranks knelt to give as many soldiers as possible clear shots, but the path was fairly narrow - even shoulder to shoulder there was only room for five between the stone wall on their left and the trees and steep hill on their right.

They didn't have to wait long.

"Stop," said Sigurdsson.

The group of people slowly skulking up the path froze. The sound of distant gunfire echoed over the city.

"We're from the castle."

The person who stepped forward was little more than a kid, and she looked dirty and disheveled even by the low standards of the rest of her group. All of them carried weapons, a mixture of civilian and military models of varying vintages and quality. The kid who had spoken didn't carry any weapon at all that Sigurdsson could see.

"I'm Karina," said the kid, wiping her nose on her sleeve. "The Prince asked me to come get you."

Sigurdsson hesitated.

"Ok, so, like Hunter thought you might be squirrelly about it," said Karina. "So, she said I should, like, tell you..."

The kid screwed up her face in concentration, apparently trying to remember the message word for word.

"Um, she was Radko's radar, but you were his anchor...? I don't get it, but you're supposed to, I guess."

"I do," said Sigurdsson, getting to her feet. Her soldiers relaxed, but not completely.

"Freyja Sigurdsson," she said, shaking the kid's hand.

"Cool. Can we go?"

"Yeah. You can lead us to the castle?"

Nodding, the kid turned and headed back down the path. One of the survivors with her, a man with some military experience by his bearing, though quite a while ago based on his age, offered Sigurdsson a shrug.

"She's in her own world a lot of the time," he said. "But she's a fantastic scout. The castle isn't far, less than thirty minutes' walk."

Signaling her team to follow, Sigurdsson headed down the path a few paces behind Karina. They were led out onto a wide street lined with buildings, some damaged and some all but demolished. Very few had remained untouched, and Sigurdsson suspected every single one had been raided for supplies or anything of value ages ago. She assigned a rear guard, given how exposed they were on the street, but as the force crossed what Karina called the North Bridge, passing over a large transit station with a caved-in roof, they hadn't encountered any resistance. The sound of sustained gunfire and the boom of icaran weaponry could be heard clearly from back in the direction of Calton Hill and Sigurdsson clenched her teeth.

"They will be all right," said Elgraphaar, as if it was he and not the Matriarch who could read her thoughts. "Aylarr is well experienced in holding defensive positions, and has more than enough personnel at her disposal. The landing site does not have any easy ground approaches for the ril-galas to exploit, and our soldiers have the high ground."

Sigurdsson grunted her reluctant agreement as she followed Karina onto a wide, old street - old enough that the centre of the street was still what she thought was cobblestone. Passing a roundabout and the remains of some kind of burned-out cathedral, the street narrowed significantly. Beyond the centuries old walls of the remaining buildings and the piles of rubble, Sigurdsson saw the high walls of Edinburgh Castle.

But in the open esplanade before the castle gates, she saw ril-galas.

23

"Have you heard this?" said Van Der Berg.

Khaifa had just dropped into a chair, her heart still pounding in her chest, hands shaking. When the adrenaline began to wear off, she knew, she was in for a crash of epic proportions. The words were out of her mouth before her brain could stop them.

"I was just in a fucking shootout," she said. "I haven't heard anything but gunfire and swearing. Most of the latter coming from me."

Though it was incomprehensible to her that anyone could have that reaction, when she glanced over at Ironhorse - who had no doubt saved her life multiple times that day - the man was smiling and laughing with one of his fellow Rangers. As much as she wanted to ask how the hell he could be happy after what they'd just gone through, Van Der Berg had taken a seat directly in front of her and was handing Khaifa a tablet.

"I know, and I'm very glad you're safe," said the spymaster. "But as we all know, no crisis is obligated to wait its turn."

"That's the truth," said Khaifa, rubbing her temples with her free hand. "What do we have?"

"Potentially something to help end one of our current crises," said Van Der Berg, pointing to the message displayed on the tablet. "I've run it through all the authentication protocols I have access to - which is most - and I'm as certain as I can be that this is real."

Frowning, Khaifa hit play and her eyes got wider with every sentence.

"We received it during your adventurous return here."

"So, the timing works for it to be real," said Khaifa. "Which means two things."

Khaifa stood, then realized how shaky her legs felt, so sat again, leaned back and rubbed her temples with both hands.

"First," she said. "The 'catch or kill' order, or whatever we're calling it, did go out and it came directly from Bianca Upshaw. Second... someone sent us this."

"And recorded it in the first place."

"So, someone who is - or was - inside Upshaw's control centre has realized she's lost her mind. Unless... is this another Ironhorse thing? You're not running some kind of shadow operation and not telling me, are you?"

Van Der Berg shook her head.

"I wish I could take credit for this, but you can be sure I'm trying to make contact with the person who sent it," she said.

"If nothing else, we need to make sure they're safe," said Khaifa. "If Upshaw finds out about this..."

"When."

"What?"

"*When* Upshaw finds out about this. She will find out about it, likely sooner than we'd hope. The recording has to be made public."

"If we make it public before we're able to ensure the safety of whoever sent it to us, we might as well shoot them ourselves," said Khaifa.

"And if we don't make it public as soon as possible, we're allowing Upshaw more time to dig in, gather support, and, frankly, have you assassinated."

"She's right," said Ironhorse.

Khaifa turned quickly in surprise. She hadn't realized the Captain had been standing behind her. The Ranger stepped out from behind her chair so Khaifa wouldn't need to crane her neck to see him.

"Sorry to eavesdrop," he said. "But Van Der Berg is right. We have a war to worry about, we can't waste time over the fate of one person given what's going on here and everywhere else."

"We can't risk throwing this person to the wolves," said Khaifa. "They've given us evidence we can use to remove Upshaw once and for all."

Ironhorse shook his head, frowning.

"I hate to sound like I don't give a shit about this informant, but I don't. Yeah, it's great they grew a spine, but where the fuck have they been for the last two years? It's not like Upshaw being a power-hungry psycho is a sudden development - this informant comes forward now, when it's clear Upshaw's nearly out of moves, and we're supposed to pretend it's for the good of the Commonwealth? Fucker just doesn't want to go down with the ship," he said. "Meanwhile, we've got shootouts happening here, the fleet's about to engage the ril-galas reinforcements, and we've launched an attempt to retake Earth. If we have in-tel that can end the situation here so we can focus on that other shit - the shit that determines whether humanity even exists anymore - then we need to fucking use it."

In the short time they'd worked together, Khaifa had never known Ironhorse to mince words, nor had she heard him so emphatic about a course of action. Still, she sighed.

"We have to protect-"

"The Commonwealth," said Van Der Berg, with a sigh of her own. "I understand your desire to protect the informant, believe me I do - it's such a core part of intelligence - but in this circumstance, I have to agree with Captain Ironhorse. What's at stake here is bigger than the life of one person."

"I know this goes against your doctor thing, to save lives at all costs," said Ironhorse, squatting beside Khaifa's chair. "But this is like the Cortez situation. Radko knew he could have come back here and saved her life, but he also knew that if he did that he'd be derailing what became our biggest victory in this war."

"The sooner we can get that Prince up here the better," said Khaifa. "You have no idea how much I don't want this job."

She stood, slowly to make sure her legs were no longer jelly, and straightened her jacket.

"Get that recording out there," she said to Van Der Berg. "If you feel it needs an introduction or if it should be broadcast without preamble I leave in your hands. Captain Ironhorse."

He stood.

"Yes, ma'am."

"Organize some patrols, please. There's the possibility people may turn on anyone in ATC Castle colours when this gets out," she said. "We need to try to stop things from getting out of hand."

"And some of those people really do just work for them," he said, nodding. "This may blindside them."

04:44:41

Whoever the Edinburgh Castle garrison had as their sniper was quite good, in Sigurdsson's estimation. Which was helpful in that her assault group had only to deal with around twenty ril-galas foot soldiers, rather than the thirty or so that had arrived at the castle gates about twenty minutes prior to Sigurdsson herself.

"Alpha Team, flank left!" she said. "Bravo Team flank right! Command Team, supporting fire!"

The Command Team was a separate entity and consisted of Elgraphaar, Udrach, and Sigurdsson herself, in addition to ten soldiers. And, of course, Jaeger.

The castle sniper must have had plenty of military training and experience, since he or she stopped firing when Alpha and Bravo closed in.

While Sigurdsson's first instinct was to lead the charge herself, she also knew what Alpha and Bravo were feeling. Tightly wound, tensed for battle, stress levels to the moon though they'd never admit it. They needed this fight, and Sigurdson allowed them to have it, with their own team leaders calling the shots.

And it was a rout. The ril-galas had been badly outnumbered with the strike team's arrival, and if they had wanted to retreat, they'd had nowhere to go, trapped between the castle walls and Sigurdsson's soldiers.

Leading her troops through the gate, stepping over the remains of the ril-galas, Sigurdsson was greeted by a Corporal from the Coldstream Guards who introduced himself as Walter

Hobson and who also seemed taken aback by her appearance. Understandably, she figured. Even back in the old days people sometimes looked at her oddly given her height, but now she not only had the arms of an icaran, but the armour of an udukiin Matriarch.

She was, she assumed, kind of scary at first sight.

And she was more than okay with it.

Her entire assault group was being given looks that varied between awe, discomfort, and fear by many of the survivors inside the walls of Edinburgh Castle, and it took a moment for Sigurdsson to understand why. Communication had been so sparse between those trapped on the Earth's surface and those on Thor's Hammer or elsewhere in space, most of the people here were likely unaware that the United Defence Force existed; that Commonwealth, Soviet, icaran, and udukiin armed forces had joined together to fight their common enemy.

And, she realized, all that aside, most of these people would have never before seen an icaran let alone an udukiin in the flesh.

"Your sniper is very good," said Sigurdsson, trying to make things a little less awkward as Hobson led the Command Group through a group of staring civilians and deeper into the castle.

"That would be Grieve," he said, nodding. "Retired from the Commonwealth Army, but he certainly kept his skills sharp."

"How long have you been here?"

"Me personally? Not very long," said Hobson. "But there have been people taking shelter behind these walls since day one of the invasion, I'm told."

Sigurdsson couldn't help but smile.

"Walls can be defended," she said.

"Hunter told us a little of Fort Hathaway," said Hobson, nodding.

Leaving Udrach in charge of the assault group, Sigurdsson and Elgraphaar followed Hobson up worn stone stairs into a tower where a Chinese woman and a young red-headed man waited. Quon Li-Chen, now known as Hunter, she knew tangentially via Radko, and she assumed the young man to be Prince Arthur.

"Welcome to Edinburgh Castle," said the Prince, stumbling over his words only slightly while taking in Sigurdsson's appearance.

"You're almost exactly as I'd pictured you," said Hunter, standing slowly and offering what appeared to Sigurdsson to be a very forced smile. The woman was either in pain or exhausted or both.

"Probably more colourful," said Sigurdsson, waggling her fingers.

"All the better to match your vocabulary," said Elgraphaar, in perfect deadpan as he removed his helm.

After a bit of a laugh, everyone became serious once more and Sigurdsson introduced herself and Elgraphaar formally, and the Prince did the same for Hunter and Hobson. Hunter nodded at Elgraphaar and smiled. Sigurdsson had forgotten that they had met in person aboard the Vimy Ridge, back before Brigadier General Locaris had generously assigned some of his commandos to reinforce Sigurdsson's garrison at Fort Hathaway.

She wondered whether the two of them felt that was a lifetime ago as well.

"I have to be honest," said the Prince. "Until we saw your ships land, I wasn't fully convinced help would actually come."

"We're here now," said Sigurdsson. "And I hate to be rude-"

"She does not," said Elgraphaar.

"-but we need to get down to business here. Ril-galas reinforcements will be arriving in Earth orbit in..."

She glanced at the countdown and swore under her breath.

04:27:57

"Less than four and a half hours."

"That could explain the reorganization of troops our scouts have been reporting," said Hobson.

"We honestly have no idea what shape these reinforcements will take," said Sigurdsson. "They may be strictly space ships and fighters, they may include troop transports to increase the occupation force. But regardless, we have a small window here where these fuckers can't call in help from above."

The Prince nodded, but seemed hesitant.

"I agree we need to strike," he said. "But as good as I'm sure your battalion is, Miss Sigurdsson, how can we expect to make a dent in the occupation with such a small force?"

"There are other assault groups," said Hunter, staring off into space, her eyes unfocused. "Other landing sites."

Sigurdsson nodded, but it was Elgraphaar who responded.

"We will be striking on multiple fronts to prevent the enemy from simply redeploying to repel a single attack."

"Strike fast, strike hard, do as much damage as possible. And then get you," said Sigurdsson, nodding to the Prince. "To Thor's Hammer. I'm not sure you've heard-"

"We have," said the Prince, swallowing heavily and looking nervous.

"Good, I've already forgotten half of the constitutional shit I was supposed to explain," said Sigurdsson.

The Prince exchanged looks with both Hunter and Hobson, looks that made Sigurdsson frown. Something was wrong, and the Matriarch knew it too. The small spikes on the symbiont armour stood up a little higher as it reacted to Sigurdsson's emotions and the energy in the room. Both Hobson and Hunter nodded, and the Prince sighed, seeming like a weight had been lifted from his shoulders.

"There are two things you need to know, Miss Sigurdsson," he said. "First, the ril-galas have regeneration pods to repair damaged units. Their strength here is in that ability – the ability to repair units and get them back on the battlefield quickly."

And then the Prince's demeanour, his bearing, his body language - even the set of his jaw changed so dramatically that he almost looked like a different person.

"Second," said the Prince, in a voice that sounded nothing like him. "Is that Prince Arthur is dead."

Sigurdsson looked at the Prince who wasn't, then at Hobson, then at Hunter, then back to the not-Prince. Pulling over a cargo crate, she sat down, and rubbed her face with both hands.

Fucking hell she was getting tired of complications. Just for once, she would have really liked for a plan to go smoothly.

Just goddamned once.

Taking a few deep breaths, Sigurdsson closed her eyes and counted silently to ten before speaking.

"Could you maybe explain that?" she said. "And maybe explain who the fuck you are?"

"She's someone who has been trying to help keep things from falling apart by doing what was needed of her," said Hunter, still staring off at nothing. "Just like you on Von Daniken's Landing."

"My name is Harley Ransom," said the Prince who was apparently a young woman. "Prince Arthur died... he was

supposed to be a symbol for us to keep people going, but he...
wasn't."

"Hunter discovered that we - my team and Prince Arthur - had taken shelter in what remained of Balmoral," said Hobson, pulling up a chair and sitting down with a grunt. "She launched a search and rescue mission to bring us all back to Edinburgh Castle, the idea being that the return of one of our Royal Family would give people hope. Give them something larger to believe in."

"He would be King Arthur," said Ransom, shrugging. "Back in Britain's hour of greatest need."

"But that didn't happen," said Sigurdsson.

"Arthur was... not what anyone hoped he'd be," said Hobson. The words seemed to cause him physical discomfort. "Even before all this, he was not a particularly caring boy. No matter what we wanted or needed him to be, he'd given up. He didn't see the point of fighting the invasion and he... chose a different path."

"A path that led off a cliff," said Hunter.

Sigurdsson frowned.

"He killed himself?"

"We couldn't come back here with nothing, we'd risked too much," said Hunter. "And if word of the Prince's death got out?"

"The people here were already demoralized," said Hobson.

"So," said Ransom. "I came up with the idea to replace him. No one knew who the hell I was - I was nobody - and the Prince wasn't really prominent in the media either, so..."

"So... you became him to become a symbol of hope for this place," said Sigurdsson.

"Pretty much. So, you see our problem?"

"Prince Arthur is supposed to take temporary control of your government as per the constitutional provisions," said Elgraphaar.

"But I'm the only Prince Arthur here," said Ransom. "And I am sure as shit not going to be running a government."

Hooray for complications.

"Does anyone outside this room know?"

"Just Grieve," said Hobson.

"The sniper? Would he talk?"

Ransom laughed.

"He doesn't like people," she said. "There's not much chance of him getting into a conversation. But regardless, he knows what's at stake."

04:15:22

"Okay, you know what?" said Sigurdsson as she stood. "Other people can figure out how to deal with this. We're on the clock right now, and I don't give a shit about Prince Arthur - what's this about regenerating ril-galas?"

"Pods of some sort," said Hobson. "One of our scouts told us about it, then I had her take me out so I could see for myself. There are a half dozen of them in Holyrood Park, by the... facility."

The pause was involuntary, but Sigurdsson knew exactly what Hobson was feeling. As far as she knew, she was the first to realize why the ril-galas were so dead set on having Earth be the first conquest of their invasion. She'd once read a quotation somewhere about an army marching on its belly, that any successful campaign depended a great deal on feeding the troops - and Earth was a source of meat for the ril-galas. Production facilities all around the planet had been converting humanity into a food source.

Hobson cleared his throat and continued.

"They lock a single unit - foot soldier, stalker, bat - into one of these pods and it somehow repairs the damage," he said. "It only works for the biomechanical parts - the units where we've killed the ril-galas pilot itself just sit and rot. Our scout says she watched for several hours and it takes anywhere from twenty minutes to an hour and a half to regenerate, depending on the extent of the damage."

"Those regeneration pods must be our first target," said Elgraphaar. "Should we be able to remove the ril-galas ability to regenerate their biomechanicals, we may severely hamper their ability to hold the planet."

"Send a runner back to Aylarr - we need the other three assault teams aware of these pods."

Without a word, Elgraphaar headed out to do so, and Sigurdsson turned back to Hobson.

"I'll need your scout to lead us as close to those pods as they can without us being spotted."

"She can do that."

She.

Sigurdsson had a sinking feeling that she'd just inadvertently got a thirteen-year-old kid assigned to the front lines of a war.

"I'll be coming too," said Ransom. "But as Arthur. The people here still need him."

The young woman's willingness to risk her life to be a symbol of hope and yet have all the credit go to a dead man was commendable, but Sigurdsson wasn't sure how much help it would be in a fight. She didn't like the idea of adding non-military assets to an assault team, but then nothing about this situation was conventional. As much as she wanted to argue against Ransom's involvement, she found she hadn't a solid reason to say no.

"I don't like the idea either," said Hunter, as if Sigurdsson has spoken her thoughts aloud. "But she's right - Prince Arthur needs to be visible. Needs to be seen as being a part of this."

Sigurdsson nodded as if was the most normal thing in the world to have her mind accidentally read. Then she looked down at her icaran arms covered by her udukiin armour and decided mind-reading wasn't so odd after all.

Hunter chuckled slightly and Sigurdsson gave her a wry smile.

"All right then," she said. "Let's get a map and figure out how the hell we're going to do this."

25

The HMCS Goose Bay, laden down with extra warheads supplied by a dozen ships, detached from the umbilical connecting it to the HMS Royal Sovereign and fired its maneuvering thrusters, positioning itself just outside the debris field of the Hornets' Nest.

Radko, cradling a steaming mug of tea, released a breath he hadn't realized he'd been holding.

The AI was working.

It wasn't that he doubted Cagliari's programming ability so much as he doubted the outdated systems aboard the Goose Bay, in conjunction with the rushed manner in which they'd had to pull it off.

"Don't look so surprised," said Cagliari, smirking. "I'm good at this."

"We're all good at this, but that doesn't stop things from going wrong," he said, chuckling.

"Can't argue that."

She was already in her flight suit, and the majority of Outlaw Squadron, having transferred over from the Vimy Ridge to the Royal Sovereign with Cagliari, were in the launch bay making sure their fighters were ready to go. At Cagliari's insistence, a wing of the Argentavis fighters led by Damianopolous - better known as Dee - had been assigned to the Newcastle's battle group. While the Newcastle was essentially leading a diversion, they would still be facing some very capable ril-galas vessels. Cagliari had been right to suggest the additional support, as far as Radko was concerned. The more damage the Newcastle and her small fleet could do, the better - and the more likely they could prevent that first wave of reinforcements from joining the second wave heading for the remains of the Hornets' Nest.

"I should get the Royal Sovereign back to the moon," he said. "And let you get out there with your fighters."

He nodded toward the debris field stretched out before them. Though still not completely used to the holographic walls of the Royal Sovereign command deck, Radko was slowly adjusting. It no longer made him dizzy at any rate, which was an improvement.

Though Cagliari nodded, she remained next to him for a few moments, frowning at what the UHUD laid out before them.

"What do you think they're after?" she said.

"I don't know," he said, shaking his head. "But if they're willing to pull their forces from so many key areas to come get it..."

Cagliari ran a hand through her short blue hair.

"Fuck."

"Yeah."

"All right," she said, giving Radko a quick hug. "I'm out. Be careful. Stay safe, aside from the whole fighting a war thing."

"You too."

As she left the command deck, Radko couldn't help but chuckle at the excited bounce in Cagliari's step. Crisis or simple patrol flight, there was nothing that could dampen the young woman's enthusiasm for getting into the control seat of her Argentavis and flying off into the black. And he realised - not for the first time - how rough a spot they would be in had Nasrin Khaifa not talked him into meeting with some rich trust fund kid who wanted her company to get a leg up on ATC Castle. Because as it turned out, while Kestrel Cagliari was indeed young and rich and harboured no small amount of resentment toward ATC Castle - which Radko couldn't judge too harshly, given his own complicated history with the military contractor - she was also a legitimate genius who had designed the Argentavis Starfighter and a third of the systems on the Royal Sovereign. Perhaps as important as all that was that Cagliari was determined to be a difference-maker in the war.

As he looked around his new command deck, he figured she'd more than made good on that desire.

Seeing Stanton-West approaching with a tablet in hand, Radko smiled.

"Once Outlaw Squadron is away, get us underway," he said. "Best possible speed to the Lunar rendezvous site."

"Of course, Captain," she said, trying and failing to tuck a stray spring of hair behind her left ear. "There's something you should hear, though."

She handed him the tablet and he played the audio file. There was a short preamble from a man whose accented voice he didn't recognize, but then he heard two voices he very much knew. Edward Vossek and Bianca Upshaw.

"It's being broadcast on a loop," said Stanton-West. "On every civilian-accessible channel."

"I don't know if this is a good thing or a bad thing."

"It has to be a good thing, right? People will know now what kind of a person Upshaw is and that Khaifa is in the right."

"I'd love to think so," he said. "But that relies heavily on people being willing and able to recognize truth when they hear it, and to not just double down on bullshit because holding on to bullshit gives them power or money or both."

Shaking his head, Radko smiled sadly as he looked out past the debris field at the blue sphere of the Earth.

"From Echo Station to now, I've seen a lot of good in people. I've seen old enemies shake hands and stand side by side; I've seen people who had every opportunity and every reason to run away, instead march straight into the heart of this war to try to make a difference; I've seen people decide to do what they felt was right, knowing that it might cost them their career or worse. But," he said, sighing, "I've also seen people let their petty jealousies control their actions. I've seen people actively make decisions that they know will hurt the war effort, and I've seen people choose money over duty - as if money even means anything right now. I've seen people so entrenched in trying to maintain the kind of me-first society we had developed that they either can't see or just don't care that all of it could be gone. Even in our darkest hour, people cling so tightly to the threads of power that they're nearly as much a threat to our future as the ril-galas. And we can't change them."

Handing the tablet back to Stanton-West, Radko felt like he needed a drink.

"They'll still be with us," he said. "Even if we free Earth and defeat the ril-galas, I doubt we can defeat human nature."

"We certainly have our problems as a species, I won't argue that," she said. "But look at what we've done here. A United Defense Force. How many of us have set aside ideological differences to serve the greater good?"

Nodding, Radko leaned against the sand table and tiredly rubbed his eye.

"I know," he said, lowering his voice. "I'm just tired. This... is hard. It's exhausting."

"This...?"

"Being *the Finn Radko*. Being the one who, somehow, is looked to for critical decisions. Who gets put in charge of a defense fleet. I'm just... it can get overwhelming. I can feel it here,"

he said, tapping his chest. "Not a heart attack or anything, just...
I don't know. I'm sorry, I shouldn't be unloading on you like
this."

Smiling, Stanton-West put a hand on his shoulder.

"Part of the XO's job is supporting the CO," she said. "And,
believe it or not, I know exactly what you're talking about. I
have an anxiety disorder. It took me years to get it under control, and yeah, the last couple years have really tested me, but
here I am."

She crossed her arms and leaned against the sand table at
his side.

"You've been under pressure from day one, before any of
the rest of us knew what was happening," she said. "Leading
any sized group is its own pressure, and your group just keeps
growing. Not that you need or want me to list your accomplish-
ments, but, you know, you've already proven you can do this."

"I appreciate that," he said. "But this is different. Bigger."

"You're commanding a starship, which is where you belong," she said. "Stop the bad guys. It's that simple."

"Stop the bad guys."

"Exactly."

"So simple," he said with a chuckle.

She stood and winked.

"That's the spirit. But seriously, Captain, just breathe and
remember that every one of us on this ship - including you -
and every member of Outlaw Squadron and every icaran and
Soviet and udukiin all know what we're doing. We all know
why we're here, and we're all here sharing this burden. Maybe
back in the beginning when it was the Vimy Ridge versus the
universe it was all on your shoulders, but that's in the past.
Now you have Rhekar, and Chu, and el Bahari, and of course
Freyja Sigurdsson," she said with a knowing smirk. "And even

Singh and his handful of pirate ships, and you have me. We're all sharing the burden now."

"Thank you," he said. "I'm usually the one giving the pep-talks, I'm not used to being on the receiving end."

"Everyone needs to be reminded from time to time that they're not alone."

"So how have you dealt with it? The anxiety, I mean."

"Well... I cut out caffeine and alcohol for starters..."

Radko made a sour face and sipped his tea.

"Yeah," said Stanton-West. "Didn't think you'd like that, but in my case it was doctor's orders. But again, in my case, a bigger part is breathing exercises and getting enough sleep."

Radko couldn't help but laugh.

"I know," said Stanton-West, also laughing. "But maybe once this is all over, you can stop drinking tea and whiskey, and start getting some sleep?"

"Freyja's a War Matriarch, so stranger things have happened."

"And stranger things have happened than humanity getting its collective shit together, so don't write us off just yet."

"Outlaw Squadron is away," announced Bell.

Radko and Stanton-West watched as the jet black fighters arced away from the Royal Sovereign as a unit, then split up and headed into the debris field, each to their pre-assigned co-ordinates.

03:43:07

They would have a bit of a wait, but couldn't risk the possibility of having over-estimated the travel time for the ril-galas reinforcements. Having the enemy arrive before all elements of the trap were in place could have been disastrous, so having Outlaw Squadron floating in low-power mode for a few hours was the better alternative. Now they just had to get through the hardest part of the plan - waiting.

The rest of the fleet, with the exception of the Newcastle's group, would have to do the same. Wait. Bide their time.

And hope like hell things were going well on Thor's Hammer and on Earth.

26

Khaifa was not convinced things were going well on Thor's Hammer.

That much was clear to Ironhorse in her body language, despite having received no information that their situation - her situation - was any worse now than it had been before they'd released what his fellow Rangers had begun calling the 'Batshit Bianca' recording. So, when the first new transmission came through, while Ironhorse was gearing up with a small squad of Rangers, everyone stopped and listened.

A civilian broadcast that had been operating on a regular basis prior to Upshaw locking down all channels had begun broadcasting again, the two hosts discussing the recent developments on Thor's Hammer.

Discussing, specifically, how Nasrin Khaifa was right to take the action she did, and how unhinged it seemed the Prime Minister had become to give someone like Upshaw such power within his government. And then they spoke to others.

Looking over at Khaifa, Ironhorse saw her staring intently at her tablet as if the audio transmission might suddenly become video at any moment.

Somehow, the hosts had managed to get man-on-the-street interviews - other civilians, purportedly chosen at random, expressing support for Khaifa. Whether they were really random interviews or not didn't matter in the slightest to Ironhorse. The important factor was that there was now public support for what had until then been a constitutional issue debated behind closed doors.

"I think Upshaw needs to tread carefully," said one of the voices on the broadcast. *"You know, because she's broken at least one law, right? You can't order people to assassinate people."*

"You *shouldn't*," said Khaifa.

"You have public support," said Ironhorse, trying to get the point through.

"Two broadcasters and three random civilians."

"And how many people will be listening to this?" he said. "It's out there now that people think you've done the right thing. That Upshaw's fucking nuts."

"And," said Van Der Berg, "how many listeners are nodding their heads privately, but keeping quiet in public because there are armed ATC Castle troops running around the station with orders to kill you?"

Nodding, Ironhorse picked up his Trondheim Arms 33A1 assault rifle and slapped in a magazine.

"I aim to go do something about that, if it's okay with you," he said to Khaifa.

"I don't want any shootouts, Ironhorse. Not when there are civilians around."

"Just going to try to contain things," he said.

At her nod, he signalled his five-person team and headed for the door, but was intercepted by Van Der Berg before he could leave.

"I'm not in a position to give orders, so consider this a suggestion," she said, handing him a small tablet. It was about a third of the size of a standard unit and it displayed what looked like the deck plans of Thor's Hammer. One particular room was highlighted.

Ironhorse looked up at Van Der Berg, a brow raised in a silent question.

"Bring her in alive, so she can stand trial."

Looking back to the map, he stared for a moment before he understood what he was looking at. No one really knew where Upshaw did most of her work, just that it wasn't in the area set aside for the civilian government on Thor's Hammer. The area of Thor's Hammer displayed on the small tablet was inside the section of the station that had more or less been annexed by ATC Castle when they'd entrenched themselves within the Commonwealth - everyone should have known Upshaw would keep her command post within a sphere where she already wielded significant power, but no one had any cause to care until recently. She was a corporate executive working in her corporate world. And then she suddenly became the second most powerful person in the Commonwealth, while actually being the single most powerful given how weak de Freitas had turned out to be.

No one knew where Upshaw's real command post was, except apparently Van Der Berg had discovered it and now Ironhorse had a map to it.

He activated the comm channel that went directly to his Revelstoke Rangers.

"Change in plans," he said. "Ashigaru, get a second fire team together and get to Fort Cargo ASAP."

He'd initially hated that the soldiers had started referring to the converted cargo bay in which Khaifa and her team of loyalists were based as 'Fort Cargo,' but he'd found himself adopting the term anyway. There was something to be said for everyone being on the same page, even if it felt like that page had been written in crayon.

Quickly informing his own team about the change in plans, Ironhorse and his sergeant, the mountain of a man named Tangaroa, began plotting an approach to Upshaw's stronghold.

"What have we got, Sir?" said Sergeant Janet Ashigaru as she led in her team.

Given all that had happened in the past two years, Ironhorse felt lucky that most of his team, including his top sergeant in Ashigaru, was still alive and still together. And though Tangaroa, the imposing Māori, had been a more recent addition to the team, drafted in to fill a hole in the roster after Tangaroa's former company had been disbanded for just that purpose – filling vacancies in other Ranger companies – Ironhorse was beyond happy to have him. The big man had been a huge help in both meanings of the term. Ironhorse waved over Ashigaru and explained the situation, stepping aside to let her and Tangaroa have a good look at the map. Part of what made a good leader was knowing when to let others do their jobs, and Ironhorse knew that the two sergeants had a better head for planning close quarters combat operations than he had.

The planning of the op took no more than ten minutes, and so the Revelstoke Rangers headed out to complete what may have been their most important mission of the war.

The public areas of Thor's Hammer were far less chaotic than Ironhorse had expected, which made him nervous. Here and there were groups of people clustered around tablets listening to those same two civilian broadcasters, but there were also people going about their lives - there was a man walking his dog, a woman bartering for some fresh bread; two little girls playing with some Commonwealth Heroes action figures.

"This is surreal," said Ashigaru.

"There was a shootout in this area not an hour ago," said Ironhorse, nodding.

Tangaroa shrugged.

"Ignoring bad shit is the human superpower."

"No kidding," said Ironhorse. "Tangaroa, take point, get us moving faster."

With a nod, the Sergeant jogged ahead and the two fire teams quickened their pace.

Leaving the more civilian areas of the station behind, the Rangers made their way deeper into Thor's Hammer, and closer to the ATC Castle-controlled sections.

Within minutes, Tangaroa called a halt and the two teams took up position.

Rifle at his shoulder, Ironhorse crept up beside him just in time to see the squad of ATC Castle operators raise their Caliburn SMGs.

"Identify yourselves!" said the leader.

"Captain Maximillian Ironhorse, Revelstoke Rangers, Commonwealth Armed Forces. Your turn."

"Major Solomon Trouba, Venom-3," said the contractor.

"The fuck does that mean?" said Tangaroa under his breath.

"No idea," Ironhorse said, just as softly, then continued louder. "What the hell is a Venom-3?"

"It's... what they call our type of unit, a Venom unit. We're the third one."

"So...," said Tangaroa. "It's like a brand name?"

There was a lengthy pause and despite himself, Ironhorse smirked.

"What's your purpose here, Captain Ironhorse?"

The smirk was gone now, replaced by a scowl. Ironhorse felt Tangaroa's body language shift as well, and he knew the big Māori was thinking the same thing he was.

"We are a unit of the Commonwealth Armed Forces operating on a facility that belongs to the Commonwealth Armed Forces, Mister Trouba," he said.

"*Major* Trouba," came the testy response.

"Yeah, sure," said Ironhorse. "Call yourself whatever you want, you're still a corporate flunky. Stand down."

"We're operating under the authority of Prime Minister-"

"No, you're not, you're taking orders from Upshaw. And you know damn well neither one is in charge anymore."

"I'm going to count to five, and you better back away Ironhorse," said Trouba. "One..."

Ironhorse squeezed the trigger twice on his 33A1 and Trouba dropped to the ground, two bullets in him.

"Whoever's in charge over there now," said Ironhorse, "do the smart thing."

There was silence, but Ironhorse took that as a good sign, because there was also no shooting.

"He's dead."

It was a woman's voice, and it was surprisingly neutral about her commander having just been shot.

"Is anyone else inclined to join him?" said Ironhorse.

"Not me," said the woman, standing with her hands in the air. She had a sidearm clipped to her belt, but her Caliburn was on the floor. "Security detail is one thing, but I ain't no enemy of the State."

"Hobart you fucking traitor," someone hissed.

"Eat it, Gladstone. You want to get killed for that psycho you go right ahead."

As she began to slowly walk toward Ironhorse's group a single shot rang out. A spray of red exploded from Hobart's neck and she dropped to her knees, her face registering shock before she fell forward.

The Rangers didn't need to wait for the order, they swarmed the hallway with Ironhorse, Tangaroa and Ashigaru in the lead and were on top of the ATC Castle operators before the latter could react.

"Leave them," said Tangaroa, as the contractors made to raise their weapons.

There was one man who held a pistol in his hand.

"You're Gladstone," said Ironhorse, reading the nameplate on the man's ballistic armour.

Gladstone nodded.

"You killed that woman who was surrendering."

"Stupid bitch didn't know what loyalty means. She deserved-"

Ironhorse swung the muzzle of his assault rifle into the man's face and fired.

"Two choices," he said to the remaining six contractors. "Leave your weapons and armour and go be useful - the hospital can always use extra hands. Or leave your weapons and armour and I can lock you in a cargo container until this situation is under control. And before you think 'oh we'll just tell him we'll help and then circle back to suckle on the corporate teat,' I don't want to waste bullets on you shitbags, but I will if you make me."

The statement was met with silence, which the Rangers allowed to stretch on for a few moments before Ashigaru prodded the nearest contractor with her boot.

"Tick tock," she said.

"I'll offer a third option," said one of the contractors. "At least for myself - I can't speak for anyone else."

Several of the others scowled at the speaker.

"Why would we let you do that?" said Ashigaru.

"Because some of us have made some bad life choices and got stuck because of them."

"Jax shut the fuck up," said one of the other contractors, who Tangaroa quickly cuffed in the back of the head.

"Jax. That your first name or last name?" said Ironhorse.

Jax just shrugged.

"Doesn't matter," they said.

"And what's your third option?"

"Like I said, bad life choices. Fucked up my first go-round with the Army," they said, meeting Ironhorse's eyes for a moment before shrugging again. "Maybe I could have a shot at fixing that."

Leaning in toward Ironhorse, Tangaroa lowered his voice so only the Captain could hear.

"We're heading into ATC Castle territory," he said. "Might be good to have someone with us who knows the area."

For a moment, Ironhorse just stared at Jax, then turned his attention to the group as a whole.

"What's your decision - be useful or be locked up?"

After a unanimous if unenthusiastic decision to be useful, Ironhorse nodded.

"Satler and Okapaso, confiscate weapons and armour, and anything we might find useful, then escort them to the hospital," he said, then pointed toward Jax. "Except this one. They can stay."

Jax looked surprised, but pleased.

"If you make me regret this," said Ironhorse.

"You'll shoot me, yeah got it."

The last of the contractors to be led away spat in Jax's face.

"You're a fucking rat, Jax. Best sleep with one eye open," he said.

"I'm an insomniac, Keller," said Jax, wiping the saliva off their cheek. "You sleep more than I do. Hint, hint."

Satler gave Keller a shove to get him moving.

Taking Jax by the shoulders, Ironhorse turned them to look him in the eye.

"You have any ATC Castle radios, or transmitters, or comm devices, or tablets on you?"

They nodded and Ironhorse held out his hand. Without hesitating, Jax handed over a tablet and their helmet, which had a built-in comm unit.

"That's it," they said. "We're a Light Company, as in light on corporate investment."

"Light on pay?"

They shook their head.

"Heavy on pay. Light on ethics."

"Sometimes the money isn't worth it," said Tangaroa, nodding.

Most days, Ironhorse forgot that Tangaroa himself had once left the Commonwealth Armed Forces to join the better-paying military contractor, but that was long before Bianca Upshaw was in control. Back then, ATC Castle had still been involved in some questionable activities, but they weren't publicly known and they hadn't involved slyly infiltrating and controlling a government. And to Tangaroa's credit, he hadn't hesitated to break from ATC Castle when the invasion hit.

"You're on your way to kill Upshaw, right?" said Jax, as Ironhorse handed them back their Caliburn SMG.

"Apprehend, not kill," he said. "We're Rangers, not a hit squad."

Jax nodded, and Ironhorse turned to Tangaroa, pointing first to his own eyes and then to Jax.

"This one's your problem, Sergeant. You get to shoot them if they step out of line."

"I won't," said Jax, shaking their head.

Ironhorse led the teams onward, taking point with Ashigaru's fire team and leaving Tangaroa's team, now with one extra, to bring up the rear. Getting to the corporate sector of the station would be the easy part, Ironhorse knew - it would be getting in to the corporate area and into Upshaw's command and control bunker that would be the hard part.

As the two teams approached the large double doors that led into the corporate sector - the section of Thor's Hammer annexed by ATC Castle - it almost made him nervous how little resistance they had encountered. Since the encounter with Trouba and their own annexation of Jax, only two security personnel had crossed their paths, and they had quickly found better places to be when they'd realized it was two Ranger fire teams heading their way.

But, outside the doors to the corporate sector, they had a problem.

"Key card access only," said Ashigaru, pointing to the flat square scanning pad beside the spot where a keypad had been removed.

With Thor's Hammer having been a Commonwealth Navy project, any keypad would have accepted the naval override codes Ironhorse had been provided by Admiral Mahoney. They should have known ATC Castle would have both been aware of and found a way to counter that approach.

"Can we hotwire it?" said Ironhorse. "Or call in for demolitions."

Tangaroa cleared his throat and Ironhorse turned from the door to see the Sergeant standing behind him with Jax, who was holding up their left forearm. Attached to the partially armoured gauntlet of their forearm armour, close to the wrist, was a small dark square.

"Or we could just open it," said Jax.

At Ironhorse's signal, the two teams readied themselves on either side of the door and Jax tapped their access card on the panel. The doors slid open to reveal...

An empty hallway.

Motioning the Rangers forward, Ironhorse again took lead with Ashigaru at his side.

Progress was remarkably smooth, even unsettlingly so. The ATC Castle section of Thor's Hammer was all but a ghost town – every room the Rangers entered in order to clear, they found empty. Some abandoned cups of coffee, still steaming; some half-eaten MREs; more than one firearm left behind.

"Rats abandoning ship?" said Ashigaru.

"Or regrouping somewhere else," said Tangaroa. "But I like your idea better."

Jax shook their head.

"We didn't have a muster point inside this section. When we needed to get a big group together, we had to use one of the cargo bays back there, in the main station," said Jax, jabbing a thumb back over their shoulder, back the way they'd come. "And I don't think the command centre is big enough to hold a bunch of troops."

"Then," said Ironhorse, adjusting the sling on his rifle, "we have to assume they're assembling in the corridor outside the control room."

Shooting through a large number of fellow humans was not on the list of things Ironhorse had wanted to accomplish that day, but life had a funny way of not giving a shit what Maximillian Ironhorse wanted and what he did not want.

As his mother had been fond of saying, life is chaos, suck it up and get on with it. And for Ironhorse, getting on with it meant going through an ATC Castle force of unknown numbers.

Except it didn't.

Cautiously peeking around the bend in the corridor that would lead his team straight to Upshaw's lair, Ironhorse had to make a second check to be sure. And then waved over Tangaroa and had the big man confirm.

"The fuck...?"

"There's no one here," said Ironhorse, filling in the rest of the team. "Let's move, but stay alert. This seems too good to be true."

Waving for Ashigaru to take point, Ironhorse fell in behind her and they lead the two teams onward, right up to the door of Bianca Uphaw's control room. While several of the Rangers covered the closed door and the rest kept watch on the corridor, Ironhorse looked at his assembled group and shrugged. The mission, to that point, had been significantly easier than any of them had expected.

"Whatever's on the other side of this door," said Ironhorse, "we need Upshaw, and we need her alive. It doesn't matter if there's a hundred soldiers waiting for us, we don't leave empty handed."

"They'll know we're here," said Jax, pointing up to the camera mounted above the doorway.

"Then there's no sense in waiting."

Jax swiped their key card, but nothing happened - and Ironhorse had expected as much. He waved in Soli, who quickly strapped one of his shaped explosive charges to the locking mechanism. Once it was set and everyone had backed off, Soli blew the charge and the door slid open with a loud bang and a billow of smoke.

There was yelling inside, but Ironhorse didn't wait. 33A1 rifle at his shoulder, he swung himself into the room, Tangaroa doing the same from the other side of the doorway, and he knew that the rest of the Rangers would be right behind.

"Weapons down!" he shouted. "Everyone on the floor!"

It would have been nice if they'd complied, but instead shots rang out and a bullet grazed the ballistic armour on Ironhorse's left shoulder. He instinctively dropped to one knee and fired two rounds in the general direction of the shooter, seeing an ATC Castle operator ducking behind a console of some sort. Then he saw Jax running low the length of the room, firing bursts from a submachine gun they had somehow acquired, and as the contractors turned to address the new threat, both Ironhorse and Tangaroa popped out from behind cover and tagged three of them. Likely not fatal shots, but the contractors would certainly be incapacitated.

At the end of the room, civilian employees of the company huddled in terror under desks, while a group of four contractors - two with Caliburn SMGs and two with Fenrir pistols - guarded two individuals.

"Bianca Upshaw," said Ironhorse, "in the name of the Commonwealth, I am placing you under arrest."

The four contractors raised their weapons.

Between them, Ironhorse could see Upshaw's face and beside her, Edward Vossek. Upshaw's jaw muscles were working overtime to contain her rage; Vossek, on the other hand, seemed calm - but then, he'd been a Commonwealth Ranger under Harlan Gray before he'd traded honour for cash.

But Upshaw was the target, not Vossek.

"You have no authority here," she hissed, "or anywhere on this station. I am Deputy Prime Minister of the Commonwealth!"

"Your appointment to that role went against the Constitution, and was at the direction of a Prime Minister who has been removed from office."

One of the contractors guarding Upshaw and Vossek twitched and moved the barrel of their Caliburn to the right as Jax approached, their own SMG raised.

"Jax, stay where you are," said Ironhorse.

They complied, which was good. Ironhorse returned his attention to the group in front of him. There was quite literally no way out for them. There were still ten Rangers plus Jax against four of them - and Vossek, Ironhorse reminded himself, who was likely armed. Regardless, there was no way this face-off ended in their favour. The only decision the contractors had to make was whether they wanted to leave warm or cold, and Ironhorse told them as much.

"Ignore him," said Upshaw. "Each of you will receive a fifty percent wage increase for standing your ground."

"Don't be stupid, Parnam," said Jax, looking to the shortest of the four. "You were always telling me to look at things logically."

"And you, traitor, are fired," said Upshaw.

"Pretty sure they already quit," said Tangaroa.

"You're a traitor as well," said Upshaw.

"Might want to look that word up before you use it again."

"An additional ten percent increase to anyone who kills one of the traitors," said Upshaw.

"Bonuses for committing murder," said Ironhorse, focusing on the contractors. "Is that really what you signed up for here? I don't know if you were ever Commonwealth military or whether you were trained up through ATC Castle, but it doesn't matter - this can't be why you joined. I get they pay better. I get they have newer toys. But are you soldiers or assassins?"

There was silence for a moment before one of the contractors tossed her pistol onto the ground and raised her hands.

"I'm a soldier," she said.

And then one of her now former colleagues put a bullet in her head before turning his gun back to the Rangers.

"Now she's nothing," he said. "Back off and give us a clear path out of here."

"Or what, you'll shoot another of your own men?" said Ironhorse. "That isn't much of a threat."

"Stand down, Vamosi," said Vossek.

It wasn't until he saw the look of shock and fury on Upshaw's face that Ironhorse realized that Vossek was holding one of the snub-nosed Starling pistols to Vamosi's head. Taking advantage of the confusion, Ironhorse and Tangaora swooped in and disarmed the remaining contractors, and Jax stepped in and took away Vossek's pistol.

"You bastard," said Upshaw, glaring at Vossek.

"Lady, you're gonna want to shut the fuck up right about now," said Ironhorse, as he directed Tangaroa to formally take her into custody. "You're under arrest. Anything you say can be used against you and all that shit."

Tangaroa, Ironhorse noticed, was barely supressing a smile while he bound Upshaw's wrists behind her back. Though he ordered Vossek and Vamosi to be bound as well, Ironhorse left the two other contractors free.

"You're not under arrest," he told them. "But if you cause any problems on this station, I will hunt you down and throw you out a fucking airlock."

They nodded and looked both shocked and relieved when Ironhorse ordered them ejected from the control centre without an escort.

Jax was kneeling beside the murdered operator, pulling something out from underneath her armour. When Ironhorse stepped toward them, Jax didn't look up.

"Not looting," they said. "Parnam looked out for a lot of us younger recruits. She carried a thing."

With a grunt of satisfaction, Jax pulled an object out from under Parnam's body armour - what looked like a small bronze tube on a leather thong.

"Some of her husband's ashes in here," said Jax. "Figured she'd want me to make sure her daughter gets it."

Ironhorse nodded before turning back to Upshaw, who still stared malevolently at him.

"Now you're going to contact De Freitas and tell him to give himself up," said Ironhorse. "For the good of the Commonwealth."

"Fuck you."

"All right, then you're going to tell me how to contact him."

Her response was the same.

"I can reach him," said Vossek, shifting uncomfortably where he still kneeled on the hard floor.

"You're very helpful recently," said Ironhorse. "You'll have to excuse me if I don't trust it."

"I went for the money, but I was also angry at the Commonwealth," said Vossek, shrugging awkwardly, hands still on his head. "Cortez killed Harlan Gray with zero consequences. So yeah, I left. And then I sent el Bahari that recording of Bianca going insane-"

"And now that your side is falling apart, you want to jump back over to the winning side. I get it. If you weren't a mercenary you'd have been fighting alongside us all along. You used to be a Ranger, and now you're turning your back on another group to try to save your own ass."

Vossek's expression darkened.

"Why do you think your path was clear coming here, asshole? I redeployed a bunch of operators. Do you want my help with the Prime Minister or not?"

"Help or don't help," said Ironhorse, shrugging. "But if you decide not to, better hope the new Commonwealth administration prosecutes treason more fairly than your people did with Anna Cortez."

Vossek deliberated for a second.

"Bring me a tablet," he said finally.

They did, and he keyed in an access code and connected to De Freitas's personal quarters before handing the tablet to Ironhorse.

"Hello Mister De Freitas," said Ironhorse, once the tired and haggard De Freitas appeared on the screen.

"Who are you?" said the now former Prime Minister. "I thought this was Vossek."

"It is," said Ironhorse cheerfully, turning the tablet to show the still-kneeling Vossek as well as the cuffed Upshaw. "Bianca's here, too! We're having a fuckin' great time. Care to join us?"

"What... what's the meaning of this? I demand you release these people at once... you can't... I'm the Prime Minister of the Commonwealth and I order you-"

"I'm going to have to stop you there. You've been relieved of your role, Mister De Freitas, and your two associates here have been arrested on charges of conspiracy to murder Doctor Nasrin Khaifa."

Even on the small screen, the blood visibly drained from De Freitas's face.

"The only question you need to ask yourself," said Iron-horse, employing the same tactic he'd used with the ATC Castle operators, "is whether when the trial starts you'll be sitting in the defendants' box, or sitting as a witness for the prosecution."

The line, supplied by Babacar, worked like magic. De Freitas deflated like a week-old balloon, and it was almost sad to Ironhorse to literally watch a man's entire world fall apart in real time.

Almost sad.

Nah, fuck it – it wasn't sad in the slightest. The guy was a piece of shit.

While the ril-galas invasion was no one's fault, everything that had been happening on Thor's Hammer from the sham trial and execution of Anna Cortez down to this moment of reckoning, was all down to Upshaw's machinations and De Freitas's willingness to go along with them.

He deserved to be prosecuted, but as Amira had figured out a long time ago, without Upshaw, De Freitas was a paper tiger.

"I... tell Doctor Khaifa I'll cooperate. I won't cause any trouble."

"See that you don't. I'll be sending men to collect you."

Before he'd finished the statement, Upshaw began yelling, hurling obscenities at De Freitas.

Stepping up to her, Ironhorse cocked his right fist back as if to strike.

"You wouldn't dare," said Upshaw with a sneer. "You're one of the *good guys*, doing everything the *noble way*. People like me win wars, you piece of shit."

"How's that going for you?" he said. "Also, if you think I'm good and noble, you clearly don't have a fucking clue who I am."

As his fist slammed into her face, Ironhorse felt Upshaw's nose crunch and she went limp.

27

02:16:26

The landing zone had held. Aylarr and her team had fended off the ril-galas attack without a single casualty and, just as important, without any of the three dropships suffering damage. The moment the runner had returned with the news, Sigurdsson set her own plan in motion.

Three teams. One led by her and Elgraphaar, one led by Udrach, and one led by Major Ustorf. All three would attack the ril-galas position in Holyrood Park from different angles, with Udrach and Ustorf tasked with destroying the regeneration pods while Sigurdsson's team hit the processing facility itself to free any people still alive inside and also cause enough damage to shut it down.

Night had fallen on Edinburgh as the three teams marched out of the Castle. Against Sigurdsson's better judgement, her team included the fake Prince Arthur, Harley Ransom, and the damaged psychic, Hunter. The former was necessary due to the Prince's symbolic status among the survivors, and the latter Sigurdsson had been convinced would be tactically advantageous. Hunter had, after all, successfully sensed approaching ril-galas attacks in space aboard the Vimy Ridge and during her time at Edinburgh Castle. Whatever problems she was having with her abilities now - and it appeared to Sigurdsson that those problems were both serious and worsening - any tactical advantage the assault teams could gain would be welcome. The young scout Karina had tried to make a case for joining them, but while Sigurdsson liked the tough and surprisingly foul-mouthed girl, she wasn't taking a thirteen-year-old into battle.

However, the biggest argument was when the decision was made that Corporal Hobson would stay behind at Edinburgh Castle. Hobson hadn't been upset so much as he felt obligated to be part of the attack, since Prince Arthur was participating. Despite the fact that the Prince was an imposter, the Coldstream Guard still felt a duty to protect him, but Ransom had explained that protection is exactly what they needed Hobson for - protection of Edinburgh Castle. Defense of the castle had to be left in the hands of someone they all trusted, and someone the military personnel being left behind would respect. Hobson had reluctantly agreed, but had still walked with them right to the gates and, Sigurdsson assumed, was now watching from atop the wall as the three groups separated and melted into the city.

Though Sigurdsson hadn't wanted to delay their departure for anything, Ransom, Hobson, and Hunter had insisted that Ransom, as Prince Arthur, speak to the assembled strike teams and everyone staying behind before the Prince led them into battle. And as much as Sigurdsson disliked speeches in general, she felt Ransom had done well, and from all she'd heard about the real Prince, probably did more to create a legacy for the little bastard in that moment that he had done in his whole life.

"While we have been safe behind these walls for the last two years - as safe as we can be in these trying times - we cannot remain this way. The walls of Edinburgh Castle have been our refuge, but they have also become a prison in some ways," Ransom had said, as Arthur. "As terrifying as I know the thought is to many of us, myself included, our only hope for survival is to strike out beyond these walls; to begin chipping away at the occupation force that not only controls our home world, but threatens our very existence."

She had looked around at the assembled crowd, making eye contact with as many as she could.

"Even now, a fleet is assembling in orbit above us to deal a decisive blow against the enemy up there. But the time for us to strike back against the occupiers here, on the ground, is now. We've been giving them a bloody nose here and there with small guerilla strikes, but now we have the knowledge, the weaponry, and the numbers to do so much more."

She had raised her arm, palm upward, toward Sigurdsson. Almost as one, the assembled faces had turned and looked at the assault group before turning their attention back to Arthur.

"None of us could ever have expected the means of our salvation to look quite like this. Honestly, I didn't know what an udukiin looked like until today," said Ransom, smiling as a number of the assembled survivors chuckled. "But here we have an alliance of three species representing four different governments, all of whom have come here. For us. For Earth. And while it is true that marching into battle against our oppressors, some of us will die, that is a fact that we will have to accept. For if we do not take the fight to the ril-galas and liberate our planet, I am absolutely certain that *all of us* will die."

The symbol of Prince Arthur had done what it had been meant to do – it had given people hope. So, carrying that hope with them, they'd left the safety of Edinburgh Castle and headed into the streets.

With the power grid for the city long since broken down, the streets were near pitch black. Their way was lighted only by the near-full moon hanging low in the sky, and Sigurdsson had made sure that each of the other three groups had an equal number of icaran commandos between them. With the advanced optics inside the faceless helmets worn by the commandos, they could serve as point men for each group, their optical enhancements making up for the darkness.

"We don't go out after dark much," said Ransom, already deep in her Arthur persona. "Our scouts sometimes, but the darkness is too dangerous."

"Then the enemy will know that," said Sigurdsson. "And the more they know about your movement patterns, the less they'll expect something like this."

"I certainly hope so."

Glancing around quickly, Sigurdsson confirmed that aside from ransom and Hunter, the only beings within earshot were icaran and udukiin - beings who wouldn't care about the imposter Prince. Still, she lowered her voice.

"So. The solution to your problem..."

Ransom nodded slowly.

"Prince Arthur has to die," she said.

"We can get you aboard one of our dropships. Hide you there, say Arthur was KIA. Find somewhere for you to lay low for a bit."

Ransom looked over to Hunter, but the woman seemed to be focusing too hard on her abilities to have overheard the short discussion. Sigurdsson was about to press the issue when she saw Elgraphaar in the lead call for a halt. She and everyone else readied their weapons and crouched low.

Keeping low, Sigurdsson fell in beside Elgraphaar, gunstaff at her shoulder. They were still a fair distance from Holyrood Park, another fifteen-minute march by Sigurdsson's estimate, but they'd be fools to assume there would be no ril-galas presence in the remains of the city. The occupation force knew the dropships had landed and Sigurdsson had to assume they would know both that a large group of soldiers had gone to Edinburgh Castle and potentially that one or more of the other assault groups over the world had begun their own assaults.

"There is movement ahead," said Elgraphaar.

Activating her own optics and immediately worsening the headache she already had, Sigurdsson followed Elgraphaar's direction and saw the movement herself. A lone ril-galas stalker, trying to get closer to their group while also trying to remain concealed behind rubble and burned-out cars.

Trying, but not very hard, thought Sigurdsson.

The street was littered with cars, and fallen trees, and large pieces of masonry. More than enough cover for a determined individual to conceal their presence - it was one of the main reasons Ransom and Hunter had suggested this route, down Cowgate and Holyrood Road, as opposed to the wider and more open High Street - but this stalker was darting between smaller bits of detritus as if it...

"It's a distraction," said Sigurdsson.

Suddenly, Hunter was her side.

"They're coming. Stalkers."

"How many?"

"I can't tell," said Hunter, shaking her head. "There are too many, they're all blending together."

Sigurdsson swore under her breath. Cowgate certainly provided plenty of cover, but it was a narrow street and they were coming up to a small tunnel, the underside of a road above. On the one hand, the other side of that tunnel would be the perfect place for the enemy to set up and ambush. On the other, it was a defensible position with only two points of egress.

But defensible positions weren't what they were here for.
02:01:47

"We have to push forward," said Sigurdsson. "We're running out of time."

Without a word, Elgraphaar began moving down the street once more, still crouched low and *aoran* assault rifle still at the ready. The assault group followed, Sigurdsson directly behind the icarans and Ransom, Hunter, and Jaeger right behind her.

When the attack came, it came from the rear.

Sigurdsson heard the gunfire first, then the swearing, as the human members of her team tried to find their targets using nothing but the flashlights attached to their rifles, and the udukiin made do with slightly better than average night vision. Most simply followed the lead of the icarans and their advanced optics.

Advancing on Holyrood Park under cover of darkness was designed to give them an advantage, but now Sigurdsson wasn't so sure.

She heard a scream to her left and swung around in time to see a stalker sink its talons into the neck and abdomen of one of the Soviet soldiers. Swinging up her gunstaff, Sigurdsson fired off a quick shot that clipped the stalker in the head, blowing off the left side and causing it to release its hold on its victim. The moment it did, Sigurdsson fired another shot and blew a hole through the centre of its chest, killing the ril-galas pilot within.

"Keep moving!" she shouted.

Through the staccato reports of gunfire and the booming shots of the icaran weapons and the softer sounds of gunstaves, Sigurdsson listened for the sounds of panic, but heard none. Despite being attacked in the dark by a fearsome enemy, the assault group was holding together.

She shot down two more stalkers and saw Elgraphaar do the same, and she turned to see a pair of stalkers charging at

Ransom and Hunter. Before she could bring her gunstaff to bear, Sigurdsson watched as Hunter clenched her fists and her teeth and squeezed her eyes shut in concentration.

"No! Don't!" said Ransom, and Sigurdsson could hear the fear in the young woman's voice.

And then Hunter screamed and the charging stalkers both staggered backward and fell as if hit by a cannon ball. Hunter collapsed and Ransom dropped to her knees and caught her friend before her head hit the pavement.

As she ran over to them, Sigurdsson leapt atop the carcass of a burned-out SUV and fired a shot from her gunstaff into each of the stunned stalkers' chest cavities, then hopped down beside Ransom. The girl was cradling Hunter's head in one hand while trying to keep her pistol at the ready in the other. Blood was smeared across Hunter's face from an apparent bleeding nose and while her eyes were open, they were glazed over and she stared up at the stars.

"The fuck just happened?" said Sigurdsson.

"Her abilities," said Ransom, voice tight. "She can... I don't know, use them as a weapon. Like punching them directly in the mind or something."

"She's done this before?"

Ransom nodded.

"It almost killed her then."

"Stay with her, we'll-"

Movement. A flicker, in the corner of her eye.

Sigurdsson spun toward it and a stalker was upon her. She raised her gunstaff only to have it knocked from her grip and as the maw full of teeth descended on her, she instinctively swung up her left forearm. The creature chomped down and though the udukiin armour prevented those teeth from drawing blood or shredding flesh, Sigurdsson still felt a painful amount of pressure. The weight of the creature and the momentum of its charge drove her backward into the SUV, and the composite material of the vehicle body buckled inward at the impact.

With a snarl, Sigurdsson began punching the stalker in the head with her free hand, the Matriarch shifting its armour over Sigurdsson's hand to both afford greater protection to her and create a more rigid impact for the ril-galas.

She felt more than saw the stalker unfold its smaller gun arms, and the heat of the two weapons powering up.

And then there was a growl and Jaeger was there, clamping his jaws around the stalker's clawed arm and pulling it backward. The distraction and the lessening of the creature's weight upon her gave Sigurdsson all the opening she needed: she drew her *vayan* sidearm and fired two superheated rounds through her attacker's chest.

It dropped to the ground dead.

Jaeger released his grip on the thing's arm, then barked at it twice to remind it he was still angry.

Retrieving her gunstaff, Sigurdsson gave Jaeger a quick scratch behind the ears before turning back to Ransom and Hunter.

"Will she be okay?"

"Fine...," said Hunter, sounding anything but. "Just... tunnel... be careful..."

"Can you walk?." said Sigurdsson, scanning the area and shooting down another stalker as Ransom helped Hunter to her feet.

"Yes," said Hunter. "Tunnel..."

"We're almost there," said Ransom.

The assault group continued onward and the stalker attack continued, but the attackers' numbers had been thinned enough to not significantly impede Sigurdsson's group.

Entering the tunnel, Sigurdsson turned back to Ransom and Hunter, who had been muttering unintelligibly the entire way and appeared even more agitated.

"Don't go in," she said finally.

"Don't go in where?" said Ransom.

"The tunnel."

Ransom looked up sharply at Sigurdsson, who in turn raised her gunstaff to her shoulder, making a full sweep of the tunnel. There was nothing, just her own team. Elgrapahaar made a sweep of his own, also coming up empty. Then Sigurdsson heard the scrape of talon on stone and slowly looked up.

Stalkers were excellent climbers.

"Oh fuck."

01:32:01

Cagliari was glad that low-power mode for an Argentavis Starfighter still allowed for near full use of the UHUD. As much as the waiting game chafed on her, she'd been using her time to create a catalogue of the larger pieces of debris present in the wreckage that served as Outlaw Squadron's hiding place so that now, in the holographic version of the space that surrounded her fighter, each of them was overlaid with a bright yellow. Using her administrator access to the networked fighters, Cagliari activated the same overlay system on the UHUDs of the rest of her flight group. When the battle was joined, the tagging would help both her and the rest of the squadron avoid impacts.

But it was not the bright yellow markings that had her attention.

Frowning, she slid the holographic window displaying her passive sensors from her far left to directly in front of her. Though the passive sensors were nowhere near as powerful as a full sensor sweep, like most things aboard the fighter, even these were highly advanced. And they were picking up a power source in the debris field with them.

"Daxma, do you copy?"

"Yes, I'm here."

The reply was crisp, but with a miniscule amount of static. The Commonwealth had learned early on that the particular brand of radiation generated by ril-galas power source interfered with the types of comm networks employed by humans.

Despite the close proximity of the other fighters, there was evidently enough residual radiation in the remains of the Hornets' Nest to cause minor interference.

"Check your passives," said Cagliari. "Let me know if you see anything odd."

There was a moment before Daxma, the female icaran who had been a test pilot on the Argentavis project, responded.

"A power source. Not strong, but stable."

"I'm seeing it, too," said one of the other pilots.

Within moments, Cagliari had confirmation from her entire flight group - they were all seeing the same thing.

Passives weren't enough to tell what the power source might be, but Cagliari glanced at the countdown clock and knew she couldn't risk doing a full scan. Their timeline had been an estimate, and she had no way of knowing whether the ril-galas reinforcements were ahead of schedule - or how far their sensors could reach. Performing a scan as deeply as she wanted to would register on most scanning technologies of which she was aware, and she couldn't risk giving away the position of Outlaw Squadron.

But they had to know. Whatever this power source might be, it was very likely the target of the ril-galas, the treasure they were willing to give up occupied planets to re-acquire.

Cagliari activated her connection to the Royal Sovereign, and smiled when Kerry Stanton-West's face popped up in a window.

"Hey Kerry," she said. "Did you send Radko to bed?"

Stanton-West laughed.

"He's just humouring me, I'm sure," she said. "But yes, he's resting in his office."

"Good, he needs it," she said. "Look, I need you to access the Goose Bay's sensor array. We've found some kind of power source in here with us, in the debris field. I think it's probably what the douchebags are after."

"And you can't properly scan without potentially giving away your position," said Stanton-West, nodding. "Give me a moment."

She was doing something outside camera range for a moment, and Cagliari assumed that Stanton-West was transferring the Goose Bay's control link to her station.

"All right, I have the sensors online - can you give me rough coordinates?"

"Yeah, just a sec."

She input the command and sent her data to the Royal Sovereign. The data packet was small enough that even the most advanced sensors would barely register the transmission.

"Thanks, got it," said Stanton-West, keying in some commands.

The program that was controlling the Goose Bay wasn't Cagliari's best work - it was clunky, and the interface nowhere near as user-friendly as the UHUD and related interfaces she'd worked on - but it was functional. It only took Stanton-West a few moments to start receiving data.

As Cagliari watched, the Royal Sovereign's XO began to frown.

"I don't understand what I'm looking at," she said.

Swearing under her breath, Cagliari tapped her fingers on her knee. She wanted to see the data for herself, but the packet would be too large, too easily picked up by any sensors - which was the whole point of having Stanton-West use the Goose Bay. If she could just get a look at...

"Hey," she said. "Can you send me an image of the readings? Just a static image, no data packet or anything."

"Sure, just one minute," said Stanton-West.

A moment later, the image popped up, floating in front of Cagliari just to the right of her passive sensors screen. She slid her own sensor readings off to the side and pulled in the image from the Goose Bay sensors closer. They had picked up the power readings the same as Outlaw Squadron, but the more powerful sensor sweep had also picked up additional detail. The object was absolutely a power source, but it also seemed to be pulsing - every so often, its power signature would increase briefly before returning to normal levels.

"Wait, wait, wait," said Cagliari. "Okay... I need you to do a series of these. I need to see it over a period of like a minute. Two second intervals if you can."

01:18:36

"And quickly," she said. "Please."

"Okay," said Stanton-West as she worked. "What are we looking for?"

"I have a thought, but I need more data," said Cagliari, just as the additional images popped into existence in front of her. "Awesome, thanks."

Setting up her UHUD to turn the thirty static images into a continually changing loop in chronological order, Cagliari chewed her lower lip as she watched the cycle. And then watched it again. And again, and again until she was certain of what she was seeing.

"Kerry, you still there?"

"Of course."

"I need another scan from the Goose Bay," she said. "Three actually - sending you the parameters now."

"Okay," said Stanton-West, then she turned and spoke to someone Cagliari couldn't see. "Bell, go get the Captain, please. He'll want to be up here soon. Okay Cags, got it. Running the scans now."

Being more detailed and with more specific goals, the two new scans took much longer than the first and Cagliari couldn't help but watch the clock ticking down the entire time.

"Got it," said Stanton-West finally.

A trio of still images appeared and Cagliari slid them around the UHUD until they were positioned around the original image of the power source. When combined, the four images showed the slightly glowing blob of the power source with three thin spokes radiating out from it.

"Shit."

Quickly she brought up a three-dimensional star chart of the Solar system, plotting first the location of the power source, then the spokes travelling outward from it.

"Shit, shit, shit," said Cagliari. "Kerry, you'd better get Radko on deck."

29

"What have you got, Cags?" said Radko, pulling his uniform jacket back on as he walked across the command deck of the Royal Sovereign and stepped up beside Stanton-West.

Before them hovered both a window containing Kestrel Cagliari and the three-dimensional star map she'd created. Stanton-West quickly filled in Radko about the power source and the scans they had been running remotely using the HMCS Goose Bay before turning the discussion over to Cagliari.

"Remember that discussion we had a while back about how well-coordinated the ril-glas always seemed?" she said.

"Yeah, the theory is that they have some kind of telepathic link within their battalion or flight group or whatever," he said.

"Right," she said nodding. "But their coordination goes a lot further than that, and over huge distances."

"They pulled out to come here almost instantly," said Stanton-West. "This wasn't a gradual thing, and it happened everywhere, all at once."

Radko's eyes narrowed.

"Like they were answering an emergency recall notice."

Cagliari was nodding.

"Look at the vectors of those spokes," she said. "Those are power surges from the source, pulses. Look at where they each go."

The star chart pulled out to show a wider area of space and the spokes extended their projected path. One shot straight down, terminating at the Earth's surface, while the other two extended at different angles into the Solar system.

"Son of a bitch," said Radko. "Bell, add our current fleet deployment to this map."

She did so, and markers popped up to indicated the bulk of the fleet in hiding on the far side of the moon, as well as Outlaw Squadron and the Goose Bay in Earth orbit, and the Newcastle's battle group.

The second spoke went straight to where the Newcastle had engaged the ril-galas feint.

The third stretched out in the opposite direction.

"That's the approach vector of the main reinforcement fleet," said Stanton-West.

"So, this is some kind of transmitter? A comm relay?" said Radko.

"I think it's a lot more than that. We also talked about how *disorganized* they've been since we took out the Hornets' Nest," said Cagliari. "Finn, what if they're not just low-level telepaths? What if they're actually connected to a hive mind?"

Radko stood up straighter as it dawned on him what Cagliari was suggesting.

"Finn... what if we've just discovered their motherfucking *brain?*"

Silence followed as everyone on the command deck of the Royal Sovereign - Radko and Stanton-West included - simply stared at Cagliari's star map and the slowly pulsing dot at its centre.

"They were in complete chaos," said Stanton-West, seemingly more to herself than anyone else. "But then they started major redeployment, on Earth and in space..."

"This power source wasn't here before," said Bell. She was quickly scrolling through window after window of what looked to Radko to be sensor scan results. "The whole area was scanned extensively after the Hornets' Nest was destroyed -

looking for survivors from our side, or anything we could use to repair our ships - but there was nothing. I can't find anything in the logs that matches this thing's power signature."

"Maybe I wasn't the only one who needed some recovery time," said Radko.

"And now it's calling the shots again," said Cagliari.

"If we're right about this, then we're wrong about the deployment on Earth," said Stanton-West. "They're not reinforcing defensively; they're doing something else. They're executing some kind of plan."

Closing his eye, Radko ran a hand through his hair.

"Which means Freyja and the others might be walking into a trap."

"And we can't get word to her without giving away our position," said Stanton-West.

"Wait, yes we can," said Bell. "The same way we did the scanning - use the Goose Bay."

"Yes," said Radko, slapping his palm again the sand table. "Do it. Brief and to the point, and send it as a blast broadcast to all four landing zones."

He glanced at the countdown clock, which he swore he could feel staring at him no matter where he was.

01:03:07

"Send all of this info to the rest of the fleet, and get all stations up and running. I want weapons hot before the Goose Bay begins her run."

"Message relayed through the Goose Bay," said Bell. "And we have an incoming from the Vimy Ridge."

It took him a moment to parse that, he was so used to he and the Vimy Ridge being one and the same, but then a floating frame containing Amira el Bahari materialized in front of him.

"Radko, Upshaw's been taken into custody," she said. "De Freitas has verbally agreed to surrender himself, but hasn't actually done it yet."

"I'm assuming she didn't surrender without a fight," he said, trying and failing to keep the satisfaction out of his voice.

"That would be correct. Several others were arrested with her, including Edward Vossek," she said. "I thought you'd like to know."

Radko nodded. It had been Vossek who had taken the ATC Castle ship Adirondack in pursuit of the Azrael's Tear and shot down Sigurdsson's transport over The Shattered World. And though he didn't have any proof of it, Radko was certain that Vossek had been a leading hand behind the scenes in the execution of Anna Cortez. While he bore no ill will to the late Colonel Harlan Gray, despite the fact that the man had tried to take command of the Vimy Ridge at gunpoint, Radko had nothing *but* ill will for Gray's former second-in-command, Edward Vossek. Gray's actions had led to his own death, and though the Colonel had appeared prepared to kill Radko, his motives were the same as those that drove Radko himself - trying to do what he felt was right and what he felt was necessary in an ever-evolving crisis. But Vossek's actions were driven by a need for revenge, a need to retaliate against the Commonwealth Armed Forces that he felt had abandoned him and Gray.

A loud beep sounded from the sand table and Radko heard it echo on the channels to both el Bahari and Cagliari.

00:59:59

Less than an hour.

"Do we destroy this thing?" said Cagliari.

"Not yet," said Radko. "We've set the trap, we have to spring it as is."

"We can't risk tipping them off that we know their target," said el Bahari.

"Once shit starts happening, I don't know if anyone in the squadron is going to have the time to target it," said Cagliari. "We're going to be on our own until you guys get here."

"Execute the plan, let me worry about the rest," said Radko. "You've more than covered your bet, Cags. Just focus on leading Outlaw Squadron - dealing with the... the brain won't change anything now."

"Yeah, I know," she said. "Just don't like knowing that thing is sitting right here... Fucking hell, we need another scan."

"What? What's going on? What's happened?"

"Nothing yet, but what if this thing has sensors?"

"And has noticed Outlaw Squadron," said Stanton-West.

"On it," said Bell, already working to get the Goose Bay's scanners on task.

After a tense few moments, Bell breathed a sigh of relief - as did everyone else.

"No sign of any activity beyond those transmission threads," she said.

"All right, send a message to Singh," said Radko. "The Azrael's Tear is small enough and agile enough to get through that debris cloud relatively unscathed. Once the battle starts, it will be his job to take out this brain thing."

The order was relayed and confirmed, and moments later a LIDAR technician spoke up.

"Captain, I'm picking up something on long range. Multiple hits," he said. "Ril-galas signatures, plus two others not far behind."

"Krellin," said Radko. "Estimated time until they enter Earth space?"

"Just over forty minutes, Captain."

"Damn it. Update the clock."

00:41:23

The countdown would automatically sync across the fleet, but the assault groups that had made planetfall would only know of the change if they were still within range of the landing craft - which Radko knew was unlikely.

He hoped it wouldn't matter.

Mostly, he hoped that Sigurdsson was doing all right.

30

Though she'd yelled a warning, Sigurdsson wasn't sure it was going to matter.

Whether it was the Matriarch sharpening her awareness and reflexes, or just a by-product of stress and borderline panic, when the dozen stalkers that had been clinging to the underside of Cowgate Bridge dropped into the United Defense Force assault group, it felt like slow motion to Sigurdsson.

She saw a stalker drop on top of one the icaran commandos and as Sigurdsson brought up her gunstaff to fire at it, another dropped directly in front of her and lunged. She swung her staff, but the thing caught it and held fast, yanking it from her grip.

Sigurdsson drew the two long knives from her armoured vest and roared. As one, the udukiin dropped their gunstaves, drew their own knives and roared.

And the ril-galas paused.

Not a long pause, just a momentary hesitation, but it was enough. The udukiin - all of them - followed Sigurdsson's lead and pounced, stabbing, whirling, slicing.

After driving one of her knives through the chest of her attacker, Sigurdsson spun to see another advancing quickly on Ransom and Hunter. With the false Prince supporting the still-unwell Hunter, neither was prepared for the attack. With a yell, she grabbed Ransom by the bicep and yanked her backward, thrusting her own left forearm forward to block the attack. Claws raked across her armour and she jabbed forward with a fist and followed with a slash from her knife. The stalker staggered backward and then its chest caved in with two shots from an icaran assault rifle.

Elgraphaar stepped up beside her and without a word, Sigurdsson retrieved her gunstaff and the two clambered up onto a car abandoned in the tunnel. Their heads nearly to the belly of the bridge, Sigurdsson and Elgraphaar stood back-to-back, taking out whatever attackers escaped the knives of the udukiin.

Eventually, there was silence, followed by the soft swish of udukiin knives being sheathed.

"Casualty report," said Sigurdsson, jumping down from the car.

They had, thankfully, only lost two soldiers - the icaran Sigurdsson had seen attacked and one of the Commonwealth soldiers - but several had injuries that were being tended to. Every single one of the injured parties claimed to be fine to continue and Sigurdsson took them at their word despite knowing at least two of them were outright lying.

She understood. She wouldn't have wanted to leave either, not knowing what they were about to do and what it could mean for the future of not just mankind, but the galaxy as a whole.

"Are you guys okay?" she said, kneeling beside Ransom and Hunter.

"Yeah," said Ransom. "Yeah, we're okay."

Hunter nodded, massaging her temples.

"Sorry," she said. "I tried to warn you. Couldn't get the words out."

Placing her hand on the woman's shoulder, Sigurdsson waited to respond until Hunter made eye contact.

"You did everything you could and that's all I ask. We would have lost a lot more people without you," she said. "But now we need to keep moving."

"They know we're coming now," said Ransom.

"Yeah. Which is why we need to keep going and try to hit them even harder. Because if they're focused on us and what we're doing..."

"Maybe the other two teams can catch them by surprise."

Sigurdsson nodded and Ransom got to her feet, helping Hunter do the same.

"Then let's go."

"Wait," said Hunter, resting a hand on Ransom's forearm. "You need to... Arthur needs to be visible. Needs to be active. Not being my babysitter."

"But Hunter-"

"No, Harley, the Prince has been a symbol and he has to continue until the end. I can still help the war effort, but I'm... damaged."

"Hunter..."

"I am," she said, shaking her head and wiping away a tear. "I have to accept it and so do you. I don't know if I can recover, I don't know anything other than we have to finish this. I can still help, but if you stay at my side I will slow you down. You won't be where Prince Arthur needs to be."

Still, Ransom hesitated.

"I will assign one of my commandos as her guard," said Elgrphaar.

"Go," said Hunter, giving Ransom a gentle push toward Sigurdsson. "Time to be a hero."

Though she didn't seem happy about it, Ransom nodded and scooped up the 33A1 assault rifle from the fallen Commonwealth soldier before falling into step beside Sigurdsson and

Jaeger. Elgraphaar ordered one of his commandos to stick with Hunter, then followed Sigurdsson, Ransom, and Jaeger as the four of them took point, a few paces ahead of the rest.

"How's the Prince holding up?" asked Sigurdsson, her voice low enough to not carry beyond the four of them.

"I'm okay," said Ransom, still maintaining her Arthur persona despite everything. "Though it's hard... not being myself. It's funny, I always felt I didn't quite know who I was, you know? Or what I wanted to be - I mean as a person, not as an occupation - but now that I have to spend so much time being someone else..."

"You've discovered who you are," said Sigurdsson. "I can understand to a degree."

"I'm really looking forward to not doing this anymore."

"Fighting a war, or pretending to be the Prince?"

"Yes," said Ransom, with a lopsided smile.

Continuing on, casting frequent glances in all directions, Sigurdsson led the group forward, crossing through an area with the remains of what looked like small apartment buildings and then further into a small stand of trees. She called for a halt. Across the narrow road before them was Holyrood Park.

And within the Park, their target.

"They're moving," said Hunter. "Away."

Sigurdsson turned to see the woman leaning heavily on her icaran bodyguard - a commando named Tyrylarr - but her eyes and expression clearer than since Sigurdsson had first arrived.

She was about to ask what Hunter meant when she heard the gunfire from further into the Park, and it sounded to Sigurdsson like it was coming from right around the area Udrach's assault team was expected to strike. The ril-galas had been so focused on Sigurdsson's group that at least one of the teams appeared to have made it to the Park unmolested, and the rilgalas were scrambling to reorganize their forces to respond.

Sigurdsson twirled her gunstaff in her hand and out of the corner of her eye, she saw several udukiin warriors do the same. She wasn't sure if it was something they'd picked up from her or something she'd picked up from them, but either way it made her smile - because the flourish shown by the udukiin led to some of the humans trying to show their own flourishes either with their knives or by twirling pistols around their trigger fingers and trying to holster them in a smooth motion. And then some of the icarans began to sing, not songs of their history as they were known to do, but songs Sigurdsson had never heard before. Songs with some very vulgar lyrics directed at their enemies.

Turning to Elgraphaar, who had removed his helmet to adjust it, Sigurdsson raised an eyebrow and laughed.

"All icarans are poets," said Elgraphaar. "But not all poets are good."

Then he bobbed his head, the icaran equivalent of a shrug.

"And some enemies deserve more scorn than respect," he added.

"This is the icaran equivalent of a drinking song, isn't it?"

"Indeed. All drunks are poets, regardless of species."

Checking her *vayan* sidearm and then her long knives... which she wasn't sure of the name for...

Hestic miroval.

The name popped directly into the centre of her mind, thanks to the Matriarch's telepathic bond. It roughly translated to 'long blades,' which Sigurdsson had to admit was mildly disappointing, so she decided she'd give hers their own name.

They had, after all, belonged to three successive War Matri-archs, and like Excalibur or Mjolnir, they deserved names.

One day. This was not the time to devote any amount of focus to naming inanimate objects, she figured.

Breaking the treeline, Sigurdsson followed Ransom's lead up an embankment to an uneven rock face that would, in the-ory, shield their advance from the eyes of any ril-galas sentries. Spreading out in a thin line, the column advanced two by two along the rock face, heading toward the sounds of battle, and the muzzle flashes lighting up the night. Grieve, the talented old sniper, broke off with five others - sharpshooters all - after giving Sigurdsson a salute, which she returned gratefully. Fi-nally, when the rock wall became too small to provide meaningful cover for their approach, Sigurdsson ordered a short charge through the long grass into the more open area where the ril-galas had engaged Udrach's company. There was no sign yet of the group lead by Major Ustorf, but Sigurdsson had to hope they, like her own group, had simply been delayed and not stopped entirely.

"Company halt!" she said. "Form lines!"

The enemy had only just noticed them in the faint slivers of dawn that had begun forcing their way through the cloud cover, and she needed to take advantage of their surprise. The UDF would be attacking uphill, which meant the enemy had the high ground. It would be a difficult proposition for them to make it to the regeneration pods at all unless they could thin the ril-galas ranks.

And she was hoping that some time-honoured tactics would do the trick.

Dropping to one knee, Sigurdsson raised her gunstaff to her shoulder. To her left, Elgraphaar. To her right, Harley Ran-som in the guise of Prince Arthur. Fanning out on either side of them, kneeling in a perfect line, were half of her combined udukiin, icaran, and human force; the other half standing three feet behind.

"Ready!" shouted Sigurdsson.

More ril-galas began to turn toward them, and away from Udrach's company.

"Aim!"

As Sigurdsson had hoped, the ril-galas began advancing toward her company. Stalkers moving quickly, darting across worn paths and through long grass, with the heavier and less agile foot soldiers moving steadily behind. Though she couldn't hear the telltale screeches of any ril-galas bats in the air nearby, those weren't her problem.

The stalkers and the foot soldiers advanced.

As the gunpods of the foot soldiers began to glow, powering up to fire, Sigurdsson almost smiled.

"Front rank, fire!"

A cacophony of weapon discharges roared across the Park, and the nearest of the occupiers were shredded by the volley.

"Rear rank fire!"

The roar was nearly deafening, but as the second volley tore into the enemy, Sigurdsson didn't stop to count the dead or evaluate her company's efficiency. Over the course of her life, even before she was military, she had learned to strike fast and to strike hard. Ensure your opponent understood that the fight, no matter who eventually came out victorious, was going to exact an enormous cost.

Before the enemy could recover or even start mounting a counter attack, Sigurdsson was ordering a march. Her front rank jumped to their feet and the two lines marched forward several paces before Sigurdsson called a halt. The front rank dropped to a knee and Sigurdsson again ordered a barrage from first front, then rear, rank.

Immediately after the second rank had fired, the company heard the bats screaming in. But they also heard the comforting sounds of sniper fire, and bats began to drop from the sky as Grieve's team made their presence known.

And just as the ril-galas began firing back at Sigurdsson's company, Udrach's company charged again.

31

00:17:42

Unclenching his fists, Radko wiped damp palms on his uniform pants as he glanced at the countdown clock, then back to the magnification window hovering over a section of the UHUD at the front of the Royal Sovereign's bridge.

To his right, the surface of Luna dominated the UHUD's holographic display and was obscuring his view of the approaching ril-galas fleet. The Lunar colonies were all dark. Mankind's first off-world colonies, they had been built inside pressure domes long before humanity had any expertise with terraforming - a science in which most would admit they were still not proficient. Due to their construction, the Lunar colonies had gone dark shortly after the ril-galas had arrived.

Pressure domes did not stand up well against attacks.

Efforts had been made at evacuation, but those efforts were largely unsuccessful. Only a few thousand of the moon's population of nearly one point two million had made it out before the domes had failed and the vacuum of space had claimed the surface of the moon once more.

To his left, the Vimy Ridge dominated his view as much as it did his heart. Seeing the ship from a distance was still a surreal experience, but one to which he was slowly, grudgingly, becoming accustomed. And past the Vimy Ridge, the remainder of the UDF, including Admiral Rhekar's Venn Shakara, Admiral Chu's Hangzhou, and the Azrael's Tear, the small but brutally efficient pirate vessel of Jagat Sohal Singh.

Though the moon obscured his real view of the ril-galas fleet, the Royal Sovereign's AI plotted their approach for him as small red arrowheads.

From one of the command stations nearby, Bell called out to him.

"Sir, incoming transmission from the krellin."

Nodding, Radko turned and pointed to the command station nearest him. As much of an adjustment as it was, going from the very old school technology of the Vimy Ridge to the cutting edge technology of the Royal Sovereign, Radko couldn't question the design of his new ship. He could access essentially anything he required from essentially anywhere he stood.

A window faded into existence above the console - the krellin transmission.

Not as contact-averse as the udukiin had always been, the krellin maintained sporadic contact with humanity. Radko had even met a krellin in person once, many years prior, when the HMCS Queenston Heights had served as honour guard to a diplomatic mission to the Ota of Krellin. Regardless, they were, as a species, so obviously non-human that the sight always made him... not quite nervous, but vaguely unsettled.

Seven limbs spaced evenly around an ovoid body with no apparent eyes or mouth. Each limb ending in a hand that was also a foot with three opposable digits, again equally spaced around its circumference. Communication was done via an organ within their body generating various harmonic waves, and by flashes of bioluminescence.

The krellin had, thankfully, developed technology to translate their completely mystifying forms of communication into various spoken languages.

"Greet," said the krellin. "Am Sossussuoa, of ship Vyrrysh Otakrel. Pass to Humanspace?"

The translation was always an adventure.

"Greetings Sossussuoa," said Radko, surprising even himself by not stumbling over the name. "On behalf of the United Defense Fleet, welcome. And thank you for your assistance."

The krellin waited a moment for the translation. As Radko understood it, one of the reasons contact was not more common between the Ota of Krellin and the rest of the galaxy was that they found it very frustrating attempting to communicate with verbal species.

"Will strike presently," said Sossussuoa. "If is so desired."

"We would ask that you hold back for now and join the attack when our full fleet strikes."

Before the krellin could respond, an alert flashed yellow across the UHUD.

Standing at the sand table, hands clasped behind her back, Stanton-West made the announcement.

"The ril-galas reinforcement fleet has passed the outer marker."

The outer marker, set by the UDF as the point of no return, the line that, once crossed by the enemy, marked the beginning of the most important space battle in human history.

Based on their current speed, the enemy would be in Earth orbit in under twelve minutes.

"Bell, fire up the Goose Bay," said Radko. "Kerry, signal Outlaw Squadron."

He heard Cagliari's confirmation and knew that on a channel for Outlaw only, she would have begun their countdown. The squadron would remain in low-power mode until the Goose Bay unleashed its fury.

As Radko watched, the ril-galas ships began to enter his line of sight, and the engines on the Goose Bay flared to life.

Under the control of Bell, the ship turned and began to sail directly at the approaching enemy fleet. An internal countdown began aboard the Goose Bay, mirrored by floating numbers above the hologram Radko watched - counting down to the simultaneous detonation of the Goose Bay's nuclear reactor as well as the twenty nuclear warheads aboard.

"Five minutes to contact," said Stanton-West, allowing Bell to focus on her work.

Radko clenched and unclenched his fist. Their own travel time to the engagement zone was six minutes.

"Get us underway, engines full," he said. "All vessels are to proceed as planned."

The order was relayed and Radko felt a slight vibration in the deck plates - much less than when he was aboard the Vimy Ridge - as the Royal Sovereign's massive engines kicked in. The moon slid away, the ril-galas fleet came into full view and its full scale became apparent.

LIDAR had been an unreliable source for info on ril-galas ships from the beginning, due to some odd materials in their biological armour, and visuals clearly showed that LIDAR estimates of ship numbers had been lacking. The reinforcement fleet consisted of two fighter carriers, a dozen battleships, another dozen of the mola-mola shaped scout ships, a trio of sleeker ships Radko had never seen before, as well as six ships that while Radko had never seen himself, he knew from intel reports to be troop carriers. Troops carriers that would, if allowed to do so, land on Earth to reinforce the occupation force.

Radko activated his communications link to Cagliari's fighter.

"Getting close to go-time," she said as soon as the link popped up.

"There are two ships in there, troop transports," he said. "They're the ones-"

"They look like angry sea turtles with sideways barrels instead of heads," she said nodding.

"Uh... yeah, actually. They're your priority target. We can't let them get past us to Earth."

"Understood. I'll let everyone know."

"Happy hunting, Cags."

She smiled.

"You too. See you for the after-party."

When the connection closed, Radko returned his attention to the Goose Bay's suicide run. Damage reports were streaming across Bell's screen as the first rank of ril-galas ships began pummeling the lone vessel, but Bell ignored the reports and increased the Goose Bay's engine outputs well beyond safety limits.

And as the first rank of ril-gaas enveloped the Goose Bay, the countdown timer on its reactor clicked to zero.

The flash of the Goose Bay's detonation was intense and Radko had to briefly look away, despite the Royal Sovereign's UHUD dimming it automatically.

"The Goose Bay reactor has detonated," said Bell, scrolling through information at her command station. "And I can confirm that nineteen of twenty warheads also detonated. The twentieth one stopped sending readings a minute ago."

"Safe to assume it's not a concern either way," said Stanton-West.

Radko remained silent. Staring intently where the bright sphere of the explosion was beginning to fade, revealing...

"Debris," sad Bell.

"Lots of it," added Stanton-West.

The strength of the explosion, the reactor plus the warheads, would have been enough to nearly vaporize a ship the size of the Goose Bay. As the glow further faded, Radko increased the magnification on the floating window before him, and finally unclenched his jaw. The Goose Bay had torn a hole through the ril-galas forces. It wasn't yet clear how many ships had been destroyed versus damaged, but by quick count, Radko knew the sacrifice of the Commonwealth ship had been worth the cost.

Hearing voice of Kestrel Cagliari from Stanton-West's position at the sand table, Radko looked just past the last position of the Goose Bay to where Outlaw Squadron was streaking out from their hiding place.

"Range?" he said.

"We'll be in missile range in ninety seconds, Captain," said Stanton-West. "Rail gun range in one hundred and twenty."

With a nod, Radko gave Bell the signal to open his fleetwide channel.

"United Defense Fleet, this is Captain Finn Radko. You know why we're here. You know what's at stake," he said. "We have a chance here that may never come again - we've already hurt the invaders by destroying their deployment hub, but now? Now we have a chance to cripple them."

Pausing, he took a deep breath that seemed, if only to him, a little shaky.

"I saw this invasion begin," he said, thinking back to those first panicked minutes of what they simply referred to at the time as 'the swarm' attacking and devastating the Third Fleet of the Commonwealth. The HMCS Vimy Ridge had been the only ship of the Third Fleet to survive that attack, and the first ship of any fleet to fight back.

"I saw it begin," he repeated. "And I damn well intend to see it end."

Falling silent, Radko brought up all the tactical information he could while Stanton-West stepped in to do her part.

"Weapons free," she said. "Unless otherwise assigned, commanders are free to select their own targets, with the condition that troop carriers must be prevented from entering Earth atmosphere and all ships attempting to enter the debris cloud of the Hornets' Nest must be prevented from doing so."

"This ship," said Radko, tapping on the UHUD to highlight one of the centipede-like ril-galas fighter carriers near the rear of the reinforcement fleet. The same would be happening on the networked sand tables across the fleet. "That's our target."

He then tapped the second of the carriers.

"Admiral Rhekar, that one's yours, if you would be so kind."

"Understood."

The two largest ships would be taking on the two largest ships, which seemed fitting.

"We're in missile range, Captain," said Stanton-West.

"Full volley from the forward batteries," he said, watching as the Venn Shakara unloaded her first volley on the other carrier. "And follow it up with a second as soon as the gunnery crews are ready to do so."

"Aye, sir."

As the battle was joined, life became barely-organized chaos.

Tearing his eye reluctantly from the holographic screens that surrounded him, Radko focused on the projection above the sand table that showed the entire battlefield. He watched the krellin, slowly approaching from behind the ril-galas, in their oddly jellyfish-like vessels, picking away at the enemy with the beam weapons at the end of each tentacle.

Outlaw Squadron, split into three separate wings, were already tearing apart three of the troop transports – one of which blinked out of existence as Radko watched – and the fighter carrier with which the Venn Shakara was engaged launched a small number of fighters before it too disappeared from the sand table projection.

Radko looked up just in time to see the brief fireball that had been the carrier fizzle to nothing. It hadn't launched even a third of its fighter contingent.

"Swing us around," said Radko, turning his attention to the ril-galas carrier with which his own ship was trading shots. "I want a full broadside of rail guns."

As the ship began to pivot on its thrusters, the point defense cannons along the flank of the ril-galas carrier stopped firing.

"They're getting clear space for their fighters to launch," said Stanton-West.

"Hold the broadside."

"Sir?"

"They're about to open the fighter bays," he said, then quickly explained the plan.

And for a moment, the two ships hung in space, flank-to-flank, neither firing.

Then, in a cascading sequence, the launch bay doors all down the side of the ril-galas carrier began to pop open.

"Execute," said Radko.

The deck plates rumbled as the Royal Sovereign unleashed its rail guns directly into the enemy's fighter bays, and then Radko gripped the sand table to steady himself as the Sovereign spun one-hundred-and-eighty degrees and unloaded a second broadside, tearing chunks out of the carrier's insides.

Without having launched a single fighter, the carrier lurched, listed, and exploded.

Radko saw a couple of high fives amongst the crew, but everyone refocused quickly.

"The Azrael's Tear advises that they are starting their run," said Bell.

On the screens, the Tear flashed blue briefly as the AI identified it, and Radko tracked it as Singh's ship swooped into the debris field, hunting the brain device.

Radko, about to order an attack on a new target, paused as a section of the holographic projection surrounding the command deck began to warp, as if the device projecting that particular area had suddenly been equipped with a fish-eye lens.

"Kerry, we're having some kind of-."

Proximity alarms blared, cutting off the statement, as within the distortion a vessel appeared. Twice the size of the Royal Sovereign and bristling with weaponry – point defense style cannons as well as three of the standard ril-galas beam weapons, each mounted on an armature, giving them a much broader firing arc.

"Finn, did you see that?!"

It was Cagliari.

"Yeah, what the hell did I just see?" he said, then turned quickly to Stanton-West. "Get us firing solutions on that thing."

"I think we just witnessed the use of an E-R Bridge drive, Finn," said Cagliari. "A temporary wormhole. We've been trying to develop that tech for fifty years."

"The power output was massive when it first appeared," said Bell, scrolling through data at an impressive rate. "But the only things generating any significant power now are its thrusters and weapons. Whatever it is, at this point it seems like it made a one-way trip."

Staring at their latest adversary, Radko shook his head.

"That means it has nothing to lose."

32

The battle for Holyrood Park had been going exceptionally well.

At least, that's what Sigurdsson had thought until the second wave of ril-galas came, their powerful gun pods chewing a hole through her line. Firing her gunstaff, she blew a hole through the chest of one attacker then quickly fired at another, blowing one of its arms clean off, while Ransom helped an injured icaran commando to her feet and Elgraphaar laid down covering fire for a Soviet performing first aid on a fallen Commonwealth soldier.

If Sigurdsson could merge her company with Udrach's, they had the numbers to weather the storm, but the ril-galas appeared to know it as well as she did, and their speedy stalkers had driven a wedge between the two groups. Where Ustorf's company was, Sigurdsson hadn't a clue, but by that point she had to assume they were either dead or pinned down as much as she was about to be.

And then the roar of engines and Sigurdsson looked up to see two of the udukiin dropships they'd left behind with Aylarr on Calton Hill roar overhead, strafing the enemy from their nose-mounted ball turrets. After taking a second pass, one of the ships flew a little ways off to set down on the summit of the extinct volcano named, ironically, Arthur's Seat. The second ship hovered over Sigurdsson's position and as the ball turret kept firing, Aylarr leapt down to the ground.

"Freyja," she said, drawing a pair of *vayan* side arms and joining the fray. "I have news."

"Hopefully good."

The arrival of the dropships had been good news in itself - their strafing of the enemy line had opened a gap in their ranks that Udrach had exploited and broke through. The two companies were rapidly forming up as a single unit.

"Some of it," said Aylar. "Brigadier Arysis reports her action is proceeding well. However, we have also received news from the fleet that may cause complications."

As briefly and concisely as she could, Aylarr explained the situation with the object hidden within the remains of the Hornets' Nest and the discovery of what it meant.

"They're not retreating to these facilities for protection," said Sigurdsson. "They're here to do something."

"But what?" said Ransom. "They may not be running scared, but we're having success. What could they be... oh shit."

"What?" said Sigurdsson, the sudden change in Ransom's demeanour immediately sounding an alarm in her skull.

"Don't retreating armies sometimes burn shit to the ground before they bail?"

Aylarr looked up sharply.

"Freyja, it is well known that the majority of ril-galas technology is radioactive."

"Possibly nuclear," said Sigurdsson, nodding. "Fuck. Fuck, fuck, *fuck*."

It was then that she realized the ril-galas were pulling back, toward the massive blight that had taken over the area by Hunter's Bog, the monstrosity that had been the last stop for many humans over the two years of the occupation: the processing facility.

The slaughterhouse.

"How many of those are there?"

Sigurdsson turned to see Hunter there behind her, standing on her own, but looking more frail than ever.

"All over the planet, I mean," she continued.

"I don't know," said Sigurdsson.

"Nor do I," said Aylarr. "But the information we were sent by the fleet indicates that the ril-galas are congregating around forty-two locations worldwide, including this one."

Hunter stared at the processing plant for a moment, swaying lightly on her feet.

"How powerful?"

Though Sigurdsson wasn't sure what Hunter was getting at, Aylarr appeared to - the icaran popped her helmet back on and did a quick scan.

"The power signatures indicate a substantial power source."

"So, if they were to blow this facility up, the blast would be substantial," said Hunter, still staring at the building. "And a massive area would be irradiated."

"You've got to be fucking kidding me," said Sigurdsson.

"We've only got four assault groups," said Ransom. "So that means thirty-eight of these that they can do whatever they want with. That they can blow up? What about fallout? If they blow them all, would that be like forty-two nuclear bombs going off all over the world?"

Sigurdsson was wishing they had brought Frankenstein - he'd probably know the answer off the top of his weird metal head. Instead, she turned to Hunter.

"You destroyed one of these, didn't you?"

"Not like this," said Hunter, shaking her head. "The one we destroyed was a small facility, not much bigger than the command deck on the Vimy Ridge. Nowhere near this large."

"Get onto one of the dropships," said Sigurdsson. "You should be able to use them to contact the fleet - see if they can give us something. We can't destroy these things if we're going to irradiate the area, and we can't let *them* destroy them for the same reason. Like... like Prince Arthur says, we need to know what will happen with those other thirty-eight."

"I'm more useful here."

Gently, Sigurdsson pulled Hunter away from the rest so they could speak privately.

"Look, Hunter," she said, smiling sadly. "I may not have your level of ability, but this Matriarch thing has given me some low-level psychic shit. I don't think the others realize how bad you are right now, but I do."

Staring at the ground for moment, when Hunter finally met Sigurdsson's gaze her eyes were wet with tears.

"I can still be useful."

"I know you can. And for starters, you can get information from the fleet, because without that info...," Sigurdsson shrugged. "I don't know what the fuck we're doing. Destroying this place? Protecting it?"

Hunter nodded slowly, but still seemed defeated.

"All right," she said.

"Hey," said Sigurdsson, placing a hand on each of Hunter's shoulders. "Look at me."

It took a moment, but Hunter complied.

"The only reason me and my people are here is because you kept up the fight. You kept people here alive long enough to be a resistance. Kept them alive long enough for victory to be an option. It may sound over the top, but the whole fucking human race owes you a debt of gratitude and the Commonwealth sure as shit owes you an apology for sticking you in a box," she said. "You have more than done your part in this war, and for you to have come from where you have, to become what you are now - a leader in the resistance against this occupation - is fucking amazing."

She smirked.

"And you know I'm telling the truth because I feel you bouncing around in here," said Sigurdsson, tapping her forehead.

"I'm sorry," said Hunter, forcing a smile. "I don't have very much control over it anymore."

"It's okay, I don't have anything I need to hide from you."

"What about Finn?"

"What about him?"

"Are you hiding the future from him?"

"You can't hide something if you don't know it yourself. You obviously know how I feel about him. He does too. But I really don't know what this means for the future," said Sigurdsson, rapping her knuckles on her armoured shoulder. "I know what I want for the future..."

"But the future has a habit of doing its own thing, regardless of what you want."

Sigurdsson nodded.

"Stay close to Ransom," said Hunter. "Prince Arthur may need to die, but I need Harley Ransom to live."

As soon as Sigurdsson nodded her agreement, Hunter headed off to where Aylarr helped her clamber aboard the waiting dropship.

33

Listing badly to one side, one of the sleek new ril-galas ships - the crew of the Royal Sovereign had taken to calling them barracudas - began to rupture along its ventral axis. As a final rail gun salvo from the Vimy Ridge tore its aft to pieces and the entire ship erupted into a brief fireball, Radko returned his attention to the enormous new entrant on the battlefield.

"We have no further data on this... this..."

Racking his brain trying to figure out what to call the monstrosity hanging in space before him, all Radko could think of was an old episode of the Commonwealth Heroes animated series - essentially five seasons' worth of half-hour toy commercials - where the HMCS Resolute encountered a giant, malevolent, and intelligent space-borne virus cloud that called itself Ultimus.

"We have no data on Ultimus?"

"Running every scan available right now," said Bell, working furiously on three separate holographic displays.

"I'm seeing identical power signatures from Ultimus as from the brainbox the Azrael's Tear is hunting," said Stanton-West. "Whatever our new friend is, it might serve the same function. Also, I get the reference."

"I'm not as old as I look. Is it broadcasting along the same direct lines as the brainbox?"

"As far as I can tell, it's not broadcasting at all," she said, pausing as a bright flare lit up the Hornets' Nest debris field.

Almost immediately, a ping sounded from the sand table and when Radko looked back toward Stanton-West, she was smiling.

"Singh confirms that the Azrael's Tear has taken out the brainbox," she said.

"Captain," interrupted one of the junior comm technicians - Radko was about thirty percent sure his name was Birch, but it may have been Flint. They looked very similar. "Incoming transmission from Earth, Sir. From the Scotland planetfall group, and they're asking to speak with you directly. Someone named Hunter?"

Radko had been about to direct the call to Bell until he heard the name.

"I'll take it over here," he said, nodding to the command station Bell herself had just vacated.

The transmission was voice only of course, the interference from the ril-galas radiation preventing something as complex as visuals from reaching to or from the planet's surface. But even without the visuals, Radko could hear the strain and exhaustion - and even a little pain - in Hunter's voice.

"I wasn't sure you and I would ever get the chance to speak again," she said.

"Same. I also didn't expect you to do the exact opposite of heading somewhere the Commonwealth and the Soviets wouldn't be able to find you."

"They still haven't," she said, a hint of a smile creeping into her voice. "But a United Defence Force has. I have a lot I want to say to you, Finn, but we're very short on time, so I'll keep it short: thank you for everything. No matter what happens from this point onward, I want you to know the chance you gave me, the choice that you gave me, was the single most important event in my life. Without that event, I wouldn't be who I am today, and I am very proud of who I am today."

"You should be," said Radko, his eye misting over. "And you should be proud of who you were when you were aboard the

Vimy Ridge, too. No matter what came before, you were an integral part in what we achieved. I couldn't have done any of this without your help to get it all rolling."

Though he wasn't certain, he thought Hunter was crying. When she spoke a moment later, her voice was steady.

"We need help from the fleet, scientific and medical information we have no way of figuring out on the ground," she said.

Quickly turning to Bell, Radko asked her to open a channel to Doctor Frankenstein.

"I am here," said the Doctor, from the other side of the command deck.

He approached and Radko gave him a quizzical look.

"I have been observing you," said the brill, shrugging his mechanical shoulders. "I am your doctor and you are absurdly stubborn in ignoring your body's frailties."

"Frailties are tomorrow's problem," said Radko. "Hunter, I have Doctor Frankenstein here - what do you need?"

With Frankenstein, Radko listened as Hunter explained the situation with the processing facilities on Earth, and ordered Bell to run as many scans as she could manage of the facilities.

The ship shuddered slightly with some kind of weapons impact, but no alarms blared, and Stanton-West still sounded calm in dealing with the situation, so Radko remained focused on the problem at hand. Or, the most recent problem at hand.

"Passive radiation levels are well below what any species would consider dangerous," said Frankenstein as he reviewed the results from Bell's scans. "However, based on the apparent size of the... I shall call it a reactor, but that is not entirely correct terminology. English can be a somewhat frustrating language for non-human species."

"Let's call it a reactor," said Radko.

"The size and power output of the reactor, as per these scans, is substantial. Passive radiation - the radiation present simply by the power source being active - is of no consequence, less than point zero two millisieverts. Should detonation of the power core occur, however, I would estimate the facility itself and the immediate radius of one kilometer would be instantly vaporized. Everything within a fifteen-to-twenty-kilometre radius would be exposed to radiation, depending on distance from the epicentre of anywhere from three hundred and fifty to five thousand millisieverts of radiation."

"Holy shit," said Radko, rubbing his face. The statement was more sigh than anything. Exposure to that level of radiation would make each one of those facilities worse than the old Chernobyl disaster - worse because there would be the equivalent of a nuclear warhead detonation first, and because there were forty-two of them across the globe. All of which would have twenty-kilometer exclusion zones.

Eight hundred and twenty square kilometers.

In addition to fallout from the blasts.

"I'll need a more straightforward explanation," said Hunter.

"Human exposure of five thousand millisieverts of radiation will generally mean death within thirty days," added Frankenstein.

"It's going to be like they dropped forty-two nukes, Hunter. Bottom line, everyone within a few kilometers will either be dead or dying the second they blow that thing up," said Radko, bringing up a model of Earth with all forty-two facilities marked. "And we don't have the manpower to get to all of them."

"What about evacuations?" said Hunter.

Looking around the UHUD, Radko saw Ultimus looming large, Outlaw Squadron still stalking troop carriers while also dogfighting ril-galas fighters. He watched the Venn Shakara trading shots with a pair of battleships while the Vimy Ridge finished off a scout ship. The Royal Sovereign itself was pummelling a battleship, and the Hangzhou was having a rough go of it against a more agile barracuda.

The two udukiin dreadnaughts were moving in on Ultimus after pounding a pair of battleships into dust.

"We're not going to be able to get there in time," Radko said, shaking his head slowly. "Not on the scale we'd need to."

He punched the command console and swore.

Gritting his teeth, he pointed his index finger sharply at Ultimus.

"Fuck you. Kerry! We're going after the big bastard," he said. "Hunter, secure what you can secure and failing that, get as many people to safety as you can. We'll be there as soon as we're able."

"We will protect as many as we can, I promise you. No matter what it takes."

She closed the transmission on her end and Radko re-focused on Ultimus. The udukiin ships were getting close and the giant ship's three beam weapons had begun to softly glow, powering up. Ultimus was about to join the fight.

"Gunnery crews can fire at will," said Radko as he removed the nuclear activation key from around his neck. "Let's arm the nukes."

34

When Hunter returned to the front lines, assisted more than she cared to admit by the icaran named Aylarr, it was oddly quiet. The ril-galas had temporarily retreated in disarray, like something had happened to cause them to lose focus, but even now they could be seen regrouping. Though she felt exhausted and nauseated and in more pain that she could even articulate, Hunter pushed through and found Sigurdsson and Ransom.

"We can't...," she paused, reaching out and grabbing Ransom's shoulder to steady herself as a wave of dizziness came over her.

"Hunter-"

"No," she said firmly. "We can't let them detonate the power core."

Breathe.

She closed her eyes for a moment. Too many thoughts. People in pain, people angry, people dying, alien thought, human thoughts, everyone and everything.

Focus!

Ransom. Find Ransom.

And she did. It took what was either a few seconds or a few minutes, but she found her. Harley Ransom, not Prince Arthur. The girl who had killed in cold blood, but cared more about the people in Edinburgh Castle than they'd ever know.

Focus.

"Radiation," she said finally. "It will be like dropping a nuclear bomb here. Devastation, and deadly levels of radiation for kilometers."

For a moment, Sigurdsson said nothing, just staring off at the processing facility, the muscles of her jaw working fiercely. In that moment, Hunter understood more about Freyja Sigurdsson than she had before. The woman's mind was clear, clearer than any she'd touched in her time on Earth, even clearer in its purpose and determination than Finn Radko's had ever been.

There was purpose there. Clear, unflinching purpose, but more than that, the knowledge that failure was not an option - and that knowledge was not something to be shied away from or to raise doubts or questions. It simply was. Failure was not an option, so she simply would not fail.

Hunter understood fully why Radko was in love with Sigurdsson.

Whether she knew it or not, Sigurdsson was the hero of this story. When people told stories of the battle for Earth, no matter what the outcome, Hunter was certain it would be Sigurdsson's name they whispered. It was her plan. She was here.

And the glimpse into Sigurdsson's mind, no matter how involuntarily, had given Hunter something she hadn't known she'd been lacking.

A belief that they could win.

No.

That they *would* win.

"We're going to win," said Hunter.

Ransom looked at her in surprise, but Sigurdsson simply turned slowly with a small smile on her lips.

"Fucking right we are."

Because she sensed something the moment before Hunter herself had filtered it through the cacophony of her mind: udukiin. There were udukiin warriors entering Holyrood Park. And humans, Hunter could feel them. Icarans, too.

Ustorf's company.

Reinforcements.

Sigurdsson began issuing orders - they were going to hit the ril-galas with everything and they were going to take control of the facility no matter what it took.

But just as Sigurdsson herself was about to join the charge, Hunter reached out and grabbed her bicep.

"We can't... We have to do more," she said.

Her tongue seemed to have a hard time catching up to her mind, and another quick wave of dizziness came and went.

"What do you mean?" asked Ransom.

Though Sigurdsson was trying to be patient, she kept glancing at her still-advancing line - advancing without her.

"There are forty-two," said Hunter. "Forty-two facilities. We can stop them from blowing this one..."

"But not the rest," said Sigurdsson. "Even if all four assault groups are successful, that leaves thirty-eight."

"Too many people," said Hunter, shaking her head. "We can't take all the facilities, so we need to get out warnings. Evacuation orders. Get them to a safer distance."

Still holding on to Sigurdsson's bicep, she tapped the woman's armoured shoulder with her other hand.

"Your connection... Matriarch... you can get a message to your soldiers telepathically?"

"To the udukiin, yes, but that only helps the assault groups."

In that moment, Hunter's own mind finally cleared. There was still the storm of outside thoughts blowing through, but they'd suddenly been relegated to background noise as she understood her role in this final battle. Coming to Earth had been her way of trying to make a difference. Of trying to become someone she could be proud of, and she'd done that. She'd done her best to protect people who needed protecting, save people who needed saving.

She looked to Ransom and smiled.

And now she would do it on a massive scale.

"Hunter...," said Ransom, a look of horror spreading across her young face. "No, Hunter, this is insane."

"Harley, I have to do this. I'm the only one who can."

"The fuck is happening?" said Sigurdsson.

"She's going to use herself as a fucking broadcast beacon! She's going to try to put an evacuation message into the heads of everyone around these things," she said, waving a hand at the facility.

"Do you think you can do that?" said Sigurdsson.

"Freyja! It will kill her!"

Reaching out, Hunter gently turned Ransom's tear-streaked face toward her.

"She knows, Harley," she said. "She knows. She also knows that was coming regardless. And so do you."

"But..."

"I can't do this anymore. I've been hiding as much of it as I can, but I know you've seen I'm getting worse. No matter what happened tonight, I was never under any illusion as to my future. I simply don't have one," said Hunter. "But that's okay. I'm a symbol of mankind's dark past. Designed to be used as a weapon against a political enemy. It's fitting that I die here."

She flicked a glance over at the advancing line of the combined Commonwealth, udukiin, icaran, and Soviet forces.

"And just maybe the attitudes that created me will as well," she said.

"No. Please. There has to be another way."

"We don't have time for another way, Harley. I can do this, I know it. I've held back on my abilities for so long... afraid of them. Now they can save so many lives," she said with a sad smile. "I was made to be a weapon, but this is the path I'm choosing."

Unsteadily, she stepped away from both Sigurdsson and Ransom, who reached out a hand to her.

"Hunter..."

"Harley, I am very proud of you. Please don't be sad for me - this is a good way to go."

Taking a deep breath, she centred her mind on herself for the first time in a very long time. Focused on her old self, Quon Li-Chen, the woman in the box, an ATC Castle prisoner aboard the HMCS Vimy Ridge. A weapon waiting to be unleashed. Then suddenly free, being treated like a person. Being shown that people were not all despicable creatures, that some were worth fighting for.

Through the fog of her mind she saw the present as well: Sigurdsson holding back a crying Ransom as the young woman tried to get to Hunter.

Felt a tear roll down her own cheek that they'd never get to explore their friendship in peace time.

Friendship.

Strangely, that was the concept that threaded it all to-gether, that allowed her to focus now on what needed to be done. Friendship shown to her for the first time by Finn Radko. Then the late Anna Cortez. Then Hutch, despite all his gruff-ness. And Hobson, who she wished she'd been able to speak to one last time. And Ransom, who had become what the people had needed, and whom Hunter now hoped could become what Ransom herself needed.

A pinpoint of light in the centre of her mind.

A blue orb.

A planet. Green and blue, swirled with the white of cloud cover.

She focused on the image, imagining it was exactly how the fleet would be seeing the planet at that moment, and re-membering how it had looked when she'd taken that Osprey shuttle from the Vimy Ridge and turned it toward the birth-place of humanity.

Behind the image she could still see the battle, still see Sig-urdsson and Ransom watching her.

And then focused on images - the facility, a nuclear explo-sion, people fleeing disaster - and embedded with those images a single thought:

Evacuate to safety.

And then she pushed it outward with everything she had, every regret, every fear, every love, every hate, every hope and dream and pity and joy. Everything she was and ever would be became fuel to push her thought far and wide, and into as many human minds as could receive it.

Her vision went first, her left eye failing a moment before her right.

The last thing she saw was a look of surprise on the faces of both Sigurdsson and Ransom and she knew then that she'd suc-ceeded. Nothing else mattered. Not the blood she could feel streaming from her nose, nor the fact that her heart was beat-ing so hard against her chest it felt like she was being punched.

Her legs gave way next, dropping her to her knees, her palms hitting the turf heavily, but still she pushed. Pushed eve-rything she had left, which, she found, was a surprising amount of one single emotion.

Despite the pain and the rising numbness in her arms, Hunter smiled.

It was love. Love for everything. And she, in turn, felt eve-rything. From everyone. Every mind she touched responded with their own love, whether it was for their spouse, their child, their parent, their pet, it was all feeding back.

Elgraphaar's love for Aylarr and hers for him.

Sigurdsson's love for Radko.

And Harley Ransom...

Hunter toppled onto her side, took one last breath and, a smile on her face, died.

The last thing she had felt was the love of her best friend.

35

As the Royal Sovereign fired its fourth barrage into Ultimus, Radko and every other human on the command deck suddenly staggered slightly as images popped into their mind with almost physical force.

Images of ril-galas processing facilities and nuclear detonations.

Then an immediate feeling of needing to get far away from those facilities.

For most of the crew it would have been confusing, disorienting, but Radko recognized the feeling. He recognized the touch of Hunter's mind. And he recognized what it likely meant when that touch slipped away.

Clenching his fists, Radko stared at Ultimus as it fired one of its beam weapons and struck a glancing blow off Her Glorious Vengeance. That was their opening. The ril-galas beam weapons required recharge time before being fired again - not a lengthy period, but long enough.

"Kerry, let's hit that thing with four nuclear warheads," said Radko. "Then I want to swing into position for a broadside."

Nodding, Stanton-West relayed the order and advised the two udukiin vessels, and Radko watched as the four warheads streaked toward Ultimus and slammed into its irregular surface. The damage was extensive, but not enough.

As the Royal Sovereign spun on its axis, Radko tracked Ultimus until he was facing to the side.

"Broadside position," said Stanton-West.

"Fire."

The entire compliment of port rail guns fired at Ultimus, throwing super-accelerated projectiles the size of a man into its flank. As he watched the projectiles tear into the enemy's hull, Radko hoped they were hitting critical infrastructure, but he wasn't going to wait to find out.

"Again," he said, and a second broadside was fired.

This time he didn't wait to see the effects.

"Again."

As the Royal Sovereign's weapons tore into the starboard flank of Ultimus, Her Glorious Vengeance and Her Divine Retribution resumed their frontal attack, and Radko watched as a wing of Argentavis fighters swooped in, effecting hit and run strafing attacks across its dorsal axis, taking out several point defense emplacements.

"Captain," said Stanton-West, "Cags confirms the last troop transport has been destroyed."

Tearing his attention from Ultimus, Radko quickly brought up the holographic battle map.

The United Defense Fleet had suffered some losses, the greatest being the crippling of Rhekar's ship, the Venn Shakara. Though not destroyed, her engines had been shut down to prevent overload and explosion, and while her weapons remained online she was a sitting duck for enemy attack. The Vor Tokar had been lost, and the Azrael's Tear had once again been tasked with picking up lifeboats. The Vimy Ridge had taken damage, but true to her reputation, had kept fighting. Outlaw Squadron had lost six fighters, including Cagliari's second in command, Daxma.

But it was working.

The sacrifice of the Goose Bay had caused significant damage to the enemy, and the destruction of the brainbox had caused a moment of confusion among the ril-galas that the

UDF had been able to exploit. The troop transports were gone. Two of the three barracudas had been eliminated, as had the majority of the scout ships. The ril-galas fighters, having ever only been powerful enough to take on a capital ship if doing so in a swarm, were so few as to be ineffectual.

A pair of ril-galas battleships still attacked the fleet, but as much damage as they could potentially do, Ultimus was the bigger concern.

"Royal Sovereign to Vimy Ridge and Outlaw Squadron," said Radko, activating the link to both. "Are you able to take care of those battleships while the rest of us focus on Ultimus?"

They both confirmed and Radko watched Outlaw Squadron peel away from Ultimus and form up with the Vimy Ridge as it turned and launched a missile salvo at the nearest of the two battleships.

"Energy readings from Ultimus's starboard beam weapon beginning to fluctuate," said Bell. "Pretty wildly, Captain."

"It's destabilizing," he said. "Give them another broadside and follow it up immediately with a missile salvo."

"Captain Radko, I apologise for interrupting your violence," said Frankenstein as he waved a robotic hand at Radko. "However, I believe this to be important."

The doctor had at some point taken up residence at one of the unused consoles on the command deck to... do something. Radko had no idea what the doctor was doing with the console, but as long as it didn't interfere with the violence the brill was sorry for interrupting, Radko figured he'd worry about it later. Though Frankenstein clearly felt it was worth worrying about now.

Waiting for the latest salvo to impact Ultimus, Radko only turned from the battle and approached Frankenstein when the enormous enemy ship's starboard beam weapon ruptured and exploded in a brief spherical fireball.

"Doctor?"

"Yes, Captain?"

Raising a brow, Radko nodded toward Frankenstein's console, which was displaying a holographic representation of Earth, with multiple points marked with red triangles. A few were pulsing.

"I'm going to say there are forty-two of those triangles," said Radko.

The processing sites.

"I am impressed, Captain. Most humans are not able to count so quickly."

"I didn't... Never mind. You have new information?"

"I do," said Frankenstein, in his incongruously cheerful voice. "After our discussion with those who made planetfall, Kerry allowed me access to the Royal Sovereign's sensor suite -- at least, those components not required for-"

"Our violence."

"Yes. Unfortunately, I can now confirm that the events feared by Freyja and her companions are indeed underway. These three locations here, here, and here," he said, pointing to each of the pulsing triangles in turn. "Are beginning to show fluctuations that indicate the beginnings of what I will call reactor overload."

The headache that had been lurking just out of sight chose that moment to step forward and Radko rubbed as his remaining eye while wishing he could scratch the painful itch that kept coming and going where his left eye used to be.

"How much time do we have before they go critical?"

The brill bobbed his head.

"I'm afraid we do not know enough about the inner workings of these facilities to make an estimate with any kind of accuracy. Though I would suggest, for caution's sake, we assume that once the process begins, the end result is imminent."

Glancing quickly back to the globe, Radko felt the tightness in his chest release -- slightly. The triangle in Scotland was not pulsing.

Not yet.

"Keep me posted on any changes," said Radko, before returning his attention to the battle.

As another salvo lit into Ultimus, Radko clenched both his hands into tight fists, then forced himself to relax. Stretching out his fingers, he felt a slight cracking in his right thumb -- that was something new, something to add to the maintenance list -- and slowed his breathing.

Inhale. Count to four. Exhale. Count to four. Repeat.

The breathing technique was helping, but it wasn't helping nearly as much as knowing Sigurdsson was safe and out of harm's way would have helped.

"Come on, Freyja, we don't have time..."

36

"We don't have time," said Sigurdsson, gently but firmly pulling Ransom away from Hunter's body. "We have to mourn later."

Yanking her arm free of the grasp, the girl -- all pretense of her Prince Arthur guise forgotten -- turned her red, tear-streaked face toward Sigurdsson. Though she seemed ready to yell and scream and call Sigurdsson all manner of names, her expression softened when she saw tears on Sigurdsson's cheeks as well.

"Later," repeated Sigurdsson. "But right now, we need to make sure Hunter's sacrifice matters."

Unsteadily, Ransom stood, wiped her tears away with both hands, but then shrugged and began crying once more, staring down at what had once been Hunter.

"But... her body. We can't just... I mean, she's lying in a field."

Though the sounds of battle filled her ears and though the instinct to run toward them and unleash her fury -- to be a War Matriarch -- was strong, Sigurdsson stood her ground, placing her hands on Ransom's shoulders. Both her own training and the desire of the Matriarch pulled her toward the front line, but not just pulled her, demanded it of her. Demanded she take up her weapon and charge into the fight, to stand beside her comrades.

And she would, soon.

Learning to be a leader had been a long, winding, and frequently uneven road. Though it was a path she thought she had been on, thought she had known, the reality was that it was a road she'd never even seen before Fort Hathaway. Prior to the invasion, the old Freyja Sigurdsson has never really understood the difference between being in charge and being a leader. And she had certainly never understood that sometimes being a leader was more about the quiet moments than it was about charging the enemy with guns blazing.

"The icarans have a very different perspective on death than most humans," she said. "If you ever hear them describe our traditions -- funerals, graveyards -- it all sounds so morbid."

Ransom's gaze drifted back to Hunter's body. As gently as possible, Sigurdsson turned the girl's head back and ducked her own head down to make sure she could meet the girl's gaze.

"When an icaran dies, the body becomes irrelevant. It's just something to be disposed of. It's nothing. The person died, they're not there anymore, but they live on in their songs. I'm sure an icaran would make this sound more poetic, but a person is the sum of all their experiences, of their memories, of the memories they help create, and of the memories they leave behind. The body is just a thing. The body is gone, but Hunter isn't."

Sigurdsson tapped Ransom once on the forehead and once on the chest, over her heart.

"We both know she's not going anywhere."

Sniffling, Ransom nodded, then slowly picked up her assault rifle from where it had fallen in the grass. Taking a deep, shaky breath, she let it out slowly, and as she did so, Sigurdsson saw her posture change as the girl disappeared into her royal façade.

"Let's finish this," said Ransom, in the voice of Prince Arthur.

With a nod and without any hesitation, Sigurdsson indulged her instincts -- she picked up her gunstaff and broke into a run straight toward the front line. There was no need to look back to know that Ransom -- Arthur -- was following closely, and her telepathic connection via the Matriarch told her that her udukiin honour guard was also with them. The heavy footfalls of armoured icarans, Aylarr and her small squad of four commandos, fell in beside her.

They came upon the battle from the side, two separate groups of UDF soldiers forming lines against an overmatched group of ril-galas directly in front of the processing facility. Another line of ril-glas reinforcements arrayed themselves in a defensive position behind their comrades, but their formation was awkward, their placement almost ineffectual to defend the facility if their front rank, already beginning to crumble, fell.

Sigurdsson slowed her run and signalled a stop.

"What have you seen?" said Aylarr.

"Nothing yet."

Kneeling down, Sigurdsson signalled her team to follow suit, and she stared intently at the battlefield. Something was missing. Something wasn't right about the scene -- they'd seen the ril-galas break and retreat before, they'd seen them lose formation and regroup, but they'd never seen them *sloppy*, never poorly positioned to attain their goals.

"How many have we killed?" said Ransom.

Sigurdsson opened her mouth to respond, then closed it again and frowned, looking back to the battle. Numerous ril-galas corpses littered the battlefield, along with more fallen UDF than she wanted to see, but at a glance, the numbers did not add up. Even taking the regen pods out of the equation -- the battle hadn't been going on long enough for any of the ril-galas to regenerate, even if they'd had the opportunity to do so -- the two lines facing the UDF and fallen ril-galas did not add up to the size of the force against whom Sigurdsson's people had begun the fight.

What wasn't she seeing?

"They've redeployed," she said. "Somewhere..."

As she trailed off, she noticed Jaeger, at her side as always, staring intently ahead, the fur along his back raised and low growl rumbling in his throat. And almost immediately understood.

"Fuck," she said, dropping to the ground, flat on her chest. "Down! Everyone down!"

As they did, Aylarr crawled over.

"Look there," said Sigurdsson, pointing to a low ridge that ran perpendicular to their position and parallel to the battle.

As he'd done many times in the past, Jaeger had proven to be a better sensor than any technology they had on hand.

The ridge, which fell off into a gully four or five feet deep and curved around the battlefield before disappearing behind the processing facility, was packed with ril-galas. A small number of foot soldiers, but dozens and dozens of the vicious stalkers, all crouched in tight balls and invisible from the other side of the ridge. The side of the ridge where Elgraphaar was leading the main assault.

Looking back to the battle, Sigurdsson saw the first rank of ril-galas fall apart and begin to retreat. And saw the hidden reinforcements tense.

"It's bait. It's fucking bait, isn't it?" said Ransom. Sigurdsson hadn't even noticed that the girl had fallen back into her own persona.

"Yeah. It is."

Sigurdsson looked along the length of the ridge, closed her eyes and swore. Opening her eyes and turning to Aylarr, she watched as the icaran slowly removed her helmet.

"I understand," said Aylarr. "And so will he."

That Aylarr understood what she was thinking, and approved of it, didn't make the ball of fire in Sigurdsson's chest any less painful. Didn't make the decision any less terrible.

"Understand what?" said Ransom. "What's going on? We need to warn Elgraphaar!"

"We can't," said Sigurdsson.

The girl just stared, mouth agape.

"Look at the ridge," said Sigurdsson, tapping her temple to turn off her optics. "It can lead us right to that facility. Behind cover. If no one can see us, no one can stop us."

"But in order to do so, it cannot be full of ril-galas," said Aylarr, turning her helmet over in her hands. "We need the enemy to launch its ambush in order for us to have a clear path to completing our mission."

Ransom looked back and forth between Aylarr and Sigurdsson three times before responding.

"But... do you know how many people could die if we don't warn them?"

"Yes, Harley. I do."

"And you still want to-."

"No, I don't fucking want to, Harley, but I have to. This isn't about what you and I want, or about what Aylarr wants. This is about what we have to do, about slogging through shit and making decisions that could kill our fucking friends and having our friends make decisions that cost them their lives, because we have exactly one option here today. We win. We fucking win, because there is no alternative for us. And yeah, this might... fuck, it likely will cost us a lot of good people. Might even cost us Elgraphaar," she said, casting a quick glance in Aylarr's direction. "But if our roles were reversed, he'd make the same call and he would know I would be okay with that."

"You'd be okay with dying?"

"Kid, if I thought it would win us the day, I'd fall on my sword right now," she said quietly. "And I think you know someone else who felt the same."

Tears welled up in Ransom's eyes, but she nodded and stayed silent.

"Our forces are advancing," said Aylarr.

Closing her eyes, Sigurdsson flinched as the hidden ril-galas erupted from behind the ridge and charged the United Defense Force soldiers. Only after she knew they'd cleared the gully did she allow the Matriarch to send out one of her telepathic bursts, a mixture of rage and encouragement to the udukiin soldiers, and then she pulled herself into a low crouch and half ran into the newly-vacated gully. The rest of her team was at her heels, all keeping just low enough to stay below the ridge line.

To not peek over the ridge to see the state of the battle was difficult, but Sigurdsson managed to do it. She knew the others would follow her lead, and they couldn't afford to worry about anything but the goal.

As they made their way close to the facility, Sigurdsson called a halt, settling in against the cool earth of the ridge. Six ril-galas foot soldiers stood guard outside the entrance to the facility, an easy number for her group to overcome, but too many to do so quietly. The udukiin gunstaves were remarkably quiet, but still.

"We cannot afford to attract the attention of the main force," said Aylarr, echoing Sigurdsson's own thoughts.

"We need a way past those guards."

"No, we don't," said Ransom, pointing further along the gully. "Look."

A back door.

Of course. Sigurdsson mentally kicked herself. Of course there was another entrance. How else had the ril-galas been able to deploy their hidden attack force without anyone noticing?

"Okay," said Sigurdsson, turning to face her team. "We take this facility and we hold this facility. No retreat."

"No retreat," echoed the udukiin honour guard.

Ransom nodded and Aaylar simply re-donned her faceless helm.

Nine soldiers to win and hold a ril-galas facility, thought Sigurdsson. The odds were long, but what else had they been from day one of the invasion? Fort Hathaway should have fallen; it didn't. The Vimy Ridge should never have made it to Thor's Hammer, let alone liberated it; it did. Sigurdsson herself should never have become Kaigor Kai Rii, and yet...

She turned back to the facility with narrowed eyes. Half building half scab, it was as monstrously ugly as every other piece of ril-galas technology she'd encountered, but it was less its design and more its purpose that imbued it with a feeling of ominousness it perhaps didn't deserve. The fact that it was just a building -- just another objective to gain and hold -- didn't matter to the growing vise-grip of anxiety in Sigurdsson's chest nor the cold sweat that she could feel on her spine. This was her endgame, plain and simple. Either she walked out of the facility having secured it and won the battle, or she never walked out period. For old Freyja, that wouldn't have been a problem, just one more situation where she'd either survive or not. But she wasn't old Freyja anymore. New Freyja had more than just herself to worry about. With no other bonded Matriarchs, she was the only leader the udukiin possessed, and if she died, she knew that not only would the Matriach with whom she was bonded also die, but the leaderless udukiin would be utterly lost.

And then there were the more selfish reasons that old Freyja had never had to face. There was now a future that Sigurdsson looked forward to, something more for her beyond the next fight. Something that made the fighting worthwhile.

"This could be a suicide mission," said Ransom, bringing Sigurdsson out of her momentary silence.

She shook her head.

"I'm not dying today," she said, pointing toward the facility. "But those motherfuckers are."

Slinging her gunstaff on her back, Sigurdsson drew her *vayan* pistol with her right hand and one of the long, curved udukiin knives with her left, and then, after confirmation from her team that they were as ready as they ever would be, she ran in a low crouch to the facility's rear entrance.

37

"An offer of amnesty?" said Truus Van Der Berg, her skepticism of the idea even more clear from her body language than her tone.

Nodding, Khaifa took a sip of her coffee before responding. Black, bitter, and so strong it could have stripped paint, the coffee was both horrible and exactly what she needed. The weight of the decisions she was having to make, the constant adrenaline, the way she had been locked into fight-or-flight mode for days... Khaifa was exhausted, mentally and physically. What she needed was some sleep, or at worst a quiet hour to herself to breathe. Instead, what she got was horrible coffee. It would have to do.

The pair were sitting on their own at one end of the now-infamous Fort Cargo – the cargo bay that had been converted to a command centre when they had begun making their moves against De Freitas and Upshaw. Now that both had been removed from their positions and Khaifa was acting Prime Minister, the operation could have been relocated to the actual command centre of Thor's Hammer, but that would have taken time none felt they had. And thus far, they had been managing well in their makeshift environs.

"Yes," Khaifa said, finally. "Obviously not for the ringleaders – they need to be prosecuted – but for the ATC Castle rank and file. I realize that 'just following orders' is a terrible defence, but we need to give them the benefit of the doubt that they truly didn't know about everything Upshaw was doing or planning."

Van Der Berg remained silent, and Khaifa understood that was the spymaster's polite way of disagreeing.

"I understand your perspective, silently conveyed by the twitch in your left eye," said Khaifa, eliciting a grudging smirk from Van Der Berg. "But the fact is, Truus, we can't afford a war on two fronts. We couldn't afford it before, but we didn't have a choice."

A commotion at the far end of the cargo bay drew their attention, and Khaifa tried very hard not to smile as she watched Ironhorse's fire team return, the hulking figure of Tangaroa with on hand on the shoulder of the cuffed – and cowed – Rocco De Freitas. Ironhorse had a quick word with his team, then he and Tangaroa headed over to Khaifa while the remaining team continued on their way with the prisoner.

Of course, they hadn't needed to come through Fort Cargo to get to the brig.

"Morale," said Ironhorse, answering the unspoken question. "Show people concrete results of their work."

Khaifa nodded, but Van Der Berg spoke first.

"Prime Minister Khaifa wants to offer an amnesty to all ATC Castle personnel."

Khaifa tried not to wince at being called Prime Minister. Though she supposed, technically, it was now true.

Unsure of how the soldier would respond, Khaifa was relieved when he shrugged.

"They may have made bad decisions, but they wouldn't be the first to find out later the company they're working for is run by shitbags," he said. "We had one switch sides and help us get to Upshaw. They're just people, like the rest of us, trying to put food on the table."

"That's an interesting perspective from someone who fights on the front lines," said Van Der Berg.

Ironhorse chuckled and shook his head.

"You know what most wars are, Van Der Berg? Regular folk like me fighting other regular folk like me over things that won't make a difference to either of us, but are of huge fucking benefit to the rich and powerful," he said. "This war, though? This war makes a difference to everyone. Rich or poor, soldier or civilian, spymaster or hot dog vendor."

"So there should be no repercussions?" said Van Der Berg, raising one eyebrow.

"For what? How many ATC Castle people actively worked against the Commonwealth and knew they were doing it?"

"He makes a valid point," said Khaifa. "Upshaw had created an echo chamber within the company. What she said was the truth for them, even when it wasn't."

"And a lot of ATC Castle people left them and joined Commonwealth forces once they realized what was actually going on," said Tangaroa.

Khaifa nodded, but said nothing. Tangaroa had been the first of those to leave the military contractor in order to help the war effort, back in the very beginning aboard the Vimy Ridge. Van Der Berg, of course, was aware of that fact.

"Captain Ironhorse," said Van Der Berg, "you're actually advocating for an amnesty for people who, until not long ago, were shooting at you."

"And now they're not shooting at me and I'd really like to keep it that way, so we can all start shooting at the alien invaders. I don't see this as a tough call."

"And if one of them puts a bullet in your back?"

Tangaroa chuckled gruffly.

"You seem awfully concerned about a risk you'll never have to take."

"Let's just step back for a second," said Khaifa, setting down her coffee with one hand while making a placating gesture with the other. "And I'd like to get Admiral Mahoney's input. Is he still in the command centre? The real one, I mean?"

Van Der Berg nodded. Since the LIDAR and communications gear in the true command centre was more suited to his needs in tracking the battle above Earth, Mahoney had, at the earliest safe opportunity, relocated with his small staff.

"All right," said Khaifa, standing. "I'm heading up there to discuss this with the Admiral. Anyone who'd like to join me is welcome."

38

Darkness. Darkness, and such an oppressive wave of heat and humidity that the group paused for a split second as they entered the ril-galas facility.

"Aaylar, take point," said Sigurdsson. She spoke barely above a whisper, and even then her voice seemed too loud. Activating her light amplification optics, Sigurdsson directed two of the other icarans to bring up the rear. With the advanced technology in their helms, the icarans wouldn't miss a beat in the dark. The udukiin would manage all right, but the humans – at least, those without cybernetics – would be at a significant disadvantage. "Slowly. And quietly. We have no idea what's waiting for us."

The atmosphere was heavy, thick, the kind that made skin feel instantly clammy, and the fabric of their clothes stick to them within minutes. A stench of sulfur and dampness and rot assaulted the team's olfactory organs, along with something else Sigurdsson couldn't identify. And something else she *could* – the scent of blood, both dried and fresh.

Briefly, she closed her eyes and took a calming breath. It was amazing how easily she could slip into combat mode, focusing on the task at hand, forgetting the larger fact of the facility's nature, its purpose. Or perhaps forgetting was the wrong word. It was more like ignoring. Blocking it out. She wasn't sure if it was her military training or just a coping mechanism her brain had developed to help her maintain her sanity.

Either way, she needed it now.

Feeling a hand lightly settle on her forearm, Sigurdsson turned to see Ransom staring her with wide eyes.

"Listen."

The young woman wasn't even using her Arthur voice, which was concerning. What had she heard? Sigurdsson closed her eyes, focused on the small sounds that surrounded them. Dripping water, or some liquid of similar consistency. A mechanical hum. The bubbling of some type of thicker liquid passing through tubing. And there, beneath it all, barely audible, a human voice sobbing and suddenly silenced. Holding up a hand, Sigurdsson shook her head to stop Ransom from saying anything else. Silence was what they needed, and no matter what other compulsions may intrude into their minds, the mission was their first priority. Their *only* priority.

For a moment, Ransom just stared, and Sigurdsson thought an argument forthcoming. But then the younger woman closed her eyes momentarily, took a deep – if shaky – breath, and nodded. And then her eyes went wide, in fear or shock, or... and she slammed the butt of her rifle into Sigurdsson's chest a split second before the slashing claws of a ril-galas stalker swiped down out of the black above. Stumbling backward, Sigurdsson watched as Ransom tried and failed to twist out of the path of the attack, the knife-like talons raking across her left shoulder and back, carving two deep channels of red.

Two shots rang out – Sigurdsson didn't know from whom – and the stalker was down.

"Ransom," said Sigurdsson, dropping to one knee beside her.

Before she could say more, she heard the skittering of sharp claws on hard surfaces. There were more. Of course there were more.

"Flare!" called one of the human soldiers – a warning to Sigurdsson and the icarans to adjust their optics. A warning

Sigurdsson just barely had time to heed before the flare burst, bathing the hallway in a pulsating yellow-orange glow.

A flash of movement to her left and Sigurdsson instinctively lashed out with the butt of her gunstaff, catching a second stalker in the teeth with an audible crunch. Aylaar had put two rounds from her *vayan* into its chest before the creature had hit the floor, but a third stalker had already taken its place. Trying to use the gunstaff as a cudgel again, Sigurdsson instead found the weapon wrenched from her grasp by yet another stalker, which had appeared behind her. Out of the corner of her eye, she saw Aylaar lunge at her rear attacker just as the claws of her forward attacker clamped down on her left shoulder. Her armour – her passenger, her protector, the Matriarch – was strong, but she still felt the pain of the grip if not the cutting sharpness of the claws. Struggling beneath the creature's weight and using her free hand to fend off slashes from the stalker's other set of claws, Sigurdsson stepped backward and immediately lost her footing, her boots skidding in something wet – she understood exactly what it was, but her brain wouldn't let her acknowledge it. Falling backward, she hit the ground hard enough to knock the wind out of her, the stalker pressing its advantage for a killing swipe with its free hand, but Sigurdsson wrenched her head to the side, the claws embedding themselves into the hallway floor – and slicing through the cartilage of her right ear – rather than piercing her skull. As the stalker shrieked its anger and tried to yank free its claws, Sigurdsson wrapped her right arm around the thing's elbow and wrenched her entire body sharply to the left. A loud, wet, snap sounded as the stalker's elbow joint snapped, its clawed hand now hanging limp and useless.

As the thing reared up and opened its toothy maw in another shriek, Sigurdsson saw it extend the two small secondary arms – the two that ended in small energy weapons. At point-blank range, she'd be little more than a smear on the ground it those weapons were able to discharge. Fumbling with the sheath for one of her long knives, the stalker's cannons began to glow as they reached full charge, and Sigurdsson drew the knife and plunged it directly into the chest cavity of the stalker and through the brain of the ril-galas pilot.

The stalker slumped forward, dead, and Sigurdsson had to use every ounce of remaining strength to roll its body off her.

For a moment, Sigurdsson just concentrated on breathing, then realized she wasn't hearing the sounds of battle.

And then remembered what she had slipped in. And was now laying in.

A large pool of Ransom's blood.

Before she realized what was happening, Sigurdsson was hauled to her feet by two of her udukiin honour guard, and she saw one of the human soldiers – a woman whose name she couldn't recall, but who had a very thick German accent – was using a spray-on medical foam to create a bandage layer over Ransom's injuries.

Taking a deep breath, Sigurdsson silently repeated the mantra: the mission is all that matters.

"Aylaar?" she said.

"Two dead," said Aylaar. "One icaran soldier and one human. Two injured, though our other injury is minor."

Sigurdsson nodded. A small butcher's bill given that she counted seven dead ril-galas stalkers. Kneeling beside Ransom, Sigurdsson put a hand on her uninjured shoulder.

"Stay with us."

Ransom's lips moved as if she were speaking, but the words were faint. Sigurdsson leaned in until her ear – the one that remained intact – was nearly touching Ransom's lips.

"Don't give me orders," said Ransom, her voice weak. "I'm the fucking king."

"Long live the king."

"No promises."

Forcing a smile she didn't even remotely feel, Sigurdsson stood and beckoned for the soldier who had applied the medical treatment to Ransom to step away with her.

"How bad?"

"I'm not a doctor," said the woman, shrugging. "She's lost a lot of blood, but the wounds don't seem as deep as I thought. I couldn't see bone, so I think mostly muscle damage. We've got to get her medical attention ASAP, though. If she stays here, she'll die – this medi-foam shit won't hold up for more than... what the fuck?"

Both women looked back to the commotion to see Ransom standing – albeit unsteadily, propped against a wall – and trying to hold onto her rifle.

"What the fuck are you doing?" said Sigurdsson, immediately taking away the rifle and steadying the king who wasn't.

"We need to... we need to finish this. The mission is..."

"Not your problem anymore. We're getting you out of here," said Sigurdsson, nodding toward the German woman and one of the udukiin honour guard. "Get her to the landing zone. They can at least give her basic treatment."

"No," said Ransom, shaking her head. "The king needs to lead."

"Fuck off. You need medical attention, and I need fully-functional soldiers. I can't have someone working at half speed to carry you around like backpack," said Sigurdsson. "You said yourself King Arthur needed to die on this battlefield. Well, welcome to his grand finale. He died here, just now, helping fend off an attack by ril-galas stalkers."

"He was very brave," added Aylaar. "It was a pleasure to have fought alongside him."

After a momentary pause, Ransom nodded. She was pale, and visibly close to collapse.

"Don't die," she said, poking a finger into Sigurdsson's chest. "That's a Royal command."

"As you wish, Your Majesty."

As she watched Ransom being gingerly led out of the facility, the udukiin supporting – mostly carrying – her while the human soldier played bodyguard, Sigurdsson scooped up her fallen gunstaff and slung it over her shoulder, then picked up the *aoran* assault rifle that had belonged to the fallen icaran soldier. Though the two were comparable in terms of power, the *aoran* was louder and left bigger holes.

"They know we're here," she said. "No need for stealth anymore – we hit hard and we keep moving forward until we've finished this."

39

"Captain," said the Brill, curling one mechanical hand into an odd little wave. "You are familiar with the mass extinction event experienced by your home planet during its Cretaceous Period?"

The brill physician had approached without preamble as Radko was checking fleet status. It took him a moment to process Frankenstein's question.

"The asteroid that wiped out the dinosaurs? Yeah, I think every kid goes through a dinosaur phase," he said.

"Some don't outgrow it," said Stanton-West

Turning his single photoreceptor toward her briefly, Frankenstein seemed unsure what response would be appropriate, if any. Turning back to Radko, he evidently decided it best to just carry on.

"Should at least thirty percent of the identified ril-galas facilities detonate, the volume of particulate expelled into the planetary atmosphere will exceed that of the Cretaceous asteroid impact."

For a moment, Radko just stared at the brill, and to his right, Stanton-West was doing the same – both processing and re-processing the information.

Thirty percent.

Hovering above the Royal Sovereign's command deck, the holographic avatar of humanity's birthplace pulsed slightly, ril-galas facility locations updating in real-time as new data streamed in. His eyes drawn to the locations flashing an angry red to indicate current or imminent reactor meltdown, Radko's heart sank.

In his peripheral vision, he saw the brill's head bob slightly.

"We are, unfortunately, already too late," said Franken-stein. "This must now be classified an extinction level event."

Radko stared at the holographic Earth.

Concentrated on breathing.

For so long, all his energy – and not just his, but the energy of so many people – had been directed at the liberation of Earth, they hadn't looked beyond the end goal. While they had, usually in silence, contemplated what would happen if they didn't succeed in liberating Earth, no one had once voiced the question what if there was no Earth left to liberate? Or, at least, no humans left to liberate.

An extinction level event.

It was not a totally accurate assessment of the situation, at least not as far as the human race was concerned. Humanity would not go extinct regardless of the situation on Earth – at last survey, the population of off-Earth colonies and installations was nearly equal to the population of Earth. Though of course the past two years had significantly altered both set of numbers. Yes, humanity would survive, but what would become of the survivors on Earth, let alone the planet itself?

"Should...," said Stanton-West. "Should I get Prime Minister Khaifa on the line, Sir?"

Radko nodded and Stanton-West set up the connection. In the few minutes it took, Radko just closed his eye and focused on his breathing. The familiar feeling of having his chest clenched by a giant warm hand was coming back, threatening to strip off the thin veneer of calm he had been projecting.

Focus. Fucking focus.

Opening his eye, he located Edinburgh on the floating globe and stared at it with laser-focus.

Sigurdsson was there. On Earth. In danger.

The clenching lessened, and was replaced with another familiar, fiery sensation.

"You look angry," said Stanton-West, her voice low enough that only he could hear.

"That doesn't even scratch the surface."

"The Prime Minister is on the line."

"Thanks. You're in command for now, not sure how long this will take."

"Captain Radko," came Khaifa's disembodied voice. There was no visual component, and she sounded like she was walking. "How are things out there?"

"Madame Prime Minister, I need you to be in a secure location for this conversation," said Radko.

After a momentary pause, she acknowledged, and then there was a longer silence.

"All right," she said, her voice clearer. "We're secure. Van Der Berg and Ironhorse are with me."

"Nasrin, the situation on Earth is grim," he said. "I can't sugar-coat it."

Briefly, he gave her Frankenstein's assessment of the situation, then waved the brill over to join the discussion.

"Okay," said Khaifa, sounding anything but. "Assuming this plays out the way we're thinking, what kind of timeline? Do we have time for any form of evacuation?"

Radko nodded to Frankenstein, who stepped into the discussion.

"With the amount of particulate expected to be ejected into the atmosphere, we can assume that within six months, the amount of sunlight reaching the Earth's surface will be reduced by between sixty to seventy percent."

"Reduced by?" said Khaifa. "Meaning we could potentially only be getting thirty percent?"

"Correct. This will result in a catastrophic drop in temperatures globally – even a currently temperate climate zone could see summer temperatures of below zero degrees Celsius. Undoubtedly, the planet would experience massive failures in food crops, and similarly massive die-offs in both terrestrial and aquatic wildlife, compounding the damages already wrought by the invasion."

"So, we're talking global famine and more or less another ice age," said Radko.

"Essentially, yes," agreed Frankenstein. "But there is also the radiation to consider. Based on current datasets, I would estimate that radiation and radioactive fallout could kill directly, or via various forms of cancer, as many as one in five humans."

Over the audio connection, Khaifa swore softly, then again with a little more vehemence.

"Okay," she said, taking a deep breath. "This is the worst possible outcome-."

"No, it isn't," said Radko. "The worst possible outcome is losing the war and the human race having no hope for survival. There's no question this is a disaster, but if there's one thing we've proven over the course our history, it's that we can recover from disasters."

"Yes, you're right. It would just be really nice if we could have a bit of a break between them," said Khaifa. "Doctor Frankenstein, based on your information, you think we have six months to evacuate the planet?"

The brill paused, and though his body language was always difficult to interpret, Radko felt it an uncomfortable pause.

"Theoretically, Prime Minister," he said. "Many of the factors I have noted – temperature, food supply, radiation – would all begin to impact the population immediately. Their effects will of course worsen over time, but they will be felt within weeks. Radiation will be the prime concern in the opening days, but mortality rate even of those who survive the initial detonations would be very high."

"How high?"

"I estimate that among those who survive the initial detonations of the facility, as many as seventy-five percent within the exclusion zone will be deceased within eighteen to twenty-four months. While that timeline is longer than the six-month window we are discussing, it is important that I point out the critically low levels of medical staffing and availability of high-end medical facilities at present, as well as the scope of the problem."

"Evacuating an entire planet is a massive undertaking, and we're still fighting a war," said Radko, rubbing at his eye. "There's no way we can get an evacuation underway now, which means by the time we can, we're looking at significant radiation exposure for a lot of the survivors."

"All of whom would require treatment, including some long-term treatment for various cancers," said Frankenstein. "We will have to understand that many of those evacuated will still become fatalities."

Again, there was silence as the information sunk in. After a moment, Radko heard some muffled words as someone on her end asked Khaifa a question.

"Doctor Frankenstein," said Khaifa, "what are the possibilities of Earth being habitable again?"

"I believe there to be a significant possibility of Earth's ecosystem recovering. However, the timeline for such recovery would be several decades, and," he said, "the planet and its ecosystem would not be the same. With the extinction of so many life forms being a likely scenario – combined with the presumed absence of humans in the ecosystem – new forms of life will evolve to take their place, just as mammals filled the void left by the dinosaurs. A recovered ecosystem would be markedly different from the present ecosystem."

"With all due respect doctors, whether Earth recovers or not is a problem for another day," said Radko. "We need to focus on winning the war and getting an evacuation plan in place – this is going to be a huge undertaking and we don't have a lot of time."

"Agreed," said Khaifa. "What are your thoughts on the evacuation, Captain?"

"To be blunt, my thoughts are that it is your problem to solve. I'm in the middle of coordinating a battle out here. If we don't win this one, then none of our other problems will be problems anymore, because we'll all be as good as dead."

"That's a fair point," said Khaifa, thankfully not sounding as offended as she had a right to. "We'll get on it. You be careful out there, Finn."

"I can't promise that."

"I know. Good luck."

For several long moments after the connection with the Royal Sovereign was closed, Khaifa stared at her tablet, slowly processing the new information.

"The amnesty isn't up for debate anymore," she said finally, looking up at Van Der Berg and Ironhorse. "Anyone willing to help the war effort, and more importantly, help with the evacuation of Earth, will be given a blanket pardon for anything they've done in the name of ATC Castle."

Van Der Berg nodded, but Khaifa continued.

"And Truus, get the word out unofficially, through your network, that if there are ATC Castle ships whose command staff are unwilling to take this offer, we will also offer pardons for crews who mutiny in order to bring their ship to Earth's assistance."

"Pods," said Aylaar, who had taken point.

Stepping up beside her, Sigurdsson wiped a hand across her sweaty forehead. The heat had become ever more oppressive the deeper the team went into the facility, and her right ear, crusted over with blood, was throbbing.

Aylaar had stopped at a railing of sorts, about chest height, curving along the contours of the corridor and out of sight down the hallway. Arrayed behind the railing was a series of six devices, large and roughly cylindrical. Though the technology was unfamiliar, the transparent face plate on each pod left no doubt as to their purpose – a ril-galas 'brain,' suspended in a viscous, bubbling liquid occupied the smaller top division of the pod, while the remainder was taken up by the biomechical construct of a ril-galas foot soldier, suspended in a similar, but lighter coloured liquid. The head of the construct had been shredded by weapon impact. At least a dozen narrow appendages that reminded Sigurdsson of a praying mantis's forelimbs twitched and stabbed within the pod liquid, rebuilding the foot soldier's head bit by bit.

"Regeneration pods," she said. "I thought that kid said she saw these *outside* the facility?"

"Perhaps the enemy had underestimated their need for these pods and the ones seen outside were constructed later," said Aylarr, pointing first up, then down.

Sigurdsson's eyes followed Ayalarr's direction and she swore under her breath. Leaning against the railing, she looked up and counted, then down, and counted again. There may have only been six pods on their level, but she could see two more banks of six above, and several more banks below, disappearing into a haze of humidity. There was no way to know how many levels there were within the facility or how far down the banks of pods extended.

"We need to find a way to shut these down, but we need to do it quickly," said Sigurdsson.

After a momentary hesitation, Aylarr turned her rifle on the nearest pod and fired repeatedly, until both the casing of the pod and the ril-galas within it were nothing but shattered and pulped remains.

Sigurdsson shrugged. About to order the whole team to unload into the pods, she then frowned and shook her head.

"The pods don't matter right now. If we don't get control of this facility, it won't matter how many pods we've taken out," she said, speaking to her remaining team while double-checking the ammunition count on her *aoran*. "Everyone split up. There's a central control room somewhere, and we need to find it."

"Should we be dividing our forces like that?" said one of the Commonwealth soldiers.

"No," said Sigurdsson. "But we have more space to search than we have time to do it."

"Doing so will also force the ril-galas to divide their own forces," said Aylarr.

With a heavy sigh, Sigurdsson looked at the faces around her. Some she knew well, some she had only known for a matter of hours; some saw her as a friend, some as a stranger, and some as the fulfillment of a centuries-old prophecy.

"This is not ideal, but it's what we have to do. Watch your backs," she said. "Radio silence unless you find the control room."

After acknowledgments all around, Sigurdsson took a moment to look into the eyes of each remaining team member.

"We're going to do this. We're going to secure this facility. Every one of us know what's been going on in here for the past two years. We know how much blood has been spilled, and we are all... fuck, probably none of us can even express the anger, the rage, that we've been pushing down into the dark dungeons of our minds. But now it's time to unleash that. It's time to take off the shackles and let that wrath run free. Do not hesitate, do not stop."

Various salutes were given, including elaborate ones from the udukiin, and each surviving member of the team headed off – except Aylarr and, of course, Jaeger. Sigurdsson wouldn't actually be alone as long as the German Shepherd had any say.

Removing her helm, Aylarr placed a hand on Sigurdsson's shoulder.

"In the event this is our final moment together," she said. "I would like you to know how much I have valued our friendship."

With a smile, Sigurdsson reached up and placed her hand over Aylaar's.

"Same. Thank you for everything," she said, then glanced quickly to Jaeger. "Especially for saving him."

Jaeger looked up at the pair and wagged his tail, just happy to be there.

Once again donning her helm, Aylarr began to head down the curving corridor before Sigurdsson called out to her.

"As the Matriarch of the Three, I'm ordering you not to get killed, all right?"

"As you command," said Aylarr, offering a melodramatic bow before turning and disappearing into the dark haze of the facility.

Kneeling beside Jaeger, Sigurdsson rubbed at his ears and he pushed his head into her chest, making a little grunting sound.

"Hey, pal. Thanks for being here for me. Through it all."

He raised his head, wagged his tail, and his tongue shot out quickly, giving Sigurdsson a light lick on the tip of her nose.

She couldn't help but grin.

"Ok, let's do this."

Standing and shouldering her *aoran*, Sigurdsson started toward one darkened corridor, but stopped when she realized Jaeger was not following. He was, instead, standing stock still, head low and ears twitching as he stared down an adjacent passageway. With a frown, Sigurdsson backtracked and stood beside him, following Jaeger's laser-focused gaze down the passage.

"This way, huh?"

The dog looked up at her briefly, then back down the corridor.

"Okay, let's go."

The corridor selected by Jaeger looked much like every other corridor in the facility – at least, those Sigurdsson had seen. There were, no doubt, corridors deeper within the facility that looked very different, and there were corridors deeper within the facility that Sigurdsson had no desire to ever see; corridors that led to charnel houses. Someone, she realized, would have to trek down those corridors to look for survivors, but there was zero chance it was going to be her. Other people could shoulder that responsibility.

Shaking her head, she swore at herself.

"Focus, shithead."

Sounds of the battle outside were faint, but continuous, and it wasn't clear whether that was good or bad.

Adjusting the stock of the *aoran* against her shoulder, Sigurdsson pressed further onward, keeping her left shoulder close to the wall as the corridor began curving to the left. There were alcoves at regular intervals, floor-to-ceiling in height, and deep enough that she had to clear each one before pressing on to ensure no ril-galas units were hiding within. Possible spots for future regen pod installations? There was no way to know, and she didn't have time to care as she notice the fur along Jaeger's spine begin to stand up in a rough ridge and his ears twitching around like tiny radar dishes as he stood as still as a statue.

Before she could ask him what was wrong, she sensed it and then heard it. Heavy footfalls, moving quickly. Ril-galas foot soldiers.

"Come on, quick!" she whispered to Jaeger as she ducked into one of the alcoves, dropping to one knee to make herself smaller. Jaeger squeezed in beside her as Sigurdsson pressed herself up against the alcove wall and readied her rifle. And held her breath.

But as the footfalls approached, the sound of gunfire from a Commonwealth assault rifle – and coming from inside the facility – echoed through the halls and the ril-galas increased their already brisk pace. Four of them passed Sigurdsson's hiding place without so much as a glance. They had eyes to spare, but none were looking anywhere but straight down the hallway, focused on finding the source of those gunshots.

Hefting the *aoran*, Sigurdsson frowned. Running a finger down the length of the barrel, she laid the weapon on the floor before standing. Jaeger glanced at the rifle on the floor, then up to Sigurdsson.

"They're deploying based on the sound of gunshots," she said, nodding down the corridor where the four ril-galas had disappeared. "And as much as I love the *aoran*, it's noisy."

Her *vayan* was still holstered on her right thigh and her gunstaff still slung over her shoulder, but instead of either weapon, Sigurdsson drew her two udukiin long knives.

"Quiet violence."

Slowly, they proceeded down the corridor, and it wasn't long before Sigursson began detecting a hum in the air – feeling it more than hearing it. And by Jaeger's agitation, it was clear he was feeling it, too, and likely more than her. The feeling immediately took her back a decade, and the evacuation efforts of the damaged civilian starliner Atavasa Dream. A similar bone-deep hum had come from its overstressed engines in the hour before they finally exploded and took the starliner with them. The feeling in the ril-galas structure wasn't identical, but it was similar enough for Sigurdsson to make the connection.

"We're on the right track, pal," she said to Jaeger.

Though while she and the rest of Commonwealth Army rescue team had made it off the Dream, along with all the civilians, well before the detonation, as Sigurdsson slowly stalked down the facility's hallway once more, she was not as optimistic of a happy ending this time.

Another bend in the corridor ahead. Another blind corner. Another in a two-year streak of potentially walking into her own death.

Shaking her head, Sigurdsson rolled her shoulders, adjusted her grip on her knives, and almost chuckled. Facing down death had become, dare she say it, kind of boring by that point. Of course something was going to try to kill her. That was situation normal. The quiet moments, the moments where she didn't have her flight-or-fight engaged, those were the shocking times.

Glancing down at Jaeger – who glanced up at her and wagged his tail – Sigurdsson realized not for the first time that she was going to need some serious therapy once they'd won the war. She was not psychologically ready for any semblance of normality. Assuming that was even a possibility for a War Matriarch.

Wiping her forehead with the back of her hand – the humidity in the facility was insane – Sigurdsson swore at herself. There wasn't time to worry about the future, just the next step. Move forward, deal with whatever comes, then move forward again. Simple.

"Sure. Simple."

Moving onward, slowly, and peeking as far around the corner as she could without revealing herself, Sigurdsson immediately drew back and pressed herself against the wall.

Two ril-galas.

She hadn't seen them well enough to know what "brand" they were, but they seemed too big to have been the sleek and agile Stalkers. Which was good. As much faith as she had in her abilities, Sigurdsson wasn't sure she'd have been able to come out on top in hand-to-hand combat with two Stalkers.

A feeling from the Matriarch washed over Sigurdsson, and she slowly extended the blade of one of the long knives past the edge of the wall. Reflected in the polished silver blade, she saw the two ril-galas, and behind them a closed door. The ril-galas weren't Stalkers – she was correct in that – but they were also not the typical bulky foot soldiers. These two were identical to the foot soldiers in every way, except they seemed scaled down by twenty percent.

"Guard units," she said under her breath.

Which meant she and Jaeger must have been on the right track. The hum was even heavier there, and what else could the ril-galas need guards for but to make sure they could finish their scorched Earth plans?

Which meant that Sigurdsson needed to get past the guards and through that door.

Which meant either using her pistol to take them, alerting any other enemies in the area to her presence... or it meant attempting to take out a pair of hostiles with her knives. And hoping that they didn't have an ability to alert their compatriots. As she pulled back her blade, Sigurdsson swore under her breath. Though neither option was particularly good, her whole war had been fought choosing the lesser of two evils. Taking a deep breath, she...

Stopped. Hearing something, a light whooshing sound that she could have dismissed as her imagination had Jaeger's ears not twitched at the same moment. Slowly, Sigurdsson extended one of her knives into the corridor again and nearly swore out loud and what the reflection in the blade showed: the door that the two ril-galas had been guarding was open, and two more guard units were stepping through. Taking on two of them would be difficult, but not unrealistic. But four?

Squinting and angling the blade slightly, she smiled despite the situation. Beyond the four ril-galas, through the still-open door, was what appeared to be a large room, well-lit unlike the rest of the facility. Though her field of view was narrowed by both the doorway and the width of her blade, the edge of what seemed to be a broad console was visible, with what looked to Sigurdsson like power level readouts on screens above.

Again, she withdrew her blade, and looked down at Jaeger and let out a breath.

"I guess one versus four it is."

Jaeger looked up at her, wagged his tail and stepped directly out into the hallway and started barking at the ril-galas.

"The fuck...?"

She'd never heard him sound so vicious, and before she could do anything, Jaeger turned, taking off at full speed down the corridor, back the way they'd come – away from the control room. It wasn't until she heard the heavy thud-thud-thud of one of the guard units chasing after him that Sigurdsson realized what Jaeger had done.

"You smart little bastard," she muttered, as the one guard unit passed by her, completely oblivious to her presence as it played an unwitting game of chase with a dog that had more situational awareness than many humans she'd met.

Another low whoosh as the control room door closed, and more footsteps, but slower this time. One of the three remaining guards beginning to follow his compatriot.

Up on the balls of her feet, knees bent, Sigurdsson twirled the knife in her left hand so the blade pointed downward.

The footsteps were right beside her alcove.

Raising her left hand to chin height – even with where the ril-galas chest cavity would be, and thus the actual ril-galas within the biomechanical construct, would be – Sigurdsson tensed her left shoulder, while dropping her right to keep it loose.

The gun pods on the guard's arms came into view.

Sigurdsson let out a slow breath.

The front portion of its head and chest came into view.

And she struck.

Lunging into the corridor, Sigurdsson swung outward with her left arm, driving the blade of her knife into the guard's chest, angled slightly upward, and in a continuous motion withdrew the blade, feeling it scrape the guard's outer shell, and spun to her right, dropping to one knee and using the knife in her right hand to slash what passed for the guard's Achilles tendon.

The first guard down and hobbled, if not dead, Sigurdsson launched herself at the remaining two. Driving her shoulder into the first, she got tangled up in its four arms, her momentum taking them both to the floor. Pulling herself free, Sigurdsson was still on one knee when the second guard swung one of its arm cannons at her head. Blocking the blow with her left forearm, she felt the weight of the impact all the way through her arm and into her shoulder, despite the Matriarch's armour, and Sigurdsson gritted her teeth as she swung around with her right arm and drove a knife blade deep into her attacker's arm. It stepped back two steps as she yanked the blade free, a viscous yellow fluid pouring from the wound, but Sigurdsson didn't have time to press the attack.

Pain shot through her upper body and stars momentarily filled her vision as a heavy impact cracked into her left shoulder and glanced off her head. Stumbling backward, she thankfully found the wall to steady herself and saw the guard she had tackled moving toward her, both arm cannons beginning to glow. Something was grinding in her left shoulder and she was still seeing stars, but Sigurdsson shoved herself off the wall and, both long knives extended in front of her, drove herself into the guard unit's chest. As the blades slid deep, the guard crumpled to the ground like a rag doll and Sigurdsson turned her momentum into a somersault – and while one of her blades slid free cleanly, the other caught on some part of the ril-galas anatomy and with the weakness in her left arm, she lost her grip.

Springing to her feet, she turned to face the lone remaining guard, which was – thankfully – still turning, off balance, trying to keep up with Sigurdsson's frenetic movement. Springing forward, she stabbed into the creature's chest just as one of its arms shot forward, catching her full in the face. Staggering backward, Sigurdsson lost her grip on the knife, which remained stuck a third of the way into the guard's chest cavity.

Feeling something wet on her face, Sigurdsson wiped at it with the back of her hand, which came away smeared with blood. Split lip, bloody nose, broken nose? Maybe all three. Tomorrow's worries.

As the thing's arm cannons raised toward her and began to glow, Sigurdsson lashed out with a side kick, the ball of her foot connecting with the butt end of her knife hilt, driving it straight into her attacker and burying it so deep the tip of the blade tore through the guard's back.

It stopped, arm cannons dropping, then toppled onto its side.

Wiping more blood from her face, Sigurdsson didn't bother trying to retrieve that knife – instead she went and yanked free her first knife and went over to the door controls, leaning on the wall momentarily to catch her breath.

And to hope Jaeger was still okay.

Her own health and well-being were tomorrow's problem, but if the ril-galas hurt Jaeger...

But first, she had to figure out how to open the door to the control room.

Looking down at the control panel, Sigurdsson couldn't help but laugh.

One button.

"You gotta be fucking kidding me."

She reached out and tapped the button with her knuckle, and the door slid aside, revealing the control room beyond.

Tightening her grip on the knife, Sigurdsson stepped inside.

The room was not as large as she had first assumed based on her narrow glimpse, the control consoles and the floating hexagonal plates that passed as monitors taking up most of the space. A second doorway stood, closed, opposite where Sigurdsson had entered. Standing at the console, apparently oblivious to Sigurdsson's entry, was a ril-galas, though of a type Sigurdsson had never seen. It was about her height, slenderer than any other ril-galas she had encountered, and unlike every other type of ril-galas construct, all four of its arms ended in the manipulator "hands" with their four tentactular fingers.

As far as she could tell, the thing was unarmed.

Quickly closing the distance between them, Sigurdsson jabbed the point of her knife into the controller's chest cavity. Not so deep as to kill the ril-galas within, but enough to let it know it was in trouble.

"Hello there."

The controller didn't respond, but Sigurdsson hadn't expected it would.

"I know you can understand me, so listen carefully," she said. "I am the Kaigor Kai Rii – I know you know what that means – and I am going to give you one chance to get out of this situation alive. Shut down all power to this facility. Stop it from blowing up."

There was a slight buzzing, similar to what she'd heard on the Shattered World when the ril-galas had communicated verbally with her, so when the controller spoke, it wasn't a complete surprise. What it had to say, however...

"Kaigor... Kai Rii... funk yours."

"It's *fuck you, you stupid shit*," said Sigurdsson as she slid the knife in up to its hilt, and let the dead controller drop to the floor with a thud. "Can't even get your last words right."

Sheathing her knife and wiping yet more blood from her face, Sigurdsson turned her attention to the control console and readouts, hoping the systems might be as idiot-proof as the single-button door mechanism.

It... wasn't.

"Shit."

But what is was, was similar to udukiin technology. A feeling passed through Sigurdsson, from the Matriarch, and she realized she could understand enough about the controls to do what she needed to do. Probably. There would be, in an udukiin reactor, controls for power inflow or generation, and power outflow, and overloading the reactor would be a matter of continuing to build power, while not releasing any of it to other systems. Theoretically, all Sigurdsson would need to do to prevent the facility from exploding would be to restore power outflow, and then shut down the reactor itself.

Glancing up at the hovering readouts, she could see that power levels were becoming critical in the power core, and that she – or more accurately, the Matriarch – was correct in that the majority of facility systems had been locked out, with minimal power flowing out from the core.

She looked down at the controls. Most were labelled in some way, but of course labelled in some spidery, geometric language she hadn't a hope of reading, even with the Matriarch's assistance. But there were multiple sets of controls that looked like sliders – odd, vaguely triangular shapes that could be moved up or down channels of varying lengths. Two pairs of the sliders were at their uppermost position, while the remaining five pairs were all at their lowermost. There were no markings along the length of the channels.

"So... I guess we just start moving things around and see what happens? Not like we could make things worse, right?"

While the Matriarch, of course, didn't respond directly, Sigurdsson also didn't feel any disagreement with the suggestion. That was – probably – the best she could have expected given how the rest of the operation had unfolded.

Taking a couple steadying breaths, Sigurdsson placed two blue fingers on the farthest set of sliders – one finger on each triangle, and slowly nudged them upward. Grimacing, she looked up at the curved screens and breathed a sigh of relief. Power levels in the reactor were still critical, but she had redirected some power somewhere else. Just *where* she neither knew nor cared. With power being siphoned from the reactor, it was edging away from overload, but not fast enough. And the results had also shown that the odds were very good that the two sets of sliders in the uppermost position were the ones controlling the reactor itself.

She quickly pushed the sliders all the way up and then moved to the first two sets of controls.

But a sound, outside-

Suddenly the closed door on the opposite wall slid open and a ril-galas stalker charged through, its clawed hands spread wide as it launched itself toward Sigurdsson, who took a step back. It was a futile move, she knew – the stalker was moving too fast – but it was all she had.

And then two loud cracks, the report of a *vayan* pistol, and the stalker's chest cavity exploded, showering Sigurdsson with gore. The creature instantly dropped to floor, its momentum causing it to slide the rest of the way. It came to rest at Sigurdsson's feet, a streak of blood and guts behind it. In the now open doorway, one side of her face covered in blood from a badly bleeding headwound, and her left hand a mangled mess, Aylarr lowered her pistol and slumped against the wall.

Rushing to her friend's side, Sigurdsson helped ease Aylarr to a sitting position, propped against the wall.

"Didn't I give you an order about not getting hurt?"

"No, you ordered me not to get killed," said Aylarr. "You did not include a provision for being maimed."

"It was implied."

"It was not," said Aylarr, who then waved her good hand toward the console. "And you have more pressing matters to attend to than my blood loss."

Preparing to argue, Sigurdsson stopped herself because Aylarr was right. Instead, she stood and headed back to the console. Placing her left hand on what she now knew to be the main power controls for the reactor, and her right on the first set of bottomed-out sliders, Sigurdsson hesitated. No matter how sure she felt she understood the controls, it was alien technology and she was taking a very large leap of faith.

She glanced over to Aylarr.

"If I do this, I could just blow us up."

"Which is precisely what will happen if we do nothing, Sigurdsson. There is, quite literally, nothing you can do that will make this situation worse."

"That's oddly comforting."

"As are you."

Brushing off the weird, but likely accurate compliment, Sigurdsson said a pair of fucks under her breath, pushed the bottomed-out sliders all the way up and the first set of power

level sliders halfway down. Then moved to the second set of reactor control sliders and moved them halfway down as well.

Glancing up at the hexagonal screens, she held her breath,
fought the urge to scream obscenities to release her anxiety,
and watched... nothing happen. The reactor levels hadn't
changed.

Frantically, she shoved the remaining few sliders from
their lower position to the top and dropped both reactor control
sets right down. And watched again.

"Come on, you fucker..."

She had to be right about the controls. There was no other
logical option to control the reactor – or if there was, it would
only be logical to someone who could read the spiky little let-
ters that made up the ril-galas language.

And still the screens did not change. The reactor was still
in a critical state.

Closing her eyes, Sigurdsson hung her head and sighed.

It had likely been a suicide mission from the start, but she'd
allowed herself to hope. Despite all her bluster, all her bravado,
she had really wanted the happy ending where her team was
successful. Where the reactor didn't explode and kill everyone.
Where she and her team managed to get back to the landing
zone, back to their ships, and back to their lives, because the
war was over.

Sighing again, she shoved herself away from the console
and moved over to Aylarr, sinking down on the floor beside the
icaran.

"I believe my head has stopped bleeding," said Aylarr.

"That's good."

"This was not your fault."

"Feels like it is."

"That's because, despite what you may feel about yourself, you are a selfless individual. You carry everyone's burdens as well as your own, and you put everyone else's needs ahead of your own. You cannot accept that an occurrence is not your responsibility, because you make all things your responsibility. Not everything need be your responsibility, Freyja. Your shoulders are strong, but they do not need to bear the weight of the universe."

For a moment, Sigurdsson just stared at Aylarr.

"You couldn't have fucking given me this advice earlier?" she said, laughing.

"I appear to be freer with my counsel due to blood loss and impending immolation."

Sigurdsson just nodded silently, their inevitable death settling over her like a warm blanket. Sure, she had regrets about things she'd done and said in her life, and just as many regrets about things she hadn't done or said... but all things considered, she was satisfied. Once upon a time, Sigurdsson had felt that the universe would be a better place without her, but now she felt, perhaps somewhat egotistically, that the opposite was true. The last few years, from Von Daniken's Landing to this moment, Sigurdsson had carved a place for herself that she'd never thought possible; she'd made a difference in people's lives and in whether they lived at all; she'd made connections she'd never thought she'd experience. It was, she supposed, as good a life as she could-

An elbow in the ribs brought her out of her obituary.

"Look," said Aylarr, nodding groggily toward the hexagonal screens of the control console.

Sigurdsson looked.

And blinked, and rubbed her eyes, and looked again.

The power levels across the board were levelling out. Power was being distributed to systems throughout the facility.

The reactor was no longer critical.

Sigurdsson shot to her feet.

"We need to let the other teams know how to do this."

"We will not be able to reach them from here," said Aylarr, struggling – and failing – to get to her feet. "The ril-galas radiation will have too great an impact on communications."

"Can you…?"

Aylarr shook her head.

"Go. I will find my own way out, at a much slower pace."

Seeing her friend's hesitation, Aylarr narrowed all four of her eyes.

"Freyja Sigurdsson, to use your own vocabulary against you, *finish the fucking mission.*"

Despite herself, Sigurdson smiled.

"See you on the outside."

Drawing her knife, just in case, Sigurdsson ran. She ran back through the door from whence she'd entered the control room, past the bodies of the guards, skidded to halt in the alcove where she'd hidden and scooped up her discarded *aoran* assault rifle, and then resumed running. As hard as she could.

Behind her, the scrabbling of claws on the hard floor. Too small to be anything but a stalker, but even then the sound was wrong. One of those tick-like creatures she'd heard about from the survivors in Edinburgh Castle?

Stealing a glance over her should, she nearly screamed in joy.

"Jaeger! You beautiful little shit!"

"Doctor, are you sure?" said Radko.

Looking back to his holographic data readouts, Frankenstein turned back to Radko and bobbed his head in his usual approximation of a nod.

"Yes, Captain. All readings indicate that the ril-galas facility in Edinburgh is no longer in a critical state – and, in fact, is reverting to normal power distribution."

Leaning on the edge of the sand table, Radko let his head drop slightly. While the news was good in many ways – not the least of which being that Sigurdsson was now one layer further removed from death – many hurdles remained before this could be a victory.

"Are any of the other reactors showing any change," he said.

"Yes," said the brill. "But not in a positive way."

Before Radko could respond, the deck vibrated beneath him.

"Primary hull breach, deck four!" someone shouted.

"Secondary hull holding, no loss of oxygen," announced a second voice. "Damage teams already responding."

A ril-galas ship – one of the ones they'd taken to calling sunfish – streaked past the Royal Sovereign so closely that some of the command deck crew ducked. It was followed by one of the Argentavis fighters, laying fire into its aft.

"Captain!"

This time, he knew the voice – Bell.

"Captain," she said. "We have a transmission from the Edinburgh team."

Without prompting, she patched it through to the sand table.

"...Edinburgh Team. I repeat, this is a message for anyone able to access a ril-galas facility on Earth," said a male voice. Again, a voice Radko didn't recognize. "Sigurdsson has managed to stop our reactor from melting down."

The voice went on to explain the steps Sigurdsson had taken, and the moment the transmission stopped, Radko snapped his fingers at Frankenstein.

"Doctor, can you create a simplified version of these instructions that we can broadcast everywhere?"

"I have already done so."

"Of course you have," said Radko, pointing at the brill and nodding. "Kerry, fleet status?"

"We've lost the Haida Gwaii. Singh has picked up most of their lifeboats," said Stanton-West. "And the Vimy Ridge has just had to shut down main engines due to damage – they're on maneuvering thrusters only."

Glancing up at the dome above, Radko quickly pinpointed the Vimy Ridge, highlighted by the UHUD as a friendly vessel. She was slowly turning, likely trying to put some space between herself and the battle, so the crew could attempt to repair the engines. But like a shark sensing blood in the water, Ultimus was turning toward her.

"El Bahari," said Radko, opening a channel to his old ship, "you're attracting attention. How are things over there?"

"Not optimal," she said, the strain in her voice more evident that Radko had ever heard it. "We have a hairline fracture in our..."

She trailed off to have an exchange with one of her crew.

"In our reactor cowling. We can't use our engines until its repaired, but we also can't repair it in the current situation –

we need a week in drydock. Best we can do is patch it, and cross our fingers we don't breach."

"Ultimus is heading right for you."

"I know," she said. "I can't get us out of its way, but I can give it a bloody nose on the way out."

"Keep its attention, we're coming to you."

Closing the connection, Radko immediately opened one to Outlaw Squadron.

"Cags, you still there?"

"Yeah, what's up?"

"How many fighters do you still have in play?"

"Enough to do whatever you're about to ask."

"Ultimus's engines. I want them on fire five minutes ago."

"Consider it done."

Within moments of the connection closing, five Argentavis fighters streaked silently above the Royal Sovereign, and Radko had to remind himself it wasn't like the Vimy Ridge – he wasn't watching them through a transparent dome, he was looking at a holographic projection, while safely ensconced in the core of the ship.

Safely being relative in his current situation.

"Move us between Ultimus and the Vimy Ridge," said Radko. "And get me connections to the Ridge, Her Glorious Vengeance, and the Tianlong."

The connections popped up almost simultaneously, and Radko began outlining his plan to the other commanding officers.

42

Holyrood Park was a disaster.

Bursting through the rear entrance of the ril-galas facility, Sigurdsson had sprinted a short distance away, dropped into a dip in the ground – which she later discovered was a crater caused by a grenade – and transmitted her reactor control instructions to the landing zone on Calton Hill for them to relay. She hadn't stopped to look around, and now, scratching Jaeger behind his left ear, she poked her head out above the crater's edge and swore.

The battlefield was on fire, plumes of black smoke rising from multiple points, and the ground was littered with dead bodies. Human, icaran, udukiin, and ril-galas. Though to Sigurdsson's immense relief, the latter seemed to far outweigh all the former combined. There was yelling, screaming, gunfire, and the booming reports of both icaran assault rifles and ril-galas gun pods; soldiers on both sides ran here and there, all semblance of skirmish order or defensive lines long having been burned away by the heat of battle.

Tired down to her bones, covered in blood, covered in dirt, Sigurdsson thought about how nice it would be to just sink back into the cool earth of the crater; to rest for a minute or twenty; to let someone else be responsible for the rest of the day. After all, hadn't she done enough? Even Aylarr had said not everything need be Sigurdsson's responsibility.

So, she'd let other people take over.

Standing, she shouldered her *aoran*.

Starting tomorrow.

After all, she was the War Matriarch.

And this was a war.

A war that could, she reminded herself, end before sunset.

"Stay close, pal," she said, glancing down at Jaeger. "This might get hairy."

Raising a fist to the sky, Kaigor Kai Rii shouted her war cry, allowing the Matriarch to pass it along through her psychic bond with the udukiin on Earth, making sure they knew their War Matriarch was still in the fight.

And then she charged onto the battlefield, Jaeger at her heels.

43

Ultimus, bearing down on the badly damaged Vimy Ridge, did not slow its pace even slightly as the Royal Sovereign moved into position between it and its target. The massive ril-galas ship itself had taken a great deal of damage, including the loss of one of its three massive gun pods, though the damage was evidently not enough to impede it to any great degree.

"Both remaining gun pods are powering up," said Stanton-West.

Radko nodded, but didn't respond otherwise.

To starboard, the Vimy Ridge dominated his view – he had ordered the Sovereign in closer than any regulations would have allowed for, barring docking procedures, at one kilometer.

To port, Ultimus, growing larger by the second.

But behind Ultimus, Outlaw Squadron.

Small explosions flared from the aft section of the ril-galas command ship, followed by larger, short-lived, bursts of flame and clouds of debris as Cagliari's flight group did their work. Again and again they swooped in, hit their marks, and wheeled away before Ultimus could bring its equivalent of point defense cannons to bear on the dark, agile starfighters.

"Ultimus is slowing," said Bell.

"We are now in position," said Stanton-West. "The Vimy Ridge is completely blocked by the Royal Sovereign – Ultimus won't be able to hit it without significant repositioning."

"We're one expensive tactical scrambler," said Bell, under her breath.

Though he was certain the comment was meant for Kerry and not him, he smiled regardless. Tactical scramblers were already more expensive than they were worth.

Warnings blared across the command deck as the gun pods of their adversary reached full charge.

"Brace for impact," said Radko, as calmly as he could, gripping the edge of the sand table.

The blast hit the Royal Sovereign amidships, a tactical error by an enemy vessel that had not yet had much experience against Commonwealth Naval ships, it seemed. Further aft, and Ultimus could have damaged engines or maneuvering thrusters, and crippled the Sovereign much like it had – apparently through sheer luck – crippled the Vimy Ridge. Still, the impact was tremendous, and proximity alerts blared as the Royal Sovereign was pushed a few metres closer to the Vimy Ridge.

"Damage?"

"Significant damage to primary hull, but hull integrity is holding," said Stanton-West. "However, it did knock out two rail gun emplacements – rail guns P11 and P12 are out of commission."

"Not ideal, but better than it could have been. Casualties?"

"None reported as yet, Captain."

"Give me a full broadside with all operable rail guns," said Radko, glancing over to the brill scientist once he saw the rail gun rounds tearing into the hull of Ultimus. "Frankenstein, any progress on the other reactors?"

"Santarém and Qala'at Sanjil teams have implemented Freyja Sigurdsson's instructions and their reactor power levels are beginning to return to normal. Jiayuguan team are still attempting to secure the facility," said Frankenstein. "And they are, unfortunately, running out of time to do so. I estimate reactor detonation in less than forty minutes."

"Captain, Ultimus will be within missile range momentarily," said Stanton-West.

"Understood. Rocketeers are to acquire locks and hold fire until my order," said Radko. "Lieutenant Bell, please signal the Vimy Ridge, Tianlong, and Her Glorious Vengeance that we are proceeding as planned."

"All ships acknowledge, Sir," she said after a moment.

"Ultimus in missile range."

"Full broadside," said Radko. "Missiles follow."

As the broadside hit home and the missiles streaked toward the enemy, Radko saw out of the corner of his eye the mass of the Vimy Ridge move, their thrusters firing on full, raising the ship upward and out of the protective shadow of the Royal Sovereign.

The moment they cleared, the Vimy Ridge let loose with their own broadside, followed by their own missiles arcing out toward Ultimus.

As the massive ril-galas ship reeled from two full broadside and two full spreads of missiles, its forward hull plating – or the ril-galas equivalent of such – rupturing in places, small jets of bluish flame briefly flaring to life before being extinguished by the void of space, the next phase of the plan kicked into action.

The Tianlong, possibly the fastest capital ship in the combined fleet, screamed in from beneath Ultimus, tearing into the ship's belly with rail gun fire and two nuclear warheads before peeling off again.

And then the final act – or, at least, what Radko hoped would be the final act.

From above and starboard, and x-shaped shadow fell over the hull of Ultimus as Her Glorious Vengeance lived up to her name, doling out the glorious vengeance of, one had to assume, Kaigor Kai Rii. Every weapon on the udukiin vessel – of which there were an incredible number, its firepower even dwarfing the considerable offensive resources of the Royal Sovereign – tore into the flank of the ril-galas command ship. Explosions rippled through the already-compromised hull of the ril-galas ship, and the two remaining gun pods glowing fiercely as they prepared another onslaught, went suddenly dark. And unlike the Tianlong, Her Glorious Vengeance did not pull up and pull away.

Radko watched as additional shield plating folded out and across the fore of the massive vessel, and Her Glorious Vengeance increased speed.

"Holy shit," said Radko.

And the udukiin dreadnaught rammed Ultimus.

With explosions rippling across the length of it, the ril-galas ship buckled and then its spine broke in a massive, brief, fireball, with Her Glorious Vengeance emerging, singed but un-damaged, from the other side. Spinning out of control, explosions tearing them to pieces, half of Ultimus drifted away from either side of the dreadnaught.

The battle, it seemed, paused for a moment as everyone – human, udukiin, icaran, krellin, and even the ril-galas them-selves – took in what had just happened.

The aft half of Ultimus disintegrated into a multicoloured ball of flame and debris first, and served to rouse Radko from his state of shock.

"Gunnery teams are to target any remaining ril-galas ships within range!" he said quickly. "Dealer's choice, just make things explode."

The crew jumped back into action, overcoming their own momentary stunned inaction, and orders were relayed. Within moments, Radko could see rail gun rounds and missiles flying, and the leaderless, confused ril-galas ships now fully on the defensive.

"Jiayuguan team has control of their facility," said Frankenstein.

"Several ril-galas ships are attempting to flee the battlefield, Captain," said Stanton-West. "Krellin ships are in pursuit."

"Leave them to it, we need to clean up here. I want reports from all vessels, ASAP, please."

It took just over six minutes for the entire remaining combined fleet to provide status updates, and the delay was mostly due to waiting for translation from the krellin.

Damages were plentiful, but only the Vimy Ridge was damaged to the point of being out of the fight.

Several ships had been lost, but fewer than Radko had realistically expected.

And all ships were reporting that the ril-galas forces were attacking aimlessly, if they were attacking at all.

Even the decoy fleet, sweeping the outer edges of the battle, reported disorganized withdrawal of ril-galas forces.

"Get me a line to Khaifa, please," he said, and greeted the interim Prime Minister with a weary smile as her face appeared in a holographic window before him. "Madame Prime Minister."

"Please tell me we have good news," said Khaifa.

"All three teams on Earth gained control of their facilities and two have successfully prevented detonation – the third is in progress. Ultimus – the ril-galas command ship – has been destroyed and their remaining fleet is in disarray. Some are even retreating."

For a moment, all Khaifa did was stare at him, and the moment stretched long enough that Radko had begun to think there was a glitch in the connection to Thor's Hammer.

"Are you…," she said, stopping to close her eyes briefly and take a deep breath. "Finn, are you saying that we actually pulled this off?"

"We still have a ways to go before I'd be willing to say those words, but as of this moment, the United Defense Fleet has control of the Solar System."

Even as he said the words, Radko felt like he was in a dream, and he realized everyone on the bridge had frozen in place for a moment after he'd spoken them.

"Captain Radko," said Khaifa, her voice thick with emotion. "I don't think I can adequately express the enormity of what you've done here today."

Radko held up and hand to stop her.

"I appreciate the sentiment, Nasrin, but we have multiple ril-galas facilities on Earth detonating and more ready to blow. We need to start organizing evacuations."

"I've issued blanket pardons to any ATC Castle captains and crews who help with the evacuations," said Khaifa. "At this point…"

She paused, shuffling papers just off-screen, before finding a handwritten note.

"At this point, we have five vessels of varying size as result of those pardons. The good news is, two of them are cargo ships with pressurized holds. They can each hold about ten thousand people – not comfortably, and without many belongings, but they'll fit. What's the fleet status?"

"Better than we'd expected, but not as good as we'd hoped. We can task a few ships with rescue efforts, but we also need to maintain our defenses here."

"Just in case they come back," said Khaifa, nodding. "Understood. I'm still waiting on reports of what other ships we have available here, civilian or otherwise, but I'm hearing we may have as many as six more."

"That's good news. Who is coordinating the rescue operations?"

"I've asked Ironhorse and Van Der Berg to handle it."

"I'll get our situation sorted and let them know which ships I'm assigning to them," said Radko. "I'll be in touch as soon as possible."

"Understood. And again, thank you."

As the connection closed, Radko realized the command deck was still as silent as the vacuum outside their hull. And he realized how exhausted he was. And the socket of his missing eye was aching terribly.

Watching what little remained of the forward hull of Ultimus tumble across the UHUD, on what looked to be a collision course with Luna, Radko took a deep breath, and then another. Echo Station seemed a lifetime ago. The chaos. The abject fear of not knowing what was happening, what to do, where to go. But they had conquered that fear. Figured out what to do and where to go. And now, he was standing on the command deck of the Commonwealth flagship, watching the ril-galas – the impossible foe that had swept through space like an angry hurricane, destroying and conquering everything its path – running away in defeat.

"Kerry," he said finally, "if you would be so kind as to reassign some of our ships to Thor's Hammer to assist with rescue operation on Earth, I would appreciate it."

Stanton-West nodded her assent, smiling.

"And... you have command of the Royal Sovereign," he said, offering a tired smile. "I'm going to find the galley and make a cup of tea."

That, as he'd hoped, elicited a round of laughter around the command deck.

Offering the crew a salute, he turned on his heel and exited the command deck.

For now, at least, Radko's war was done.

44

In the chaos of the evacuation of Earth, it took a full twenty-four hours for Radko to learn that Sigurdsson had survived the battle of Holyrood Park, and another forty-eight before he had the chance to speak with her over a tinny, static-laden comm line. It was, they agreed, oddly fitting, given that was exactly how they had first met.

Strolling slowly down one of the main corridors of Thor's Hammer, Radko reviewed the latest updates regarding... regarding everything. Of the ril-galas facilities on Earth that had been set by the invaders to go critical, the ground teams had stopped four, and three others had failed to detonate for various reasons, which was excellent luck. However, thirtyfive had still exploded, meaning the scenario presented by Frankenstein was still occurring, just on a marginally reduced scale. Loss of human life over the course of the occupation had been severe, though loss of life directly due to the explosions had been minor in comparison to what they had predicted. Quon's... *Hunter's* psychic warning burst had worked. Prince Arthur had died on the battlefield, much to Khaifa's disappointment – she would be interim Prime Minister for a little longer.

What remained of Ultimus was in the process of being taken apart by Singh and his band of pirates. The Commonwealth was looking the other way, both as an unofficial thank-you to the corsairs for their assistance in the war effort, and because it was an open secret that they were being paid by Cagliari Aerospace to look for anything connected to the supposed jump drive Ultimus has used to materialize in the thick of battle.

As he had several times over the past few days, Radko found himself standing in front of the makeshift memorial wall that had been put up in the main corridor. In easier times, it would have been a large screen displaying duty assignments, or anything else station command needed to convey. But some enterprising civilians had covered it with thick white paper, and provided a table full of tape and markers. Photographs of those lost had been taped up, names written beneath them. But more common were just the names. Countless names, written in various colours. The memorial wall has only gone up two days ago, according to Khaifa, but it was already a third full.

Reading the names, a few were familiar, but most weren't.

Setting his tablet on the table, Radko picked up a thick marker. Blue, appropriately enough, given how many of the names on the wall had laid down their lives in defense of the blue planet that birthed humanity.

Taking a shaky breath, he added four names to the wall.

Harlan Gray.

Locaris.

Hunter.

Anna Cortez.

There could have been more. His eye began to tear up – he could have added so many names to the list, so many people who died so others could live. So many who would lie in unmarked graves or whose remains weren't even recoverable to be put in a grave at all.

"I added a few names this morning."

Wiping his eye, Radko turned to see El Bahari, her own eyes wet.

"In the middle of everything, it was hard to see beyond hitting our next target. Reaching the next goal. Seeing this," she said, nodding to the memorial wall, "puts things into perspective."

"It does."

"Without you, I'd have been on that wall."

"And without you, I would have been."

El Bahari didn't argue the point, but she didn't agree either.

"I just got out of a meeting with Admiral Mahoney," she said. "Are you sure about this?"

"Yes," he said, putting back the marker and picking up his tablet. "I can't keep going like I have been. Even if I didn't have more than one doctor telling me I needed rest, my body is telling me the same."

It was true – aside from the constant ache in his empty eye socket, after more than two years of having a near-constant flow of adrenaline through his veins, Radko was crashing and crashing hard. Even the simplest of tasks like making tea, as essential as that was to his well-being, made him feel like Sisyphus pushing his boulder up the mountain. No matter how he tried to argue with himself, Radko knew he was in no condition to continue in his role with Commonwealth Armed Forces – at least not for a while.

"It's only three months," he said. "And then based on the repair timelines, that gives me another two months of desk duty before I get back onto the command deck."

El Bahari nodded, extended her hand, which Radko shook. And her face did that thing he'd only seen it do once before.

"Again, thank you," she said, smiling. "If you need anything, just let me know. I mean it."

"I will. And congratulations on the promotion, Captain."

"I just hope I can live up to the standards of the person I'm replacing."

"He's not the giant everyone makes him out to be," said Radko, chuckling. "And your XO, Stanton-West, is one of the better officers I've served with. Lean on her when you need to and you'll be just fine."

"Still…," she said, pausing for a moment as if deciding whether to continue the thought. Instead of continuing, she changed topics. "We're not supposed to make this widely known, since people are still so much on edge, but Her Glorious Vengeance has been given docking clearance. Airlock thirteen."

Though Radko tried to maintain a neutral expression, he had clearly failed.

"Go," said El Bahari, laughing.

So he did.

Airlock thirteen was disgorging a stream of refugees from earth – a phrase Radko never expected he'd ever use in his lifetime – who were quickly being directed to the makeshift medical and housing facilities set up by Ironhorse and his team in several unused cargo areas of Thor's Hammer.

Through the flood of humanity, weaving between the legs of those stunned souls, was one who would be too stubborn to be directed anywhere by anyone.

"Jaeger," said Radko, smiling and dropping to one knee.

An excited *merf* and a quick bound, and the big dog was burying his head into Radko's chest while having his ears rubbed.

Among the last to come through the airlock, alongside a young redheaded woman being wheeled out on a wheelchair, was Freyja Sigurdsson.

"I'll come and check in on you soon," Sigurdsson said to the redhead, who nodded in acknowledgement before she was wheeled away.

For a moment, alone at the airlock entrance, Radko and Sigurdsson stood in silence.

"We did it," said Sigurdsson, finally.

"Yeah. That bitchy soldier from Von Daniken's Landing turned out okay."

"So did that stuffy prick of a Naval officer."

Neither tried to hide their tears as they quickly embraced, and stayed that way for a long time.

How they made their way to the little pub, or how they'd managed to get a secluded booth to themselves, was a blur to Radko, but there they were, sitting across from each other at their usual booth, but this time with Jaeger curled up like a canine croissant and snoring softly on the bench beside Sigurdsson. And everyone else in the half-full pub was leaving them in peace, seeming to understand that what he and Sigurdsson needed was each other. Holding Sigurdsson's blue, three-fingered right hand in his left, Radko lightly rubbed his thumb over her knuckles as she took him through her side of the final battle with the ril-galas. And when she'd finished, as he told her of the battle in space, she'd taken his left hand in both of hers.

"Finn…," she said, after the stories and after a toast to the fallen. "I can't stay."

There were tears in her eyes.

"As much as I want to, and fucking hell do I want to, this," she said, exaggeratedly shrugging both shoulders to indicate the Matriarch, "means I can't. With the ril-galas having killed the other Matriarch, the one who would lead the species, I'm all the udukiin have. Right now, Kaigor Kai Rii isn't just the War Matriarch, I'm the only Matriarch."

A tear slowly rolled down Sigurdsson's cheek, and Radko reached out to wipe it away with his thumb.

"And Khaifa has asked the udukiin to clear out any ril-ga-las stragglers," he said.

"Yeah. And after that, work out plans for a defensive perimeter until we can get some kind of unified fleet officially organized."

"I know."

"Of course you do," she said, smiling sadly and nodding. "You were probably involved in the planning."

"Well, yes, but what I meant is that I knew all along you wouldn't be able to stay. You're Kaigor Kai Rii. You have... you have responsibilities on par with Khaifa right now, trying to keep a civilization together. Humanity wasn't the only species that suffered in this war, and I think on the human side, we tend to forget that. Udukiin, icaran, krellin, and I'm sure others we haven't had contact with since before the war – we've all suffered tremendous losses, and we're all about to start putting the pieces back together."

"Yeah. It's just... we're only here for forty-eight hours. Then I'm taking Her Glorious Vengeance out to start the patrols, and at this point, I have no idea when I'll be back."

"How big are your quarters?"

"Aboard Her Glorious Vengeance?" she said, frowning. "Enormous. Why?"

"Want some company?"

"Absolutely. I'd hoped we'd be able to spend as much time as possible together before I have to leave."

"Not what I meant," he said, lifting her hand to his lips and kissing her knuckles. "I had a meeting with Khaifa and Mahoney. I requested – and was granted – a three-month medical leave. So, if you want, I could tag along while you-."

"Yes, I want!" she said, grinning and wiping away tears with her free hand. "But I can't guarantee we'll be back here in three months, Finn. And what about the Royal Sovereign?"

"El Bahari has been promoted to Captain and put in command of the Sovereign," he said. "And I spoke with Singh. He's almost done his work for Cags, then the Azrael's Tear will be doing recon, looking for survivors of the original invasion – ships, stations, colonies that weren't completely destroyed. He's agreed to rendezvous with us and bring me back, if we don't think Her Glorious Vengeance will be back in the area. I've also arranged for remote counselling sessions, so I can try to work through a metric tonne of trauma. I know three months isn't *that* long, but we've got three months to figure out what's next."

He figured he had covered most of his bases in trying to set the plan in motion. The tricky part was whether or not he could adjust to both living on an udukiin vessel, and not having any duties on the ship. Though Radko had been relatively confident in Sigurdsson's acceptance of the plan, the smile on her face left no doubt. They were going to do this.

"Marry me," she said suddenly.

"Okay."

"I mean, not like Commonwealth official marriage," she said quickly. "The udukiin don't have marriage, like we know it. When two udukiin decide to be together, they just *do it*, no government bullshit to... wait, did you...?"

"I said okay. Yes. Udukiin equivalent, krellin equivalent, whatever," said Radko, smiling.

Sigurdsson's grin got even wider.

"Um, just so you know, a Matriarch choosing a mate is a huge deal to the udukiin. We will, at some point, need to go to the Shattered World, and there will be a party. For about a week," she said. "But not until we've finished our mission here."

"So would I be a Prince or something?"

"Honestly, you'll probably just be called Kaigor Kai Rii's mate. Sorry."

"It's all right, I know you're kind of a big deal," he said. "And the idea of being in the background and not the one everyone looks at... has its appeal these days."

"I can understand that."

"I'll make sure Mahoney knows there will be another leave request coming at some point."

Leaning across the table, Sigurdsson grabbed a fistful of Radko's jacket and pulled him into a kiss.

"I love you," she said, when she finally released him.

"I love you too."

And then reality intruded once more.

"Captain Radko, please report to Fleet Ops," came the echoing voice from the station's intercom.

Both Radko and Sigurdsson shrugged, smiled, and stood.

His nap disturbed, Jaeger raised his head and grunted his displeasure.

"Cags probably wants to go over some stuff before my leave starts," said Radko. "We talked her into overseeing repairs and refits of my ship. I suspect she'll be getting creative."

"I thought El Bahari was in command of the Royal Sovereign now?" said Sigurdsson as they left the pub and headed down the corridor.

"She is. My ship is probably in drydock for six months or more. She took quite a beating in the battle, and let's be honest, she was badly in need of some upgrades anyway."

Sigurdsson's confused frown slowly turned into a smile as she connected the dots.

"The Vimy Ridge," she said, nodding.

He smiled.

"Well, Captain," she said, with feigned formality. "Her Glorious Vengeance will be departing in forty-eight hours. Make sure you get all your shit on board, and I'll let the udukiin know to put another toothbrush in my quarters."

"Aye-aye, your worship," he said, laughing and saluting.

Laughing, Sigurdsson pulled him in to another kiss.

For a moment, it was nice for the entire universe to consist of just the two of them. Two people whose life paths kept colliding until they got the hint.

The End

ABOUT THE AUTHOR

David Whale lives in Stoney Creek, Ontario Canada, with his spouse Mandy, his step-daughter, and their beloved boxer, Gus. He has been telling stories in various forms since he was a kid, from writing and drawing his own comic books to creating photo-stories using his old Kenner Star Wars action figures to script doctoring on a televised sports show. *Radko's War* – the first installment of the trilogy now completed by *Cry Havoc* – was his first published novel.

When not writing, Whale enjoys reading, action figure photography, and creating custom action figures and dioramas.

Follow him on Instagram and Threads @whale.david